M000238475

THE BOOK OF HARMONY

THE LAST ORACLE, BOOK 7

MELISSA MCSHANE

Night Harbor Publishing

This book is dedicated to the fans.
Thank you for loving this bookstore as much as I do.

Wind lashed frozen rain against the plate glass window with ABERNATHY'S stenciled on it in big, gold-highlighted letters. The chill didn't extend into the store, which had an excellent climate control system, but I pulled my sweater more closely around myself anyway. It was one of those bleak January days that made me wonder why anyone had wanted to settle in Portland in the first place, way back in the nineteenth century. Even hardened trappers and lumber-jacks must have hated the incessant rain.

I turned the page of my cookbook and skimmed down the recipes. Slow cooker pot roast. Too late for that today, but I could start it tomorrow morning before leaving for work and it would make the house smell incredible when I got home. I was never going to love cooking the way my mother did, but I was competent after six months' practice, and Malcolm never complained or insisted on cooking more often than he already did. I added the ingredients to the shopping list on my phone.

One more meal, and I could send the list to Ingrid, who would do the shopping and have it all put away before six.

I suppressed the usual twinge of guilt I felt when I thought about Ingrid. She represented a compromise between me and Malcolm, who'd wanted a housekeeping service when we moved into our new home. I'd challenged him on it—we'd already learned our lesson about letting wealth dominate our lives with our last apartment—and Malcolm had pointed out that I worked six days a week, usually nine to six, and didn't have time for all the chores a house that size required, not to mention shopping and all the little errands that have to happen during the day. But I didn't like the idea of someone else doing all the cleaning when we were both perfectly capable, not to mention I felt it was a little too upper-upper-class for upper-middle-class me. That was something Malcolm could understand, and agreed with.

So we'd settled on Ingrid, who was a Warden with a tragic past in need of a job. She ran errands and did the shopping and left the cleaning and cooking to me. I'd realized how wise a choice we'd made when the dishwasher broke and the repair place had given us one of those "we'll get there when we get there" time estimates. Ingrid hadn't minded waiting for them at all. Even so, employing her felt so odd, even if Ingrid wasn't at all servile. We might even become friends if I was ever home long enough to get to know her.

I turned another couple of pages. Fish, maybe. I could use more practice poaching fish. I made another note and pressed Sync to upload the list so Ingrid could download it, then texted her a heads-up. A few seconds later she responded with her usual smiley face emoji. I closed the cookbook and stretched. 3:45. It felt much later, thanks to the rain.

Someone hurried past the window, and seconds later the

door flew open, sending the bells jangling. "Sorry," said the woman who entered. "The wind took it out of my hands." She had a carton covered with a big plastic garbage bag tucked under one arm and a brightly colored scarf covering the tight black curls of her Afro.

"Hi, Juliet," I said. "I didn't think anyone would come in today."

"I was running errands and figured I'd stop by, drop these off," Juliet Dawes said. She set the carton on the counter and removed its plastic cover, revealing a disorganized pile of leather bound tomes. "I don't have an augury request today, so if you could put them on my account?"

"Sure. Judy!"

Judy's muffled reply was unintelligible, but shortly she emerged from the stacks. Her knee-length smock in vivid green and yellow made her look as if she'd stepped from the pages of a '70s fashion magazine. "Oh, hi, Juliet," she said. "Sorry, I was updating software. I didn't think anyone would come in today."

"That's what I said." I grabbed a handful of books and set them in an irregular stack on the glass-topped plywood of the front counter. "I half expect to see Noah and all his animals poling the ark down the middle of the street."

"Three days of nonstop rain is excessive," Juliet agreed. "You still think it was a good idea to plan your wedding for January?"

Judy snorted with indelicate amusement. I lifted my chin defiantly and said, "Malcolm begins four months of training new teams in April, my parents are going to France in May, and I didn't want to wait a whole year. And nobody gets married in January, so I didn't have to compete hard for a venue. It was a smart decision." How many times had I made that little speech? It was amazing the number of people who felt entitled to comment on how nuts my wedding plans were.

"If you say so," Juliet said doubtfully. "I'm impressed you were able to pull it together so quickly."

"That was Deanna Forcier," Judy said. "Wedding planner extraordinaire. She makes Marine Corps sergeants look like indecisive dilettantes."

"A wedding planner? What, you didn't have everything already decided?" Juliet leaned on the counter and propped her chin on her palm. "I had a wedding binder years before Elliot and I even met."

"I never daydreamed about my future wedding," I said. "I was just as happy to let Deanna come up with options and point and click the ones I liked best."

"Helena's not a romantic," Judy said. "Surprising, given her taste in movies."

"I am so a romantic," I protested.

Judy rolled her eyes. "Your idea of a romantic evening is pizza and a movie. And since you put jalapeños on your pizza, you smell like hot peppers the whole time."

"Well, there's nothing wrong with that. And you're not romantic either. You're the most sensible person I know."

"Thanks. I think." Judy hauled another stack of books out of the box. "Hang on, I'll get Juliet's file so we can record these."

"It's going to be beautiful, though," Juliet said when Judy was gone. "Are you nervous yet?"

"I still have two weeks before I can justify feeling nervous. Everything's planned and on schedule. I just have to show up."

Juliet shook her head in mock despair. "I think half the Wardens were betting you'd turn out to be a Bridezilla, with how relaxed you are all the rest of the time. I should have started a pool."

Judy returned with a manila folder and a pen. "My money is on Viv for that."

"Is she engaged?" Juliet exclaimed. "I hadn't heard!"

"No, she's not engaged." I opened the book at the top of the stack. "Viv doesn't believe in marriage. And no, I don't know what Jeremiah thinks about it. It's not something I want to ask her. Or him. This one's $100, Judy."

We went through the rest of the books and added the total to Juliet's account. While Judy carried a stack of books away to shelve them according to Abernathy's rigorous system of not having a system, I said, "So you're coming to the wedding, right?"

"Of course. Even Elliot is excited about it—well, not *excited*, most men don't feel that way about weddings, but he's looking forward to the dinner. The Warwick does a great spread." Juliet wadded up the garbage bag and stuffed it into the carton atop the few books Abernathy's had rejected. I had no idea how it decided how much books were worth in trade and wasn't inclined to pursue the question.

"I sort of wish it was over already. I feel as if I'm in limbo," I said. The truth was I felt like Malcolm and I were married already, what with sharing a house and joint finances and all the rest. I already had trouble not referring to him as my husband. The wedding ceremony was just a formality as far as I was concerned. But my parents were thrilled, my sister had already made plans to bring her little family from New York for the big day, and everyone around me acted as if I should be eager for it, so I put on a good face and reminded myself that all the important things had happened months ago.

"That's how I felt," Juliet said. "Don't worry, it will be here before you know it." She waved goodbye and pushed her way through the door, ducking her head against the rain as she ran for her car, parked in Abernathy's magically reserved spot.

"Maybe you'll get lucky, and it won't rain on your wedding day," Judy said, emerging from the stacks to retrieve another pile of books. "Even if the ceremony is indoors, rain is still gloomy."

I picked up the third pile of books and followed her to the shelves. "Or I could get really unlucky, and it will snow like it did last year and no one will be able to reach the hotel because the streets will be impassable."

"Let's just hope for the best, shall we?"

The bells over the door rang again. When I reached the front counter, the newcomer had shed his hat and scarf and unbuttoned his coat. "It's really coming down out there," he said. He looked surprisingly overheated and was breathing heavily.

"Welcome to Abernathy's. Can I help you with something?" I'd never seen the man before, and it was possible he was one of the rare ordinary people who sometimes found their way to the store. I always let those customers browse until they realized the store wasn't organized at all, at which point they generally left without any prompting from me.

"Augury," the man said. "I usually send my requests by mail, but I'm in town on business and I wanted to see the store." He made a big show of turning around in a slow circle, his head tilted back. "It's not at all as I pictured it."

"I hear that a lot," I said. Well, not a *lot*, but often enough that I was used to the reaction. Abernathy's shelves weren't aligned in neat rows, but stood at odd angles to each other on the ancient linoleum floor spangled with gray blisters that had once been silver stars. Books were crammed onto those shelves sideways, or on their faces with the spines poking out like tiny staircases for book-loving pixies. Though the store never smelled the same two days in a row, the oracle being fond of experimenting with fragrances, underlying the scent of the day was always the smell of dust, no matter how often I cleaned the shelves. The high, white ceiling kept the place from feeling claustrophobic, but it was definitely no ordinary bookstore.

"Did you write your question down?" I asked. The man dug in his rear pocket and came up with a much-folded sheet of lined paper. "I'll take care of this right away, Mr....?" The oracle didn't need to know his name—it seemed to know without being told—but after the time the oracle had come under the influence of a confusing illusion, I always asked the customer's name so I could compare it to the one on the augury. It might be paranoia, but I wasn't interested in taking a chance.

"Sean Willis," the man said. "Thanks."

I nodded, and took three steps and entered the timeless peace of the oracle.

The air was blue-tinged, not with the chill of a rainy winter afternoon, but with a clear light like that of a full moon, if moonlight could be as bright as the sun. Even so, the oracle felt darker than usual, and I couldn't figure out why. I strolled among the shelves, not dawdling, but not in a hurry either, my shoes making quiet taps against the linoleum. Spending time in the oracle always left me relaxed, and I sometimes used my recently developed ability to enter its space without an augury slip to calm myself after a long, demanding day. "I wonder why you let Mr. Briggs keep the temperature so cold, back when I first arrived," I said conversationally. "Do you not feel it the way a human would? And it stank of onion, too. That's a smell you've never used since."

I sometimes wondered about Mr. Briggs, custodian before me, who'd been murdered when he refused to falsify an augury. He'd chosen me as his successor despite my knowing nothing about magic, or the war between humanity and monstrous invaders from another reality, or how to be a custodian of an oracular bookstore, for that matter, and I'd never figured out why. It might be as simple as my apparently innate ability to see through illusions, or as complex as how I'd twice become the oracle to defend the store against attacks. Or it might just have been that Mr. Briggs needed someone who wouldn't ask questions about his blackmail activities. It probably didn't matter, but I didn't like mysteries and I really didn't like mysteries centered on myself. But I had no idea how to solve this one, so mostly I just idly wondered.

Ahead and around a corner, I saw a brighter blue light, like the corona of a star. The augury stood on a shelf in a gap where several books ought to have gone. Juliet's trade-ins were just in time. I walked toward it, my mind already drifting to what I'd make for dinner. Soft tacos, probably. I hated the mess the hard-shelled ones made.

Something was niggling at me, something more than my idle thoughts about Mr. Briggs and soft tacos. I took a few more steps and stopped a couple of feet from the augury. Footsteps. My steps never made noise when I was in the oracle, but the tapping sound had followed me all the way from the front of the store. I experimentally took a few steps in place. *Tap, tap, tap.* That was weird. I backed up and listened to the sound of my shoes on the pale pink linoleum. Weird, in the oracle, was never good.

Pale pink linoleum. Abernathy's floor was yellowish cream.

I dropped to my knees and ran a hand over the floor. It was cool and slightly bumpy to the touch, and very definitely pink. Grit clung to my fingers. I'd swept inside the stacks that morning, but this felt as if it hadn't been cleaned in a few days. This wasn't my floor. I looked around and finally registered what else was different—the bookcases, normally made of yellow 2x8s, were oak, solid and sturdy, making everything look darker by comparison.

I stood and tried to calm my breathing. All right. So the floor and shelves were different. Maybe this was Abernathy's new way of exerting control over itself, the way it produced a new fragrance every day. Maybe it was tired of the gray blisters, and who could blame it? *Or maybe something is seriously wrong.*

I left the augury where it was and walked away, heading for the heart of the oracle. If the oracle needed to communicate with me, it could do so wherever I was—even, as I'd learned six months before, through my dreams. But I always felt most comfortable when I was at its heart, the center of four bookcases facing each other like ancient monoliths. I imagined it let the oracle focus its attention on me, if that's what it was—that sense of being looked at by some entity stranger than I could comprehend.

I rounded a corner that should have led to the center. Three bookcases stood there, aligned sideways to each other, not four forming a square. I turned and went back, taking a different route. Bookcases laden with books surrounded me, mazelike, the smell of dry paper and old leather filling the air. It had smelled like ripe apples only moments before. The new route took me to a dead end, one I'd never seen before. I backtracked and sidled through a narrow gap, brushing up against a couple of oversized gazetteers bound in yellow buckram.

The feather-light touch sent a thrill of fear through me. I was lost inside the oracle.

My hurried steps turned into a run as I took turn after turn, desperately looking for an exit. I felt as if I were trapped on the set of some experimental film, built entirely of books and plywood, hidden cameras recording my increasing terror. Finally, I came back to the same dead end and leaned, panting, against the shelves, not caring that I was getting dust in my hair. I closed my eyes and breathed in the smell of the books. It calmed me somewhat. This was ridiculous. Abernathy's wasn't big enough to get lost in, and I needed to calm down and think rationally. The augury. I'd left it on its shelf, and when I looked up I could see the blue glow a few "rows" over.

I wiped my sweaty palms on my pants and made myself walk slowly through the aisles and around the corner. The augury sat patiently waiting, its blue glow undimmed by my fear. I reached for it slowly, approaching like I might a wounded animal, assuming I were stupid enough to try to touch a wounded animal that might well bite my finger off.

My hand closed around the spine. The blue glow faded, disappeared, and the book tingled with the live-wire buzz of a live augury. The smell of ripe apples brushed my cheeks and nose. I looked down to see the familiar dull yellowy cream and gray blisters of the linoleum. Silence fell over the space where I stood, surrounded by unfinished pine shelves.

I took a deep breath, let it out slowly, and took a few steps. No noise. Swiftly I walked through the aisles, taking familiar turns, until to my relief I stood in the heart of the oracle. The four bookcases, taller than I could reach even with my step stool, towered over me. "So what was that?" I said. "I would swear this place vanished. Is there something wrong? Something I should know about?"

Silence. A ray of sunlight passed between two of the book-cases, high above me. Dust motes floated lazily within it like constellations in an alien sky. I felt nothing, not the terrible pressure of becoming the oracle's body nor the nagging sensation that something was trying to communicate with me. No glowing books floated off the shelves, rearranging themselves to spell out a message.

My neck and shoulders were sore with tension, and I suddenly longed to be home, soaking in a hot bath, maybe with Malcolm rubbing my feet. Maybe it was just tiredness. Maybe I'd overreacted. It could be nothing, but I'd been through a lot with the oracle and I was disinclined to laugh any strange behavior off. I just didn't know what to make of it, and since I was the custodian of Abernathy's, I was the expert I might otherwise consult.

I made my way out of the oracle, not getting turned around even once. This time, as I retraced my steps, my feet were silent. I stopped once and hopped up and down a couple of times, and even that made no noise. I handed the augury to Willis, then had to take it back because in my disquiet I hadn't looked inside to see how much it cost. "$1000," I said. "Judy will write you a receipt."

"*On Wings of Eagles,* huh?" Willis said, turning the book over to read the back cover copy. "I always think it's weird when the oracle produces a book I could easily buy online."

"You could say that about any book these days," I said. "I guess what you're really paying for is the oracle's services in choosing the right book."

"Oh, I hope you didn't take that as a criticism. I appreciate the oracle." Willis took the receipt and handed over a thousand dollars in hundreds. "It's just...weird."

"I understand." I waved goodbye and walked back to the

office, where I put the cash in the bottom drawer of the file cabinet. "And it is weird."

"I don't think it's weird," Judy said. "I mean, technically the oracle could sell the title of the book and make people go to the bookstore for their own copy, right? So this is just making sure people appreciate what they're getting by giving them something tangible. Even if it is a copy of *Harry Potter and the Sorcerer's Stone.*"

"We don't know that's how it works."

"We don't know it isn't."

I sighed. "I guess it doesn't matter." The unsettled feeling wouldn't go away, but I didn't like to tell Judy I'd seen something strange when it might just be me. And when I didn't have any idea what it might mean. How much of this mysterious behavior was down to me being keyed up? Sure, I didn't think I was nervous about the wedding, but maybe I was tense on a level I wasn't aware of. Not that I was trying to explain the mystery away, but it made sense to eliminate the possibility that the strange behavior was all on my side. And *then* I could worry about the other possibility—that the oracle was once again under attack.

2

No one else came in that afternoon. The rain didn't let up. Malcolm texted me to let me know he'd be home late and not to wait dinner on him. I revised my dinner plans to be leftovers rather than cooking just for myself, which I disliked. It wasn't an aversion that made sense, but there it was.

Remembering the gritty feel of the pink linoleum floor, I got out the broom and swept, though it really was unnecessary. As I steered the wide-headed broom around the bookcases, I kept glancing over my shoulder, expecting the shelves to transform between one look and the next. But nothing happened. The distant sound of rain and the swoosh of cars driving past on the wet road made a quiet background to the whisper of the broom on the floor.

From closer to hand, Judy cursed, startling me. "What's wrong?"

"Stupid Wardens are what's wrong," she said, and a moment later came around the corner, brandishing her phone.

"I just got a text from Valerie Dutton saying she won't be at your bachelorette party. She made some feeble excuse about prior commitments, but it's really that she doesn't want to make nice with Ambrosites. It's disgusting."

I leaned on the broom handle. "They all used to get along just fine. I hoped having a common enemy would make a difference."

"It did, for a while." Judy patted her hip as if looking for a place to stuff her phone, but her dress had no pockets. "Don't take this the wrong way, but I'm afraid your wedding might be stirring up tensions."

"I've got friends in both factions. I'm not going to ignore half of them just to keep the other half happy."

"I'm not saying you should. I'm just saying—I don't know. If they can't put their differences aside to celebrate a wedding, what's it going to take? More mass murders of Wardens by the Mercy?"

"Let's hope it doesn't come to that," I said, and took the broom back to the basement.

Judy left at five to have dinner with her father, and I wished I could do the same—leave early, that is, not have dinner with William Rasmussen, who was no friend of mine. But I still had to worry about not giving Timothy Ragsdale, Board of Neutralities member and my own personal millstone, grounds to haul me in front of the Board for failing to uphold my duties. It had been nine months since I'd been penalized for breaking the Accords, but Ragsdale hadn't let up on his campaign to see me punished further. Another three months, and what I thought of as my probation would be over. I tried not to think about how long three months could be.

At five minutes to six I went through the store to lock up. Since I'd moved out, Judy had taken possession of the upstairs apartment, so I no longer had a key to that door, but I checked the others so the store would be secure until Judy returned. I even made sure the keys to the safe deposit boxes hung in their proper place, though no one but I could touch them. Then I sat behind the cash register, stared at its antique keys, and traced the outline of the Victorian lace valentine appliqued to its top.

Judy was right that we didn't need tensions increased. In the six months since the Mercy had made their big push to capture every Neutrality in South America, and attempted to destroy the oracle, they'd completely disappeared. They'd drained the nodes they'd captured and abandoned them, vanishing as completely as if they'd been erased from existence. A few Wardens, primarily conspiracy nuts like Doug Schrote, believed they *had* disappeared, gone off into the reality where the invaders came from, never mind that it wasn't a place humans could survive in. Mostly people thought they were hiding out, regrouping their forces and preparing some new and horrible attack on the Wardens when they'd become complacent. In either case, the Mercy wasn't a present threat.

Unfortunately, that meant the tentative peace that had broken out between Nicolliens and Ambrosites had unraveled, leaving the factions at each other's throats once more. Each side blamed the other for the losses sustained in the fighting against the Mercy, however irrational that was. Lucia had had to crack down hard on factional fighting, and for once I'd been grateful that the Board of Neutralities had altered the Accords to forbid Nicolliens and Ambrosites using a Neutrality at the same time. It angered me that they couldn't set their differences aside. Couldn't they see how they were weakening themselves against the day the Mercy came back?

I realized it was well after six o'clock and locked the front door and turned the sign to CLOSED. Ragsdale would have no grounds for criticizing me today. Then I scraped ice off the windshield of my old but meticulously maintained Honda Civic and headed for home. I was hungry, but even more than food, I wanted that long, hot soak in my enormous tub. I went over the contents of the refrigerator in my head, wondering what leftovers I might re-heat. Malcolm hadn't said why he was going to be late, nor what "late" meant in real time. Maybe I'd eat in bed, watching a movie. After the day I'd had, I was in the mood for dark comedy, maybe *Kind Hearts and Coronets*. Alec Guinness in drag...yes, that would do nicely.

The house was dark when I pulled into the driveway, illuminated only by the antique street lamp in its decorative island in the front lawn and the lights at the side of the garage. I parked the car and hurried inside, away from the wet chill and into the welcoming warmth of my home. I stood inside the mud room without turning on the lights and breathed in deeply, feeling tension drain away with the indefinable smell of home. The giant house never felt overwhelming, possibly because it had seen families grow up in its shelter and was used to wrapping people in comfort. It had been Malcolm's childhood home, and despite the extensive renovation it had gone through before we moved in, I could still picture him as a child running around inside, sliding down the bannisters or making a blanket fort in his bedroom. Sometimes, when I was feeling sentimental, I imagined Malcolm's and my children doing the same. That was years in the future, but it was fun to pretend.

I flipped on the light switch and kicked off my shoes, then walked down the short corridor to the kitchen. It felt like my domain now, even with Ingrid sharing the space. She'd left me a note—*roast in fridge, bought more rice*—rather than texting me. I liked seeing her handwriting. It made her seem more real.

Somewhere during my drive, hunger had won the battle over fatigue. I rooted around in the refrigerator and came up with a container of baked ziti, heavy on the cheese, and a bottle of beer. While I watched the plate go round and round inside the microwave, I peeled off my stockings, standing on one foot at a time like a flamingo, and wadded them up and stuffed them in my pocket. Bathing could wait. The smell of tomato sauce and melted mozzarella made my stomach rumble loudly.

I carried my meal upstairs to the bedroom and put it on my bedside table, then shucked my clothes and got into stretchy pants and a ratty T-shirt I was sure Malcolm wished I'd get rid of. It was decidedly unsexy, I knew, but soft and comfortable, and it wasn't like he was home. I took a moment to lie back on the wonderful bed, one of the few pieces of furniture we'd kept from Malcolm's old apartment, then turned on the television and settled in to watch and eat.

After about half an hour, when the food was gone and I was trying to get up the resolve to move to the bathtub, I heard the back door open. Voices—*voices?*—drifted up the stairwell, indistinguishable as more than a masculine hum. I paused the movie and called out, "Malcolm?"

"We're here," Malcolm replied. *We? Who is "we"?* Had he brought his team home? I suddenly wished I'd chosen a different T-shirt. Quickly I rooted through my dresser, looking for an alternative.

I heard someone coming up the stairs. "There you are," Malcolm said, "I was—oh." He'd caught me with my shirt off, midway to changing into something nicer. "Well," he went on, coming forward to put his arms around me, "I almost regret that we're not alone in the house."

"Who did you bring home?"

Malcolm released me so I could put on my new shirt. "You forgot."

"Did I? Forgot what?" Memory slapped me upside the head. "Oh, is that *tonight?* I didn't forget, exactly—no, it's all right, but I'm so glad I cleaned yesterday!"

"Come downstairs and meet him," Malcolm said, taking my hand.

A sturdy-looking man with sandy blond hair cut military short sat on one of the couches in our living room, a duffel bag at his feet. He stood as we came down the stairs, smiling pleasantly. "Mike, I'd like you to meet Helena," Malcolm said. "Helena, this is Mike Conti."

"I'm so pleased to finally meet you," I said, extending a hand. "Malcolm's told so many stories about you, I wanted to hear your side."

Mike Conti grinned and clasped my hand firmly and not too hard. "Don't believe his version?"

"He just won't tell stories about himself."

"Don't you dare," Malcolm said.

"Hey, you wouldn't want me to disrespect my hostess's wishes, would you?"

"Do I need to remind you about Antwerp?"

Mike groaned. "Low blow, Mal."

"What happened in Antwerp?" I asked.

Malcolm glanced at me. "Ah…possibly that is not a story that makes either of us look good."

"I'm sure I can come up with something," Mike said. "You're sure you don't mind putting me up? I really can go to a hotel if you're too swamped with wedding plans."

"You're our first house guest, and I'm so glad we have room for you," I said. "It's really no trouble."

"I can't believe you agreed to it. Aren't brides supposed to be completely insane at this point? And you're willing to play hostess to a total stranger."

I smiled. "My wedding planner is amazing. And I guess all the plans are at such a distance, they don't feel urgent. Maybe *Deanna* is insane by now."

Malcolm put his arm around me. "She seems calm enough to me. At least, she was patient when we were choosing the cake. And the invitations. And the venue. And the hundred other things that went into the wedding preparations."

I sighed and leaned into him. "Promise me we'll never have to get married again?"

Malcolm smiled and put his hand over mine briefly. "Promise."

"Well, I'll try not to be underfoot too much. I'd like to visit Abernathy's tomorrow some time, if you don't mind," Mike said.

"Of course not. Though there's not much to see."

"You're likely to be bored until the wedding," Malcolm said. "I'm sorry I can't take time off to show you around."

"I'm good at entertaining myself," Mike said, which sent both men off into gales of laughter. I tried not to feel annoyed at being left out of the joke. Mike was Malcolm's best friend, a paper magus and a former Navy SEAL from his unit, or what-ever they called SEAL teams, and they had a long shared history I had no need to be jealous of. It just reminded me that Malcolm and I had only known each other a little over two years and didn't have nearly so many stories to laugh over. Well, that was the point of getting married, you planned to spend a lifetime together creating those kinds of stories.

"What was her name? Brigitte? Betty?" Malcolm said.

"Bethany," Mike said, "and believe it or not, she sent me a wedding announcement a year ago."

"I'm guessing she did not tell her fiancé about you."

"Probably not."

"Did you eat?" I said, hoping it didn't sound too abrupt. "There's lots of leftovers—I didn't want to cook just for myself—"

"We stopped on the way from the airport," Malcolm said. "Mike, let me show you your room."

I let Malcolm lead the way and trailed behind the men, down the hall to the guest suite. When the house was remodeled, I'd discovered in myself a hidden love of interior decorating, and had enjoyed creating different looks for different rooms. The guest suite was warm with mahogany and mulberry curtains coordinating with the pale gray walls, the large bed making a nice contrast with its creamy white bedding and pillows. A little table and a plump, well-padded chair stood in one corner, opposite the sliding door that let out on the back patio. The bathroom door stood ajar, and I hurried over and turned on the light so he could see it better.

Mike set his bag on the bed and whistled, low and appreciative. "This is much nicer than a hotel."

"There's towels in the cabinet over the toilet," I said, conscious of my hostess's duties, "and an extra blanket in the top of the closet if you need it, and…I can't think of anything else."

"That's more than enough. Thanks."

"Well, if you need anything, just ask." I squeezed Malcolm's hand. "I was going to take a bath, unless you wanted to do something?"

"We have some catching up to do," Malcolm said, "and I

intend to take Mike on the hunt with me. I hope you don't feel abandoned."

His saying that reminded me of what had happened at Abernathy's that day. Much as I wanted to share my fears with him, this wasn't the right time. "Of course not. Good luck." I kissed Malcolm, waved to Mike, and retreated to my bedroom.

I turned the movie back on while I waited for the big tub to fill. *Kind Hearts and Coronets* wasn't usually my favorite, because I couldn't help wishing Louis didn't have to kill Henry D'Ascoyne—he was such a good-natured guy. But black comedy had its own rules, and by the time the tub was full, I was caught up in the story again. I paused the movie and stepped into the deep tub, sinking in until the water reached my chin. I'd become addicted to hot baths during my time living in the apartment over Abernathy's, and my enormous garden tub was one of my favorite luxuries. I rested my feet on the opposite rim so my toes stuck out, chilly by contrast, and closed my eyes. Perfect.

But I couldn't relax. Now that nothing else demanded my attention, my memory of being lost in the stacks resurfaced. I'd been Abernathy's custodian for over two years, I knew the store as well as anyone could, and yet I'd seen corridors and shelves that hadn't been there yesterday. Weren't there now, since the store seemed to have gone back to normal. I wasn't stupid enough to assume that meant the problem was gone.

Unfortunately, I had no idea what to do next. If this… transformation…meant some new disaster unfolding, I didn't dare wait to see how it played out. But I didn't have a clue where to start asking questions. I didn't even know what to call it, so using the Athenaeum would be difficult. Not for the first time, I wished I could call on Abernathy's other custodians, or at least their recorded knowledge. But while most of them had kept journals, their ideas of what constituted important information about the oracle varied wildly, and as far as I knew, none of them had ever faced a problem like this one.

I sighed, and submerged entirely, then opened my eyes to look at the watery world around me. Their records would still have to be the first thing I checked, and then…I didn't know what "then" would be, but I'd come up with something. And hope nothing catastrophic happened in the meantime.

3

Sunlight, weak and watery but still bright in the clear, cloudless sky, made the street outside Abernathy's gleam like late March instead of mid-January. I withdrew a creamy sheet of thick paper from its envelope and unfolded it. *Where is Miranda Velasco?* "Is it just me, or have there been a lot of 'where' augury requests lately?"

"I wouldn't know, I haven't been reading them," Judy said absently. Her finger swiped across the screen of the cheap little tablet she'd brought in from Best Buy this morning. "Wow, some of these custodians were seriously long-winded."

"I downloaded all the custodian diaries the Athenaeum had stored, and it turned out to be a lot. At least someone transcribed Elizabeth Abernathy's diary from the handwritten original so it's searchable now. I tried reading her handwriting and just got confused."

"Nobody learns handwriting anymore. I wonder how long it will be before cursive is obsolete?" Judy swiped again. "I haven't found anything by searching for 'transform.'"

"I don't expect to find much of anything, but we have to try." Holding the paper two-handed in front of my chest like a shield, I walked into the oracle.

The cool blue light soothed my nerves, as did the sight of the worn yellow linoleum. I'd done five auguries since the one yesterday where I'd gotten lost, and none of them had been strange in any way. I still felt keyed up, jumpy and prepared for the worst. "I'd like to think you'd warn me if something were wrong," I said, searching for the bright blue glow of the augury, "but suppose whatever is wrong affects your ability to communicate, the way those illusions did? And if this is a new attack by the Mercy…" I couldn't think of a way to end that sentence, and let it die away.

The augury was a battered copy of *To the Lighthouse* that looked as if it had been someone's college textbook, judging by the notes scribbled in the margins. I flipped through it idly, wondering if the answer to the question would be found in those marginalia rather than the text. That would be one instance where the physical book mattered. I folded the paper, tucked it between the book's pages, and took the long way back to the front of the store, daring Abernathy's to change as I walked. Nothing happened.

The store front was crowded when I emerged. Ten o'clock, opening time and start of the Nicollien morning rush. I set *To the Lighthouse* on the counter and greeted the first person in line. "Such a pretty day," I said.

"I suppose," the man said with a shrug. "I'm off to Hawaii in a few days. Can't wait to escape this place."

"That sounds wonderful." The idea of a trip appealed to me, but I was tethered to Abernathy's and a trip anywhere more than a day's travel away was impossible. It was the one thing I regretted about our wedding plans, that I couldn't have a real honeymoon. I'd never been to Hawaii and the idea of spending a week on the beaches was lovely. I tried not to think too hard about what I couldn't have. We'd have our wedding night in the honeymoon suite of the Hotel Warwick, and that would be more than enough.

I glanced over his augury request—*How should I promote my business?*—nodded, and walked into the oracle.

This time, alert to any possible changes, I immediately knew something was wrong. Once again the sound of my footsteps rang out on the pale pink linoleum. I folded the augury request and put it in my pocket, not moving from the spot, listening, sniffing, and staring at the shelves. The place, whatever it was, smelled of old books and dust, not freesias as Abernathy's had smelled when I entered that morning. The bookcases were different again, too. Abernathy's bookcases, most of them, were little more than yellow 2x8s slapped together with plywood backs. Now they were solid maple or oak, deeper than the ones I was used to and more solid.

I took a few steps and examined the contents of the nearest shelf. The books were all hardbound, about half of them in worn leather, not a single Tom Clancy paperback in sight. I touched one, ran my finger along its spine; it came away grimy. So whatever, or wherever, this was, it was old and not very well cared for.

I walked through the corridors, which were as haphazard as I was used to, exploring the place. My footsteps tapping across the floor disturbed the silence not at all. The lack of noise felt almost tangible, pressing on my ears the way a really loud rock concert might, but in the opposite direction. Abernathy's was always as silent, but the silence was companionable, like the oracle was aware of me and simply chose not to speak. This silence unnerved me.

Ahead, I saw the blue glow of an augury. When I'd prepared myself for this to happen again, I'd resolved not to take it immediately, wanting to explore further, but the sight comforted me so much I realized how on edge the place had made me. I hurried around the corner and took the book off the shelf. At least that was normal; the blue glow faded, replaced by the electric tingle of a live augury. The title was *This Side of Paradise*, imprinted on the spine in gold letters, some of which were chipped away so it read *Ths Sid of aradse*. I checked inside the front cover: *Barry Henderson, $2500*. I'd forgot to ask the man's name, but my more pressing concern was—how did I find my way out?

I tried not to dwell on my earlier notion that this was a movie set, with hidden cameras tracking my movements and recording my fear. Forcing myself to breathe normally, I set out through the stacks, hoping I wasn't just making myself more lost. It was eerie, familiar and yet strange, and I clung to the augury with cold, aching fingers, praying this wasn't a permanent change.

Between one step and the next, the bookcases shuddered. I had my eyes on one as if taking a bearing in the woods and therefore saw it change from dark oak to yellow pine. I stopped, closed my eyes, and let out a long, thin stream of breath. The faint smell of freesias drifted past me. "So what was that?" I said, not opening my eyes. "Did I go somewhere else? It feels like it, but where? And why?"

I strained to hear a response, though I doubted it could be that simple. I heard nothing but quiet, not the deep silence of the oracle but the more usual stillness of the bookstore, the distant sound of cars rushing past and a low murmur of people talking. I opened my eyes. "I think," I said, "if this were a serious danger, you'd warn me. At least that's what I assume from what happened when the Mercy tried to destroy you. But maybe that's not a safe assumption."

I made my way to the front of the store and handed the augury to the customer. "$2500," I said. "Judy will write you a receipt. I'll be right back."

I left Judy giving me a curious look and trotted back to the office, where I found a legal pad and a plastic ballpoint pen in the drawers of the desk. At the top of the first page, I wrote *Barry Henderson—How should I promote my business—This Side of Paradise*, then, after some reflection, the book's author, F. Scott Fitzgerald. Maybe the augury questions were what triggered the bookstore's transformation, or whatever it was. Normally we didn't keep track of all that information due to privacy concerns, but I'd been through too many threats to the oracle to quibble over that now.

When I returned, Henderson was gone. Judy said, "Something I need to know?"

"I'll explain later," I said, accepting the next augury slip.

Abernathy's didn't misbehave once the rest of the morning. Around 12:45, when the throngs vanished, I said, "It happened again. Just the once, but it was unsettling. I wrote down the question and the augury, just in case."

"That was smart," Judy said. "I don't suppose you remember the other one?"

"No. I was too rattled."

"Well, let's eat, and then...I don't know what else to do." Judy shook her head. "There has to be some explanation. I'll keep searching the custodian diaries."

"Thanks. I guess I'll finish these mail-in auguries." There were three left from the morning's mail. "I don't know whether or not to hope it happens again."

"You're getting married in less than two weeks. You'd better hope it stops happening," Judy said.

The bells over the door jangled. "I guess it's too much to hope this weather holds out," Viv said, unwrapping a long multicolored scarf from around her neck. "I have a feeling it's going to storm on Friday."

"Everything is happening indoors. It doesn't matter if it storms," Judy pointed out.

"Way to be rational," Viv said. "Anyway, I came to get the —" She glanced at me, then loudly whispered behind her hand, "The *you-know-what.*"

I rolled my eyes. "I don't know why you bother. I don't get excited about surprises."

"Well, I do, and it's my party."

"It's *my* bachelorette party, Viv."

"Judy and I are hosting it, that makes it ours."

"I left it in my car," Judy said. "You can pull around back and Helena never has to see it."

"Please tell me it's not an inflatable sex doll," I said.

"As if," Viv said. "No booze, no sex toys, no strippers. The last two aren't any fun without the first, anyway."

"*I* wanted strippers," Judy said. "I have to live vicariously through the two of you now I'm single again."

"Why don't you pick up lunch, so long as you're going to the car," I said. "I've got these auguries to do, but I'm getting hungry."

But when Viv and Judy had gone, I stood behind the counter, shuffling the three augury requests and pondering the oracle's mysterious behavior. If I couldn't find an answer in the custodian diaries, I wasn't sure where else to look. It still produced correct auguries, that was something, but could I count on that lasting? I didn't want to make assumptions.

The oracle stayed normal for all three auguries, at which point Judy and Viv reappeared, toting paper bags full of cheeseburgers. Viv handed me a large fountain drink and said, "Sorry that took so long. We took care of a few other things on the way."

I took a long pull on my Diet Coke. "Well, I'm starving and it's nearly the Ambrosites' time."

"You'll thank us later," Judy said, smirking.

Outside, a queue was forming. I saw a familiar face and set my drink on the counter. "Be right back."

Mike Conti stood peering through the plate glass window, dressed casually in jeans and a forest green T-shirt with no logo under his leather bomber jacket. "Hi, Helena," he said. "Is it okay if I come in if I don't need an augury?"

"Sure. People come in to chat all the time. Sorry I can't let you in early, but—"

"I don't want any special favors. It's fine." He seemed not to notice that the other Wardens in line were eyeing him speculatively.

"Okay, good, that's…good. We open in five minutes." I went back into the store and tore into my cheeseburger. One of these days I'd have time to eat my lunch without Wardens breathing down my neck.

"Who's that?" Viv asked.

"Mike Conti. Malcolm's best man. He's staying with us for the wedding."

"That's presumptuous," Judy said, scowling. "You're going to be way too busy to play hostess."

"I don't mind. It was my idea, actually." I wiped my mouth and took another big drink.

"Even so." Judy gathered up napkins and cheeseburger

wrappers and stuffed them into a bag. "I hope he doesn't expect to be entertained."

"I doubt it. He and Malcolm went on the hunt last night, but he said he'd find stuff to do on his own until the wedding." I walked over to the door and opened it, greeting the first woman in line.

Mike didn't line up with the others, just wandered around looking at the shelves. It made me almost as nervous as if he'd been Ragsdale monitoring my adherence to the Accords, though I was sure he wasn't judging me. I tried to stay focused on the auguries. Only once did I enter the strange other space, and I hadn't even retrieved the augury before the shelves shuddered back into what I now thought of as normality. As before, the oracle seemed not to care which reality was active, producing an augury whose glow didn't falter even as the world shifted. I wrote down the title—*The Opposite of Fate*, by Amy Tan—but couldn't see any relation to the first book. Well, two wasn't enough to come to any conclusions.

When I finally emerged with the afternoon's last augury, Mike was still there, reading a book he'd taken off a shelf. Viv perched on the stool behind the counter, fiddling with the cash register. Judy stood next to the last customer, though they weren't speaking—right, it was Gideon Randle, an Ambrosite high in Ryan Parish's organization and a long-time enemy of Judy's father William Rasmussen, head of the Nicolliens in the Pacific Northwest. Judy was as neutral as I was, but she'd grown up in a Nicollien household and there were Ambrosites who couldn't get past that.

"$3750, Mr. Randle," I said, offering him the encyclopedia of North American birds the oracle had produced for him. "Judy will write your receipt. Please excuse me."

Mike looked up as I approached. "Busy day?" he asked.

"No more than usual. Are you bored yet?"

He waved the book at me. "I wouldn't want to shop here for real, but for serendipity you can't beat this place."

"That's how it works, yeah. Let me introduce you to my friends."

Mike shook hands with Viv and Judy when I made introductions. "Mike, how long have you known Malcolm?"

"Since high school," Mike said, "and then we went to college together, then there was the Navy...we just kept falling into each other's orbit. Though we don't see each other often nowadays. Before yesterday, I hadn't seen him for over a year. Not since he was in hiding."

"Oh, did he go to you?"

Mike shrugged. "For a couple of nights. We hunted together. He didn't mention you, though."

"We were still a secret back then." It felt like ages ago instead of more than a year.

"I can imagine. News that the Accords had changed rocked Chicago. You weren't the only ones who'd been keeping your relationship secret, by the way. One of the prominent neutral magi at the Barrington Node turned out to have been dating a Nicollien. Stockwell fired him immediately, of course."

"Why 'of course'?" Viv asked.

Mike's pleasant expression gave way to a frown. "Keeping secrets like that can be deadly. Damned Nicolliens take advantage of that, too."

"Excuse me?" Judy said, her voice icy.

He didn't hear the warning in her voice. "He was accused of slipping confidential information to his girlfriend, who was using it to give the Nicolliens an unfair advantage on the hunt. Typical."

"Hunting isn't a game," Judy said. "It's not like you're scored on how many invaders you destroy, or how often."

Mike waved a dismissive hand. "We all know who's most successful. There's nothing wrong with that. It's those familiars that make the hunt so lopsided. Invaders should be destroyed outright, but these Nicolliens—and after what happened a year ago—"

"The Nicolliens fixed that problem with the harnesses," Judy cut across his words. It surprised me to hear her say that, given that she was more in favor of destroying all familiars than I was.

"Doesn't change the fact that they were responsible for the problem in the first place." Mike took a step toward Judy. He wasn't very tall, but he was still taller than her petite frame, and he loomed over her.

"My father," Judy said, "is William Rasmussen." She stood her ground, not even a little bit intimidated.

Mike's eyebrows went up. "And you're working *here?*"

"Judy's neutral," I said, "but she understands Nicolliens better than any of us." I hoped he'd take the warning.

He didn't. "Don't bother defending them to me," he told Judy. "It was Nicollien stupidity and vindictiveness that sent Malcolm into hiding for months. If they didn't want revenge for Amber Guittard's death—"

"Ambrosites would have done the same," Judy retorted.

"Not without better reason than that."

"If you—"

"*Judy,*" Viv said, "I need to talk to you about the party. In the office, maybe?" She hopped off the stool, grabbed Judy's upper arm, and towed her away toward the back of the store. I let out what I hoped was an unobtrusive breath of relief.

Mike shook his head. "I'm sorry. I shouldn't have started a fight."

"We try to make Abernathy's neutral ground, even if we have to divide its time between the factions," I said. "I agree with you that Nicollien hatred kept Malcolm away from home for several months, but not every Nicollien wanted his head. It's that kind of thinking that weakens all the Wardens."

Mike shrugged. "Maybe. I've never known a Nicollien I could respect."

"Then I'll introduce you to the Kellers, and you won't be able to say that anymore."

I showed him the basement, filled with its wooden file cabinets and the safe deposit boxes, pointed out the office but didn't enter it, and led him back to the front door. "I told you it was boring."

"It's weird, thinking of what comes out of this place, and how little it looks like an oracle." He smiled. "Look, can I take you and Mal out for dinner tonight? To say thanks for putting me up?"

"Um...sure, that would be fun! Why don't you work out the details with Malcolm? I'm sure he can suggest a good restaurant."

"I'll see you tonight, then." With a wave, he left the store.

I walked back to the office. "He's gone."

"Good riddance," Judy snarled.

"I hoped you'd have calmed down by now."

"That *is* calm," Viv said. "You weren't here for the swearing."

I shook my head, feeling exasperated. "Judy, you know how most faction members think. And Chicago has more reason than most—they actually had a war in the streets between the factions only about twenty-five years ago."

"Malcolm's more sensible than that, and I thought his friends would be the same." Judy sighed and slumped against the desk. "I can't believe I'm saying that about Malcolm Campbell. Two years ago I detested him as much as any Ambro—" She closed her eyes. "And now I'm doing it."

"It's hard to break an old habit," I said, "and I'm going to introduce Mike to Harry and Harriet and open his mind a little."

"Well, I plan to stay as far away from Mike Conti as I can," Judy said, "in the interests of keeping harmony in the bridal party."

"Um," I said.

Judy eyed me. "Um, what?"

"I think…you may be partnered with him. In fact, I'm pretty sure you are. The height thing, you know. Viv and Ewan, Cynthia and Derrick, you and…"

Judy swore again. "He's still six inches taller than me. Make Viv be his partner."

"Come on, you can be polite for the space of a walk down the aisle," Viv said.

"Of course I can." Judy scowled. "But I won't dance with him."

"I wouldn't make you," I assured her.

4

I climbed the long ladder leading from the Athenaeum, carefully not looking down. I wasn't afraid of heights—much—but the tall, narrow chimney made me feel claustrophobic despite how brightly lit it was. I wondered, not for the first time, how very large people got in and out. And how long ago the access point had been built. It always reminded me of the set of a cheesy '70s science fiction movie, but maybe it was newer than that and someone had just been nostalgic.

Guille, the technician, held the trap door open for me as I emerged. "You find what you were looking for?"

"No, but I think it's just that I don't know the right questions to ask," I said with a sigh. "Thanks again."

"No problem." Guille walked with me to the front door, past a couple of browsing customers. They might have been ordinary people who'd come in to what looked like a florist's shop. I certainly didn't recognize them, but I didn't know more than a fraction of the magi in the Pacific Northwest despite my position.

Unusually, Guille followed me out of the store and closed the door behind us. The chill wind ruffled my scarf, and I tucked my hands into my coat pockets. Guille stood as if the wind didn't touch him. "If it's not confidential business," he said, "you could maybe hire someone to do the research for you. There are plenty of Wardens who do that. They charge for their services, obviously, but they're experts. Might be something to look into."

"Thanks, Guille, that's a good idea." I hunched my shoulders against the cold. "Where could I find them?"

"Ask anyone at the Gunther Node, they'll tell you." Guille nodded at me and ducked back inside.

I trudged off toward my car, parked a few streets over. It looked like it was coming on to rain again, or, as cold as it was, maybe snow. I wasn't sure which to wish for. Snow would be pretty, but harder to drive in. Rainwater runoff trickled down the gutters I skipped over, wishing I'd worn more sensible shoes. For the briefest moment, I wished I'd planned my wedding for June like a normal person.

Safely in my car, I headed east toward Abernathy's. Could I hire a researcher? All right, that was a stupid question, of course I could. The real question was, would a researcher have any more success than I had if I was barely able to articulate what was going on? Since the truth was I didn't know what was going on. Maybe a fresh perspective, a new pair of eyes, was what I needed, even if the information I had to start with was thin.

A familiar little white van was parked in Abernathy's magically reserved parking space as I drove past on my way around to the lot behind the building. I caught a glimpse of Dave Henry sitting in the driver's seat. Lucia must have some particularly confidential request this morning, and an urgent one if she was sending him to the store well before opening hours.

Judy hadn't come downstairs yet, so I walked through the store and opened the front door. It was 9:33, but even Ragsdale couldn't criticize me for favoritism if it was another Neutrality that needed help. I crossed the sidewalk to the van and said, "Oh! Lucia!"

"You sure take your sweet time," Lucia said. Dave shut off the van and the two of them got out.

"You could have texted Judy to let you in."

"I didn't feel like loitering in the store. And I have an augury request, so it's not like Rasmussen could help me." Lucia strode ahead of me and opened the store's front door with the same forceful energy with which she did everything. I trotted after her, trying not to feel annoyed. It wasn't like Lucia was going to change, ever.

"Three augury requests," she said, waving at Dave, who carried a familiar briefcase. He pulled some folded papers out of his jeans pocket and handed them over.

I glanced at each. *Where is Everett Stratemeyer?*
Where is Gloria Slocum?
Where is Peter Pritchard?

"I sense a theme," I said.

Lucia smiled, a thin little twist of the lips that didn't look very amused. "All three of them have disappeared in the last eight days," she said. "Two of them mine, one an Ambrosite. None of them are the type to go haring off without a word to anyone. Stratemeyer in particular has a work ethic that makes you look like Beetle Bailey. I've had my people searching, but no luck."

I wished I dared ask who Beetle Bailey was. "The oracle is

good about helping find people. If they're in danger—you don't think this is the Mercy, do you?"

"I don't know what to think. Those disappearances back when the Mercy first was outed were mostly men and women fleeing justice. If they've started kidnapping people…" Lucia shook her head. "The only thing they have in common is they're all glass magi."

"So…what does that mean? Someone wants to locate something? Can a magus be compelled to do magic?"

"As well as anyone can be compelled to do anything, which is to say all people have their breaking point. It disturbs me."

"Me, too." I took up the slip with Gloria Slocum's name on it. "I hope this is useful."

None of the auguries took me to the other place, for which I was grateful. All of them were for less than $100. That was less encouraging. Usually if an augury for a missing person was that cheap, it meant the oracle believed the person was in danger. When I brought out the third book, *A Troubled Peace,* and handed it to Lucia, she said, "This better mean these are easy to interpret. Pritchard's been missing for seven days already. The longer that goes on…"

"I'm sure they'll help," I said.

Dave handed over a couple of bills. "I guess we didn't need the briefcase, after all."

I wrote up their receipts, wondering where Judy was. It was almost ten o'clock, and the Nicolliens were lining up outside. "I had a question, as long as you're here?"

"Shoot," Lucia said.

"If I had something I needed to research, but didn't have time to do it myself, who would I talk to? Guille said you'd know."

"Depends on the topic. What's the question?"

I quickly summed up what I'd observed the oracle doing, ending with, "I'm not even sure what questions to ask. But I need to figure this out quickly."

Lucia nodded as if in thought. "You definitely need an expert. I'd start by calling Kenneth Gibbons at Meryford University. He's a non-magus Warden who's involved in updating the Athenaeum. He knows more about the history of the named Neutralities than anyone else alive. Wrote the book on the Labyrinth, for one. If the oracle is tapping into some other place, he might know where that place is. Might even know why it's happening."

I made a note to myself on my phone. "Kenneth Gibbons. Thanks."

"Let's hope you have better luck than we have," Lucia said darkly, and let herself and Dave out.

It was 9:55 and still no sign of Judy. I ran for the office, intending to go upstairs and pound on her door, but she was seated at the computer, typing furiously. "Where have you been?" I demanded.

"Got a late start. Sorry." She pushed away from the computer and stood.

"What were you doing?"

"Personal stuff." She brushed past me and left the office. I followed her, though for a moment I thought about calling up whatever she'd been working on—but that would be tacky, plus I didn't know how to figure out what app she'd closed down.

It felt as if a city's worth of Wardens was trying to beat the storm, because the store was more than usually thronged with people wanting auguries. Two of them took me to the strange alternate version of Abernathy's, which looked even grimier than it had before. The books it chose still didn't tell me anything. I hurried out of there as quickly as I could.

I finished the last of the augury requests by 1:30 and slumped against the front counter, rolling the tension out of my shoulders. I hadn't even started on the mail-in requests. The day was looking grimmer every minute.

Judy emerged from the back with a steaming plate. "You look like you could use this," she said. I sniffed. Beef stroganoff. One of the things I was best at cooking, and it reheated well.

"*Thank you,*" I said, and fell to eating.

"So I was talking to a friend who lives in Chicago," Judy said, a little too casually.

"Oh?" I mumbled around a mouthful of noodles and sauce.

"And she had some things to say about Conti."

"Oh." That didn't sound good.

"He's been bouncing around teams for the last two years, never sticks with any of them more than a few weeks. He's got a reputation for being sloppy."

"That can't be true. He's a former Navy SEAL, Judy, they don't let their people be sloppy."

Judy shrugged. "I'm just saying what Em told me. She heard he got someone killed."

I gasped. "That *really* can't be true. Malcolm would definitely have mentioned that."

"If he knew. Conti said they hadn't seen each other for a while."

"Judy, do you have a point with all this?"

Judy's face was pinker than usual, and she had the intent

look she got when she felt like arguing. "I'm just saying maybe you shouldn't let him get too close."

"Malcolm trusts him. That's enough for me." Though now I was wondering if there were any way to bring the subject up with Malcolm. "Is Em a Nicollien?"

Judy's pink cheeks reddened. "Well…yes."

"So she might be biased. Or at the very least have the wrong perspective." I took another bite of stroganoff, but it had lost its appeal.

"She says even the Ambrosites talk about it. He used to be a top hunter, but things have changed."

"It has nothing to do with us, or with my wedding. And if he *is* untrustworthy, he'll be gone in a week or so and we don't have to worry about it." I finished my stroganoff and headed for the break room. "I need to make a call. I'll be back before two."

I rinsed my plate and fork and set them aside to dry, then went to the office and settled in the chair behind the desk and did a search. Meryford University…it was in Virginia. Three hours' time difference, but he might still be at his office. I did a search on the faculty directory. Gibbons was a history professor, Dr. Gibbons with a Ph.D who'd been at the university for many years. I dialed his number and, unfortunately, got his voicemail. "This is Helena Davies at Abernathy's Bookstore," I said when it beeped. "I have some questions about…about the store's history, and Lucia Pontarelli thought you might be able to help. Please call me at this number." I recited my phone number, said, "Thanks," and disconnected.

I sat and stared at my phone's screen until it went black. It felt like progress, but at the same time I felt more worried than ever. I thought about it for a while and traced the source of my disquiet to what Judy had said about Mike Conti. Her description didn't sound anything like the man I was coming to know. Last night's dinner had been fun, and I hadn't minded at all when Mike and Malcolm started swapping stories. But now that I thought about it, they were all stories about the distant past. Malcolm had talked a little about things that had happened when he was on the run, but Mike hadn't said word one about his recent life.

Maybe I was overreacting. Okay, *probably* I was overreacting. I trusted Malcolm's judgment, and this was his best friend. He wouldn't continue to support someone who'd done something seriously wrong. But I had to wonder about the possibility that Mike's actions, or maybe inaction, had gotten someone killed. You didn't have to stop being someone's friend for a moment of carelessness, but you certainly couldn't trust them fully anymore.

I pushed back the chair and rose, stuffing my phone into my back pocket. This was all ridiculous. I wasn't going to judge Mike based on second-second-hand information from someone who might well be inclined to think the worst of him.

There weren't as many Ambrosites that afternoon as there'd been Nicolliens that morning, and by 5:30 I'd finished not only filling their requests, but almost all the mail-in auguries as well. "This is one of those days where it feels like I've run a marathon," I told Judy when I emerged from the oracle the second to the last time.

"Is it because of the weird auguries?" She was twirling the broom, spinning it so its heavy, long head made a circle against the linoleum.

"I don't think so. It's not like when the oracle was under that illusion, and it felt like slogging through mud to produce each augury. This is just normal tiredness. I didn't keep track of how many auguries I did today, but it must be nearly a hundred. I'm looking forward to an early bedtime."

My phone rang. I checked the display. "I have to take this," I said, and, "Hello?"

"Is this Ms. Davies?"

"Yes. Dr. Gibbons?"

"This is Ken Gibbons, yes." He had a melodious voice, not what I expected of a history professor. Not that history professors had to sound a certain way.

"Thanks for returning my call."

"Not at all. Is there something I can do for you? Or for Abernathy's?"

I leaned against the counter. "I hope so. Lucia said you knew everything there was to know about the named Neutralities."

He laughed, a rich, ringing sound that made me smile. "I'm not sure we'll ever know *everything* about them, but I have made it my life's study, yes."

"How do you make that work with your, um, mundane career? Don't you have to publish or perish? You wouldn't be able to make most of what you know public."

Gibbons cleared his throat. "My specialty is the history of sacred places. I conceal my research about places like the Sanctuary and the Labyrinth in the more mundane, as you say, study of the ways in which sacred space developed over the years. There's some overlap with anthropological research, of course, but for the most part I've been able to maintain my cover without any difficulty."

"So do you consider Abernathy's sacred?" It was a new concept for me. I didn't know much about religion, and the idea that it might be holy—that I might be stumbling around not being properly respectful—made me nervous.

Gibbons chuckled. "Not in the strict sense of being consecrated to deity, no. But in the more general sense of being set apart to a purpose higher than the quotidian, the named Neutralities function as sacred spaces. But that's not what you wanted to ask me, I'm sure."

"It's fascinating, but no, I have a problem I was hoping you could help me with." Once again I summed up what I'd experienced and seen and even smelled, straining to recall even the smallest details that might be helpful. "Has this ever happened before? Does it happen to the other named Neutralities? I don't even know where to begin."

There was a pause, then Gibbons said, "I'd...have to do some digging. I'd rather not mislead you by guessing, and anything I told you now would be a guess. I can tell you that no one's ever reported experiencing anything like that before."

I tried not to feel discouraged. What were the odds, after all, that Gibbons would know the answer right away? "I've read the custodian diaries, the ones in the Athenaeum. None of them said anything about it either."

"I have access to some records that aren't in the Athenaeum. I'll check those. Give me a few days, and I'll let you know what I find."

"I don't want to put you to any trouble." I did, really, but I wasn't going to be selfish out loud.

"It's my life's passion, my dear, it's no trouble. I might even get a paper out of it." He chuckled. "I can assure you the oracle is in no danger, but you should be careful nonetheless. If you're entering some other space, or some other time—"

"*Time travel?*"

"I'm sorry. I told you I could only guess. But that's a possibility."

I thought of the old books, the grimy bindings, and the elegant bookcases. "It makes sense."

"It's still just a guess. I promise to call you when I can be more certain."

"Thanks, Dr. Gibbons."

"Please, call me Ken."

We exchanged a few more pleasantries, then I disconnected. Judy, who'd been waiting nearby, said, "Time travel?"

"He said that was a guess. But…could you imagine it? What if I went back to Silas's time? What if I could talk to him?"

"I thought time travel was impossible." Judy leaned the broom against the wall and dusted off her hands.

"Is it one of those things magic can't do, like mind control?"

"I don't know. I think, if it were possible, people would do it all the time."

"Suppose it's only possible under certain circumstances? If we could figure out what makes the difference, what triggers the effect—"

Judy shook her head. "It would be pretty limited. A one-way passage back in time."

"Even just a one-way passage would be amazing." I picked up the last of the mail-in augury requests. "I wish I weren't so afraid of the consequences of Mr. Ragsdale finding me disregarding the Accords, because I want to go home early. Though this new idea has me too excited to be tired."

"Don't get too excited," Judy warned. "Isn't it more likely Abernathy's is connecting to some other place?"

"Yeah, but what place? Where else would it go?"

"I don't know." Judy picked up the broom. "I'm going to start tidying up."

As if in response to my excitement, the final augury of the day took me into the other place. I paused to smell the books and run my fingers across one of the shelves, then regretted it when my hand came away dirty. "Can you hear me?" I whispered. "Are you still there?"

Silence. I looked around at the old bookcases, at the leather and buckram bindings of the books. The place felt empty, without the intangible presence of the oracle pressing lightly upon me like a soft blanket. "If I'm back in time," I added, "I wonder what time it is. Could you reach all the way back to the time before Abernathy's was in Portland?"

The eerie stillness echoed in my ears, overriding the sound of my blood pulsing through them. I turned in a slow circle, and as I did so, the scene shuddered, and I was back in Abernathy's. Instantly I felt the oracle's presence, invisible and inattentive, like it was paying attention to something else. Ahead, the blue glow of an augury shimmered like heat haze. I headed toward it. "I hope Dr. Gibbons—Ken—can figure this out," I said. "If it is time travel, if the Wardens can figure out how to make it work beyond the oracle, imagine the possibilities!"

Though now I'd said that, I couldn't think of any possibilities that wouldn't create some kind of paradox. Suppose, for example, they were able to stop the attack that had left thousands and thousands of steel magi dead worldwide. If Malcolm hadn't lost his aegis, he would never have undergone the Damerel rites a second time, Darius Wallach would not have developed the improved steel aegis, and Malcolm might not have survived his fight against the weavers. Were those things an acceptable sacrifice for all those lives? Not that I wanted those men and women dead, but it seemed an impossible comparison.

Even so—maybe *I* couldn't think of a good way to use time travel, but I was sure there were people who could. I took the fat little augury off the shelf and checked inside the cover. *Stuart Kelig, No Charge.* It felt like a fitting end to a difficult day.

5

F riday morning I rolled over in bed and gasped in surprise. Malcolm lay there propped on one elbow, watching me. "Is something wrong?" I said.

He put his arm around my waist and pulled me close, brushed a kiss across my forehead. "I've been debating whether to wake you, or let you wake naturally," he said. "Undressing you while you were sleeping struck me as creepy."

"And watching me sleep isn't?"

"I was thinking about how beautiful you are, and remembering the way you look at me like I'm the only man in the world."

"Mmm," I said, pushing back the hair that lay across his forehead. "I like the sound of that. Of course, I'm awake now."

"We should take advantage of that," he said, leaning down to kiss me.

I'd never been so grateful that the guest suite was at the other end of the house.

We showered together afterward, enjoying the feel of wet skin against skin, and eventually ended up in bed again. "You're awfully amorous," I said later, breathing heavily. "Is there some special occasion?"

Malcolm kissed me, then rolled out of bed and began hunting for his clothes. "I was thinking," he said, "we're running out of opportunities to have sex without being a married couple. Or I might just have been thinking it's been a while. I'm not sure."

"I doubt sex will be less exciting once we're married," I said, rising to dress. "I know I felt better once we didn't have to sneak around anymore. This is just another form of security."

"True." Malcolm went into his closet. "Is your party tonight, or tomorrow?"

"Tomorrow. I have no idea what to expect. Judy and Viv have been very closemouthed about the whole thing. I would suspect them of trolling me, except I've known Viv too long not to expect her to do something wild."

"After nixing the alcohol, sex games, and strippers, I can't imagine what's left to be wild about."

"That's what worries me."

Mike was in the kitchen eating cereal when we went downstairs. "It's really okay if you cook, you know," I told him.

"I have trouble eating heavily in the morning. My stomach doesn't wake up until around 10:30." He waved his spoon in the air for emphasis.

"It's true," Malcolm said. "And then he demands a full meal. Any time we were on active deployment and in a hostile area, half his pack was MREs."

"I have a healthy appetite. Nothing wrong with that."

I sat at the counter opposite him while Malcolm whipped

eggs and poured them into the heated frying pan. "How long have you been out of the Navy?"

"Five years. I'd always meant to stay longer, make it a career, but things in Chicago heated up around then and I was needed more in the field than in the Navy." Mike scraped sugar sludge off the bottom of his bowl and sucked on his spoon happily. I tried not to look revolted. "It's been a long five years."

"Have you been with your team that long?"

Mike's expression grew guarded. "I've been a temporary member of several teams for the last year or two. Usually I come on board when a team needs some extra illusory support. Then, when the crisis is over, I move on."

"Oh. Is that…I've never heard of that before. Is that something you enjoy?"

Mike laughed. "Fighting the Long War isn't generally about enjoyment," he said, but not harshly. "I go where I'm needed."

"It's not uncommon for specialists to have temporary assignments," Malcolm said. "Though more often those are non-magus weapons specialists like Canales." He handed me a plate of scrambled eggs with cheese, and I dug in happily.

"The temporary assignments are usually more challenging," Mike said. He carried his bowl to the sink, rinsed it, and put it in the dishwasher. "So there's that. I love a challenge."

"Are you still planning to spend the day at Campbell Security with me?" Malcolm asked.

"If you're sure I won't be in the way. I'm interested in trying out some of the tools you mentioned."

"It's no problem." Malcolm took a seat opposite me and forked up some of his own eggs. "I'd like your opinion on the illusions set on the more specialized weapons."

"What sort of illusions?" I asked.

"To make them look less like guns when people are carrying them around in the open," Malcolm said. "Changing their appearance is easy, but deciding what to change it to is the difficult part. I'd show you, but there would be no point."

"No, they'd all just look like weapons to me," I agreed.

"You can see through illusions?" Mike said. "You're only the second person I've met who could."

I sat up straight. "You what?"

"You and this swami in Mishawaka. He was a long way from home."

"But—" I struggled to find words. "I thought it was just me! Tell me more!"

Mike seemed startled at my reaction. "He was a student of some Indian art of meditation, and I assumed that was how he did it. Attuned himself to reality, or something. I take it you aren't a practitioner?"

"No, of course not. We think it's something I was born with." I realized I had a forkful of cold eggs raised halfway to my mouth and set it down. Food seemed suddenly unappetizing. "I need to meet him."

"I don't know where he is now. I can call the Barrington Node and see if anyone's heard from him lately. He was a stone magus, and a traveler—renewing wards, you know."

"I do." Silas Abernathy, in his second life as a stone magus, had written a book about his travels doing exactly that. "This could be so important, Mike."

"I get that. Have you read *A History of Magic*? There's a chapter about magical sports that might interest you."

Stunned at the sudden change of subject, I said, "Ah... there are magical sports? Like Quidditch? What does that have to do with seeing through illusions?"

"Not sports as in athletics, sports as in genetic outliers. Weird abilities that crop up out of nowhere. There have been a few people, over the ages, who have the ability to tap their own magic without the benefit of an aegis. Some have magical traits like finding objects or seeing glimpses of the future. Seeing through illusions seems like one of those."

"Why hasn't anyone ever told me about that?"

"They occur among the general population, not just within those who have aegises, so the odds of one showing up where the Wardens would know about it are pretty slim. And it's been decades since there were any among the magi. I imagine nobody thought anything of it."

"I never made it through *A History of Magic*." It was at least five very thick volumes long and drier than week-old bread. "But if it's relevant—I mean, it's not like I've had time to look into this, what with how busy I am, and the wedding and all, but if I could learn more about people like me…"

"I'll bring home a copy," Malcolm said. "Digitized for your carrying convenience."

My excitement over the possibility of uncovering more of the mystery of my ability carried me all the way to the store, even overriding my impatience over the mystery that was closer to hand. I knew Ken hadn't said he'd call immediately, but the instances where I was transported elsewhere, or into the past, weren't abating. Even though they also still weren't interfering with the auguries, I disliked not knowing.

Despite what Ken had said about guessing, I was increasingly convinced I was stepping into the past every time it happened. The look of the place, the fact that there weren't any modern books, was more evidence for my theory. As excited as that made me, it also made me nervous—what if I stepped outside the oracle's boundaries and was trapped in whatever year it was? In the two days since talking to Ken, I'd become more cautious about my explorations. So far, I hadn't found the limits of the oracle's space, but I was sure that couldn't persist.

"—can't do that," Judy was saying into her phone as I entered the office. She glanced at me and said, "She's here. I'll talk to you later," and hung up.

"More secrets?" I said.

"You'll find out tomorrow," Judy said. "Not very many mail-in auguries this morning."

"I'll get started anyway," I said. "I'm running a little behind."

But when I reached the front of the store, I saw two figures waiting outside the door. One was tall, the other stocky, and both wore heavy trench coats. Detectives Acosta and Green. In the past nine months, they'd gone from being enemies to tentative allies, though I was sure their loyalties weren't as solidly with the Wardens as Lucia would like. Even so, they'd turned out to be an excellent resource within the Portland police department, and came in every couple of weeks for an augury related to whatever case they were working on.

I thought about pretending I hadn't seen them. They weren't Nicolliens or Ambrosites, and I couldn't get in trouble for letting them in early. On the other hand, I didn't think I was obligated to open early just because they were detectives and unwilling to wait for ten o'clock like normal people. On a third hand, though, I'd never known them to abuse my time, at least not since they'd discovered the truth about Abernathy's. I suppressed a sigh and went to let them in.

"Thank you, Ms. Davies," Acosta said. His lean, dark olive complexion was only a little lighter with his winter pallor. "It's getting colder out there. I think it might actually snow."

"I hope not," I said. "Is there something I can help you gentlemen with? Because if it's not official business, I'll have to ask you to wait until we open."

"It's not about an augury," Green said. "When's the last time you saw Harriet Keller?"

I blinked. "Um…maybe a week? Why?" Chill dread struck my heart. "Is she all right?"

"We don't know," Acosta said. "Her daughter reported her missing yesterday afternoon. Her and Harry Keller both."

I put my hand on the counter to steady myself. "They're glass magi. Lucia said the glass magi were being kidnapped."

"It's premature to make that conclusion," Acosta said, "but we're keeping it in mind. Right now we're trying to establish just how long they've been missing. The most recently anyone reports seeing them is five days ago. That's a long time to be out of contact with anyone, particularly for senior citizens."

It struck me as odd to think of Harry and Harriet as senior citizens just because they were in their seventies, but of course that's what senior citizen meant. "So how did Amelia find out?"

"Mrs. Perkins had arranged a short stay with her parents, according to her report," Green said. "She arrived at their home to find them gone, but their car was still in the garage. The house doors were unlocked and there were some lights still burning. It was as if they'd just walked away, though the likelihood of them having done that in this weather is small."

"They wouldn't have done that," I agreed. "So are you investigating this as police, or as Wardens?"

"Both," Acosta said. "Lucia called us, and we arranged to be assigned to the case. We're looking into the disappearances of three other glass magi as well."

"Lucia came for auguries about them. I thought they'd be easy to interpret."

"We weren't given them." Acosta shoved his gloved hands into his pockets, an uncharacteristically impatient gesture. "So we're also here for an augury of our own."

Green extended a slip of paper to me. *Where is Harriet Keller?* "I'll be right back," I said.

The oracle chose not to transport me in time, and I hurried through the stacks, looking for the blue glow. "Please make this an easy one," I said. "Harry and Harriet…if they've been kidnapped…I don't know what to think."

The book was *The House of Dies Drear*, by Virginia Hamilton. I tucked it under my arm and returned to the detectives. They waited patiently, not pacing or fingering the books. "$500," I said. "I don't know what to make of that."

"Let us worry about the detecting, Ms. Davies," Acosta said, but with a smile that told me he wasn't serious. He accepted the book while Green counted out hundreds. They always paid cash. Acosta had told me once there was no space on the reimbursement forms for mystical prophecies.

"You'll let me know if you learn anything?" I said. "The Kellers are friends of mine."

"We can't make any promises," Acosta said. "If we stopped to update everyone who has an interest in finding the Kellers, we'd do nothing but call people." He hesitated, then added, as if taking pity on my obvious distress, "Lucia will know. I'm sure she'll arrange for the news to spread."

"Thank you. And—good luck."

When the detectives were gone, I slumped against the counter and dropped the sheaf of envelopes on its glass top. My desire to do any auguries had vanished. It couldn't be coincidence that all five of the missing people were glass magi, even if, in Harry's case, one of them was a former magus. They couldn't all have gone missing for innocent and unrelated reasons. Someone was kidnapping glass magi, and if it wasn't the Mercy, well, that was another too-big coincidence. But what did they want? And how did they propose to force the magi to do whatever it was? My eyes ached, and I rubbed them hard with the heels of my hands. Whatever the kidnappers intended, it couldn't be good.

It wasn't until midafternoon, the third Ambrosite augury, that Abernathy's sent me into the other place. I stopped where I was, inhaled deeply, and closed my eyes. This place felt so empty, without the oracle's familiar, distant presence. And yet it was still the oracle, or there wouldn't be any auguries for me to find. I strained all my senses, willing the oracle to make itself known.

Somewhere in the distance, footsteps sounded, faint taps on the linoleum.

My eyes flew open. I wasn't alone here.

I stood rooted to the spot by indecision. Should I try to confront the other person? He or she might know what was causing this. Or—suppose I *had* traveled back in time? Maybe interacting with someone from that time would cause a paradox, or something, that might mean catastrophe. I wished I knew more about time travel. I wasn't a big science fiction reader, and I was pretty sure movies didn't get it right. *The Time Traveler's Wife* had just confused me. But I had to make a decision.

Quietly, pretending I was Malcolm with his preternatural gift for moving silently, I took a few steps, casting about for the augury. The footsteps stopped, then started again, coming closer. I ducked around a bookcase, keeping close to it and hoping I was still concealed. The footsteps grew louder, and I heard humming. It was off-key, but still recognizably the theme from the first *Superman* movie, the one with Christopher Reeve.

I took a few sidling steps around another bookcase and saw a distant blue glow. The humming was louder now. Whoever it was stood between me and the augury. I stepped toward it, then stopped as the humming cut off. Silence fell, with no footsteps to disturb it. Then someone whispered, "Who's there?"

I kept my mouth shut. The person took two steps. He, or she, wasn't more than a few yards away. "Who's there?" came the whisper again.

Then the bookcases shuddered, came into focus, and I felt the presence of the oracle swell up around me. I let out a deep, frightened breath and shook out my fingers, which I'd had clenched into fists. The blue glow shifted, flicking from somewhere ahead of me to somewhere to my right. I breathed in the scent of lilacs and calmed myself. Lilacs. Did the oracle know how unsettled I was?

Almost without thinking, I turned toward the new location of the augury. That was different. Either the oracle had an answer for a question, and produced a single book, or it had no answer and the light turned red like the rays of a dying sun to let me know. It didn't change its mind mid-stream, so to speak. Yet when I took the new augury off the shelf, it behaved exactly as if it were the only augury the oracle had chosen. Maybe it was a single book that happened to be on different shelves in each of the locations? We moved books around sometimes to keep me from becoming too familiar with the bookstore's contents and layout. If I were traveling to Abernathy's in the past, it wasn't impossible that there were books still in the store in the present that had been there since it came to Portland in 1938.

I carried the augury to the front of the store and handed it over absently, still mulling over the problem. The book certainly looked old enough to have been around for eighty years. Maybe I should call Ken and let him know about this new development. It might be important information.

"Helena?" Judy said.

By the sound of her voice, she'd addressed me at least once already. "Sorry. What?"

"Jonathan has an augury request."

I glanced at Jonathan, who was a short, round man with a normally cheerful expression that at the moment looked concerned. "Oh. Sorry. Yes, just a minute."

The oracle seemed as placid as always this time. It hadn't yet transported me, or whatever, twice in a row. I paced the aisles, reassuring myself that I was the only person there before retrieving the augury. Jonathan looked only slightly relieved when I emerged. "Wedding plans making you crazy?" he said.

I half-smiled. "A little."

"Well, nothing to worry about. It's not until *after* the wedding that the real challenge begins!" He laughed and waved goodbye.

I looked around, but saw no one other than Judy. "Weren't there more Ambrosites here a minute ago?"

"That was at two. It's nearly 4:30 now," Judy said. "Are you all right?"

"There was someone else in the oracle just now. Someone from the other place."

Judy's mouth went slack with astonishment. "I thought that was impossible."

"If I'm traveling back in time, there'd be another custodian. We'd both be able to enter the oracle, and who says we couldn't do so at the same time?"

"Did you talk to him?"

"No. I was returned here before we encountered each other. I'm not sure that wasn't the best outcome. What if meeting each other means we'd, I don't know, annihilate each other? Like two identical versions of a person canceling each other out?"

"But you're not identical. It would be you and the earlier custodian." Judy leaned against the counter and rubbed the toe of her ankle boot against her shin. "Even so, if you *are* traveling in time, you shouldn't give away knowledge of the future. That's the one thing all the books agree on."

"I hadn't thought of that. I wish Ken would call."

My phone rang. I jumped, startled, then pulled it out of my pocket. It was Malcolm, not Ken. I tried not to sound disappointed when I answered. "Hi, love."

"It's good to hear your voice. Everything well?"

I decided not to have the conversation about the oracle over the phone. "Fine. You?"

"Actually, something's come up, and my team is going on the hunt tonight. Mike is coming with us. I hope you don't mind being abandoned. Again."

"I'm abandoning you tomorrow night, so I guess that's fair. Is anything wrong?"

"It's not an invader problem. We're pursuing some leads Lucia and the detectives came up with that might tell us who kidnapped the missing glass magi."

A pulse of excitement shot through me. "You think you might find the Kellers?"

"Unfortunately, no, but if we can find their abductors, that's the next step to finding them."

It was still a reassurance. "Then you have my blessing. Not that you needed it."

Malcolm laughed. "Having your support means more to me than you know. Don't wait up."

We exchanged a few more endearments, then I hung up. Judy had a strange look on her face. "What?"

"Is he taking Conti with him tonight?" she said.

"Yes. Why?"

Judy's lips thinned. "Conti's bad news, Helena. I'd be worried if I were Malcolm."

"Judy, Malcolm trusts Mike with his life. They've been friends for a long time. I'm sure Malcolm knows him better than your Nicollien friends."

"Are you saying I'm biased?" Judy said irritably.

"No, I'm saying your information sources might not be reliable."

"I'm only concerned for Malcolm's safety. And Derrick and Hector's."

I sighed, wishing the conversation was over—or, better yet, had never begun. "What do you want me to do about it?"

Judy shrugged. "I don't know. Talk to Malcolm? Ask him what he knows about Conti's reputation in Chicago?"

Shocked, I said, "I can't do that. Malcolm would feel so betrayed that I listened to gossip about his best friend."

"Then how is he going to feel if Conti gets him or his teammates hurt, or killed?"

I shook my head. "I don't know, Judy. I guess it makes sense, but it feels wrong."

"It's up to you," Judy said. "I know what I'd do." She turned and headed for the office. I leaned on the counter and stared at my phone. I knew what mattered—that Malcolm and his team could count on each other, that they didn't have to worry about a teammate betraying them, even accidentally. But it was even more important that Malcolm and I trusted each other, which meant trusting each other's judgment. Malcolm believed in Mike, which meant I should too. Maybe. I put the phone away. Why couldn't life ever be simple?

6

S aturday morning, I woke before Malcolm for a change—well, he must have come in late, and he, unlike me, didn't have work today—and decided to take advantage of the extra time to go to the Athenaeum and do a little research. I was tired of not knowing how time travel worked, or didn't, and now that I knew there had been other people like me, I wanted to learn more about them. Maybe there were some living now. I showered, dressed, ate quickly, and was out the door by seven.

The florist's shop was empty when I arrived, but before I could do more than take a few steps toward the counter, the long grass on the back wall parted. A woman with blonde dreadlocks and a pierced eyebrow emerged from the hidden door. "Good morning, Irina," I said.

Irina nodded acknowledgement and held the grass aside for me like holding back a velvet curtain. She and I weren't enemies, but we'd never become friends. By now I was used to her brusque manner.

The small, low-ceilinged room beyond the grass smelled richly of loam and green growing things. Irina hauled up on the trap door and let it fall heavily to the floor. I smiled in thanks and began my descent, hoping to be far enough down when she closed the trap door that I didn't feel closed in.

At the bottom, I chose one of the sliding doors in the aluminum wall and set my purse on the floor beside the column at the center of the room. I'd brought plenty of *sanguinis sapiens*, since I had no idea how much the information I wanted might cost. Gone were the days when I had to worry about acquiring it; Malcolm took half his salary in the stuff, and he'd told me it was mine to use as I wished. I set the little honeycomb case on the flat top of the column and placed both my hands flat on the rubbery disks to either side. "I want to search in English," I declared, and my vision filled with white light that seemed to come from within me.

Welcome to the Athenaeum, a familiar woman's voice said. *What would you like to learn about today?*

"Time travel."

The whiteness filled with gray specks like bees, whizzing around like a demented Etch-a-Sketch. *There are ninety-five million, three hundred fifty-six thousand, two hundred seventy-one records relevant to [time travel]. How can I narrow your search?*

"Um...how about factual records? Records that aren't fiction or speculation?"

There are no records matching those search parameters. Would you like to alter your search terms?

That was disheartening. "You mean there's no solid evidence for time travel?"

That query is outside the parameters of the search algorithm.

"I mean—search for records about experiments on time travel."

A pause. *There are seven hundred sixty-six records relevant to [time travel] + [experiments]. Would you like to narrow your search?*

I thought for a moment. "Did any of those succeed in sending someone or something through time?"

There are no records matching those search parameters. Would you like to alter your search terms?

That was discouraging. Or maybe it wasn't. "How about... of those experiments, how many were carried out in the last... ten years?"

There are seventeen records relevant to [time travel] + [experiments] within that time frame. Would you like to narrow your search?

"Can you display the records in electronic format, along with the contact information of the people who conducted them?"

Please insert payment to continue.

To my surprise, a single tube of *sanguinis sapiens* was enough to pay for my information. A door at the base of the column slid open, revealing a flash drive. *What would you like to learn about today?*

"New search," I said. "I want information on people with unusual magical abilities that don't come from having an aegis."

There are seven thousand, five hundred and eighty-one records relating to [unusual magical abilities] − [aegis]. Would you like to narrow your search?

"Were any of them able to see through illusions?" I didn't know why it had never occurred to me to ask this question before.

There are two records relating to [unusual magical abilities] − [aegis] + [illusions]. Would you like to narrow your search further?

"No. Could you display those in electronic format? But I'm not done with these search terms." I closed my eyes, not that it made a difference. "In the subset of unusual magical abilities without an aegis, how many of those records are about people, or instances, in the Pacific Northwest?"

There are no records matching those search parameters.

So I was rare, if only for this part of the country. Interesting that there weren't any records about me. "How many of the records in those search terms are from the…let's say the last fifty years?"

There are seventy-six records relating to [unusual magical abilities] – [aegis] within that time frame. Would you like to narrow your search further?

"No—wait, yes. I want just the ones in North America." I was going to have enough trouble tracking these people down without having to make a lot of international calls.

There are thirty-eight records relating to [unusual magical abilities] – [aegis] within that time frame and geographical restriction. Would you like to narrow your search further?

"No. Please display all those files in electronic format." The cubby door slid open again. "I'm done searching."

Please insert payment.

One more tube. It felt like such momentous information ought to cost more. Then again, it was only momentous to me. "Thanks," I said without thinking.

Have a nice day.

It wasn't the first time the Athenaeum had addressed me as if it were a person who knew me. After the events of six months ago, when I'd actually spoken with the oracle, I'd asked my fellow custodians if they felt their charges were sapient beings rather than just magical places. Claude Gauthier, custodian of the Athenaeum, had told me he'd sometimes received responses from his Neutrality that suggested it was, in fact, self-aware, but those communications had always been on its terms and not in response to anything he could do. "I think, me, it is a secretive and stubborn creature, if it is a creature," he'd said. "But it is the keeper of many secrets, so perhaps that is not so strange." At any rate, I chose to behave politely to the Athenaeum, just in case.

The trap door was open when I emerged, but Irina was gone. I shut the door behind me and listened carefully at the grass curtain before pushing through it. Irina, arranging flowers in a tall Grecian vase big enough to hide a body, did little more than grunt a farewell when I left. Outside, rain was coming down in hard, fat drops, and I stopped to pull my collapsible umbrella out of my purse, silently cursing the cold water spattering my head and face. Hawaii was looking better all the time.

When I trudged into the office, trailing water, Judy said, "This is one of those days I wish we could just stay home."

"You *are* home, practically. You didn't have to run through the rain to get here."

"Yes, but you know how damp it gets up there. I wish I could cuddle up with a mug of hot chocolate and a book."

It was such a lovely, compelling image I sighed with pleasure. "Instead, there are mail-in auguries."

"But tonight's the party! I hope it stops raining before then."

I gathered up the small stack of envelopes. "So do I."

The rain didn't let up all morning, though, and only a few Nicolliens showed up, all of them drenched and irritable. I kept a pleasant smile on my face through willpower alone. Didn't any of them realize grousing only made things worse? The thought made the smile real. I'd certainly done my share of grousing over the weather, not caring that it worsened my bad attitude. I was better at giving advice than taking it.

Malcolm called around 12:30. "I wish I could take you to lunch," he said.

"I wish you could, too." I went into the break room and sat in one of the chairs, leaning with my elbow on the table. "Did the hunt go well?"

"Not as well as we hoped. We did eliminate some possibilities, which is good, but not as heartening as if we'd found evidence that would lead to our missing people."

"I can see that. Didn't the auguries help at all?"

"Lucia's magi are still interpreting them. She won't tell us anything until she's sure. But I think she has a guess she's waiting for confirmation of."

"I'm so worried about Harry and Harriet. You don't think…they might be dead?"

"I doubt it. There would be no point, and considerable danger, to abducting them only to kill them elsewhere. If the point were to eliminate glass magi, we would have found bodies. No, someone wants them for a purpose, and we must assume that means they're still alive."

"That's a relief." I hesitated, then said, "Is Mike working out all right?"

"Very well. Why do you ask? That sounded like the kind of question where you already have an answer in mind."

I hesitated again, then came out with, "Judy said his reputation in Chicago wasn't the best. I was sure that couldn't be true, Malcolm, but I did wonder if something had happened to him there."

"He had some trouble, yes," Malcolm said, but he didn't sound angry, and I relaxed. "It's not my story to tell, though. Did Judy's information come from Nicolliens?"

"That doesn't automatically make it suspect." I conveniently ignored how I'd made that same objection.

"She should keep in mind that among the Nicolliens here, my reputation doesn't look good either. I trust Mike with my life, Helena. He's a good man who's had some bad luck."

"I know you couldn't be friends with someone who'd done something seriously wrong."

"That, too." Malcolm sighed. "Mike and I are heading out to lunch now. Will I see you tonight?"

"Maybe. I'm coming home to change and then the party starts at 6:30, with dinner. I love you."

"I love you, too."

He hung up, and I put my phone away. It rang again barely two seconds later. "Hello?"

"This is Ken Gibbons. I hope I didn't catch you at a bad time."

"No, I—actually, could you hold on for a minute?"

I ran across the hall to the office, where Judy was just rising from the computer. "It's Ken Gibbons," I told her. "Would you let me know if anyone comes in?"

Judy nodded. "You're probably safe," she said, "but don't get so caught up you forget to eat."

I settled myself into her vacated chair and said, "Thanks for calling back. It's still happening, but it hasn't gotten any more or less frequent. I hope you have good news for me."

"I hope you'll consider it good news," Ken said. "Unfortunately, there's not much of it. You say the incidences haven't changed in frequency?"

"No, there are still about three to five a day, and they're always to the same place. I've started to become familiar with it."

"It's not a place," Ken said. "You're definitely moving through time."

I caught my breath. "You're sure?"

"In order for you to move through space under these conditions," Ken said, his voice becoming more mellow and unctuous, "there would have to be another, identical place for you to move to. Imagine two transparencies—do you know what those are? You're young enough, you might not."

"I don't. Is it important?"

"It might help you envision the problem. A transparency is a sheet of flexible plastic the size of a sheet of paper that's completely transparent, hence the name. We used to draw on them and project the resulting image onto a screen for our students to see. Imagine Abernathy's as a picture on a transparency. Now imagine yourself as a fly on that picture, capable of moving around inside it. If there were a second, identical transparency, you could step from one to the other if they were perfectly aligned. If not, or if the image weren't identical, you'd be stuck in your own image."

"I can sort of picture it. So you're saying there would have to be another Abernathy's somewhere?"

"Yes. And that's impossible."

He sounded so certain I suddenly wanted to argue with him. "Couldn't someone build another oracle? Don't they have information on how Elizabeth Abernathy did it?"

"Elizabeth Abernathy was a very lucky woman. No one's entirely sure why she succeeded where someone else failed only fifty years before. At any rate, even if someone built a second oracle, it wouldn't be identical to Abernathy's. So the analogy holds."

"Okay. And that means…time travel?"

I could almost feel the smugness coming through the phone. Ken might be a smart man, but he was also a proud one. Maybe his pride was justified, if he knew so much. "I don't know how it happened, but somehow the oracle must have connected with its earlier self, which *is* identical. I can only speculate as to the cause, but it's possible when the oracle selects a book it's chosen in the past, the two auguries create a resonance—a harmony, so to speak—that bring the two times together for a short period."

"But I know it's chosen the same books before, and this has never happened until now." It had brought out copies of the same book when warning us about the Mercy, for one, and there were all those atlases when it told Silas Abernathy to move the store to Portland.

"I said I could only speculate. It may have to be an augury that happens at a particular time, or one where the books in question were located close to one another in the store's physical location. Have you noticed anything in common with the relevant auguries?"

"I've been writing down the titles and the questions people ask, but I haven't seen a pattern yet."

"You might want to write down more information than that. Time of day, day of the week, affiliation of the person asking—the more information you can gather, the more potential you have of a pattern emerging. I'll continue searching, but I thought you would like to know what I'd learned so far."

"You said you have records that aren't in the Athenaeum. How is that possible? I thought it had everything."

"The Athenaeum doesn't automatically contain every word ever written by men. Records have to be added, a process that takes time. Much of what I have is in the process of being added—things I uncovered during my research, for example. Lost manuscripts and diaries. With time, they'll all be available in the Athenaeum."

"Oh." I wanted to ask how records were added, but felt

that would take the conversation too far afield. "That makes sense."

"I also have a warning."

His voice dropped low on those last words, and I shivered. "A warning about what?"

"Be very careful when you travel to the past. If you move outside the oracle's boundaries, you could be trapped there. And you shouldn't give away information about the present— the future—to anyone in the past. That could be deadly."

"Wow." I shivered. "I almost did meet someone there yesterday. I don't know what I would have said to him if I had. Or her."

"You saw someone in the oracle?" Ken sounded startled. "Did they see you?"

"No, I only heard footsteps. And someone whispering. I think they heard me, too."

"Be more careful. You will have trouble explaining your presence to anyone from the past."

"I *was* careful," I said, feeling a little annoyed. "It's not like I stood up and announced myself."

"Sorry. I'm simply concerned for your safety." His deep voice sounded even deeper and more reassuring.

"That's all right. And thanks for everything. Do I...how can I repay you? You shouldn't have to do all this for free."

"It's been my pleasure. I haven't had a challenge like this in years." He chuckled. "Let me know if any new developments arise."

"I will. Thanks again."

After Ken hung up, I sat at the desk staring at the computer screen, displaying its usual starscape background. How *would* I have explained myself to whoever had nearly caught me in the past? Or...was he a fellow traveler, another custodian caught out of his time? Part of me wanted to disregard Ken's instructions, because what could be more fascinating than talking to someone else like me? But he was the expert, and if he thought it was dangerous, I should probably not ignore that.

Since Judy hadn't returned, I decided to take a look at my findings from the Athenaeum. I hadn't kept track of which flash drive was which, so I chose one at random and plugged it into the computer. A browser window popped up, displaying a list of files with meaningless alphanumeric names. Each was tagged with the abbreviated name of a source and a short description. I'd chosen the one about time travel experiments, and the names all looked very official, like the titles of abstracts from scientific journals. Bracing myself for a world of boredom, I opened the first file.

It wasn't as bad as I anticipated. While some of the files were, in fact, excerpts from scholarly journals, filled with strange mathematical symbols and therefore beyond me, many of them were written in a casual, readable style I could easily follow. At first. The ones I could read still contained references and vocabulary that assumed the reader knew some basic concepts about time travel I'd never heard of. I got out a pad of legal paper and a pen and started taking notes. The ones that most interested me had made actual attempts at sending things through time, or bringing things from the past. None of them referred to sending *people* through time, and I wondered if that meant it was impossible, or if it was like pharmaceutical trials where they put the drug through extensive testing before giving it to humans, and they just hadn't gotten that far yet.

By the time I'd worked my way through the nine files I was able to understand, I had three sheets of notes and the beginnings of a headache that cried out for Diet Coke. I flipped back through the notes, bemused. Black holes, singularities, Einstein-Rosen bridges…they all sounded way too big to be testable on Earth, yet these experimenters had made the effort. Most of them had tried to take advantage of Einsteinian physics to send things forward in time, but couldn't prove their experiments had succeeded. A few had tried to send things backward in time, but only succeeded in breaking their equipment. And two of them had used magic, making their objects (a red rubber ball and a toy car respectively) vanish without reappearing. None of it was reassuring.

On the other hand, I had a better idea of what might be happening with Abernathy's. If it was time travel as these experimenters understood it, it seemed likely that some kind of wormhole—a term I liked better than the offputtingly long Einstein-Rosen bridge—had connected my present with one of Abernathy's pasts, allowing me to step from one to the other. Given how little success other experimenters had had with the concept, it seemed absurd that Abernathy's had done it with no effort. But Abernathy's was unique, and probably had more magic at its command than either of the other research teams had.

The very last file included a name I knew. Darius Wallach, the self-styled mad scientist of Gunther Node, had been part of a team researching ways to send objects into the future using magic. It was one of the files written in horribly complex language I couldn't understand, but the opening paragraphs explained that they'd tried to create a singularity under laboratory conditions and failed. Maybe Wallach knew something I didn't—okay, yes, he knew a lot of things I didn't, but maybe one of those things was how time travel worked. I decided to find some time to pay him a visit.

It was almost two o'clock, but I figured I had enough time

to glance at the other files, the ones about unusual magical abilities. The Athenaeum hadn't separated out the two records about seeing through illusions, and it took me a minute of searching to find them. The first was a review of a book about practical uses of magic, which referred, among other things, to creating objects that would allow ordinary people to see through illusions. I skimmed the document and discovered the book it referred to had been written in 1947. That made sense. I already knew Wardens had these objects; I'd seen Malcolm's team use them a couple of years ago when we were trying to find the origami illusion attacking Abernathy's. How disappointing.

The second item was an obituary. Sort of. It wasn't from any newspaper, just a single document, but it read like the obituary my mom and uncles had written for my grandfather when he died. Except this had clearly been written for the eyes of Wardens only. It referred to the deceased, Aaron Azoulay, having attended the Université Magique, and mentioned his long service at a node somewhere in Europe. It looked old, older than the other record, and sure enough, the death date was 1807.

I read on in fascination. Aaron Azoulay hadn't been a magus, just a scholar-Warden who'd lived an ordinary life and raised a family and been in almost every way unexceptional. But he could see through illusions. The obituary made a big deal about this, how Azoulay had used his ability in the service of the Long War and contributed to destroying many invaders despite not being a magus. According to this, he'd had the ability all his life, and no one among the Wardens had ever figured out where it had come from or what about him was unique. It was also disappointing, but knowing I wasn't the only one, even if my comrade in magic was two centuries dead, kept the disappointment from being too severe.

I printed the page out and folded it to put in my purse. I wanted to show it to Malcolm, not that I expected him to learn any more from it than I had. It was hard not to feel excited, though I remembered what Mike had said about magical sports like me showing up mostly where the Wardens wouldn't know about them. Finding others was probably nearly impossible. But knowing about Azoulay gave me hope.

Two o'clock. Just a few more hours, and I could go home for the weekend—no, I could go to my bachelorette party. I closed my eyes and said a brief, heartfelt prayer that Viv's plans weren't too outrageous. Judy would have kept her in check, I hoped. Probably God didn't answer prayers that frivolous, but it never hurt to try.

7

I opened the door to Viv's house and nearly walked into Malcolm's arms. I gasped in surprise, then started laughing. It wasn't the real man, but a life-size cardboard figure of Malcolm wearing his workout clothes and a sexy smile. I turned to Judy, who'd come in behind me, and said, "Is this what you were both so secretive about?"

"Part of it, yes," Judy said with a satisfied smirk. "Like it?"

"I love it! When did you get him to pose for this?"

"A few weeks ago. He thought it was hilarious. Insisted on showing off his chest, which I have to say is spectacular. No wonder you don't care about strippers, if that's what you go home to at night."

I felt smug at my soon-to-be husband's gorgeous physique. "He looks even better shirtless."

Judy rolled her eyes. "Come on in and let's get this party started."

We were a few minutes late, traffic coming through downtown being heavier than usual, and several women were already there, including— "Cynthia!" I exclaimed. "I thought you weren't coming until Wednesday!"

My sister came forward to hug me. "Surprise! I decided we needed a few extra days off so Mom can spoil her grand-daughter. And when Viv told me about the party, I knew I had to be here."

"I'm so glad!"

Viv and Jeremiah's living room was comfortably sized for a few people, but crowded with thirteen. The overstuffed recliner had been decorated like a throne, clearly intended for me, and my friends Linda, Poppy, and Allie sat on the sofa. Viv had dragged her dining room chairs into the living room to provide more seating, and Sue and Pen, both magi, sat on two of these chatting with Betsey and Ruth, both non-Wardens. The room smelled deliciously of tomatoes and creamy chowder.

"Get some soup," Viv directed me, "and have a seat. We're going to see how well we all know you."

There were four soups in warming pans on the dining room table. After a little dithering, I chose tomato with basil and a couple of soft rolls, then carefully sat in my throne, not wanting to spill on myself. Viv produced a bunch of tray tables for our convenience. I ate, and felt the day's tension drain away.

"Helena, look over here," Pen said. "I don't know what color your eyes are."

There was a pause as everyone in the room tried to gaze into my eyes, which made me blink at the intensity of the stares. "Couldn't I just tell you?" I asked.

"You're not allowed to give any answers," Viv said. She

dragged a chair next to me and put her bowl on my tray table. "This is an icebreaker. Gets us all warmed up for the main event."

"Which is…"

"Hah. Not telling. You'll find out soon enough." Viv took a large bite of clam chowder as if to prevent herself from saying more. I shrugged and listened to the conversations. It was funny the things people knew about me, or didn't know.

"Okay, who was her first crush? Cynthia?" Linda asked.

"Don't you dare," I said.

Cynthia's eyes glinted with merriment. "She was going to marry Zac Efron and live in England with him and their four blue-eyed children," she said. Everyone went "ooooh" at the same time. I blushed, though I wasn't sure why. Zac Efron was cute.

"And she had a poster of him on her closet door," Cynthia went on, "and—"

"Cynthia, I'm going to kill you if you don't stop!"

"And she kissed it goodnight every night for six months."

The ooooohs were louder and mingled with laughter this time. I blushed harder. "I did not!"

"Hey, you wouldn't want me to lie for you, would you?"

"Cynthia!" I threw a roll at her head. She ducked, grinning.

"I want to know about your first date," she said. "You and Malcolm, I mean."

The laughter died down a bit. "Wait," said Poppy, "doesn't anyone know about their first date?"

All eyes turned on me again. Viv said, "Actually, I don't think *I* know what their first date was. Helena, you might have to break the rules and tell us."

"I, um," I said. The truth was, we hadn't really had a first date, if you didn't count some extremely satisfying sex in my old apartment. We'd been unable to be together publically for so long, we'd had to snatch moments of privacy where we could. "We didn't really date for a while because Malcolm was, um, traveling for several months after we were together. I guess the first official date was—" The first official date, when we could be together openly? "My birthday last year. He set up this elaborate experience with a beautiful dress and a fancy restaurant, and he gave me this—" I touched the diamond solitaire pendant I wore as often as possible. "It was so romantic."

The magi in the room, and Viv and Judy, exchanged glances. They knew as the others did not that our first date marked the day I'd convinced the Board of Neutralities to change the rules that prevented Malcolm and me from dating. It had been momentous for more than just us personally. The Board, we'd all thought, changed for no one.

"You're so lucky," Juliet sighed. "Elliot's not nearly so romantic."

"I don't mind if all we do is pizza and a movie," I protested.

"This is true," Viv said. "But tonight, we're going to shake our boring Helena up a bit. Eat, everyone, and then we'll move to the real party venue."

"Which is…?"

"Helena, try to get into the spirit of being surprised."

I genteelly slurped down soup and laughed at some of the answers my friends came up with—really, who didn't know my favorite food was lasagna?—and occasionally glanced at the cardboard cutout Malcolm and wondered what the real thing was doing. He'd said he didn't want a bachelor party, but I thought he might be out with friends tonight. I'd been so preoccupied with wondering what Viv and Judy had planned, I hadn't really paid attention. He really was incredibly hot, but that wasn't why I loved him. And we were getting married in just over a week. How lucky was I?

"All right, and when we add up the totals, we see that… Cynthia, who probably has an unfair advantage, is the winner!" Judy announced. "Though I think Pen gets a bonus prize for being the only one who knows Helena's dream vacation is a week in Maui."

"You should tell your bosses you're just leaving," Ruth said. "It's so unfair of them to keep you from having a honeymoon."

"It's a demanding job," I said awkwardly, "and they… really need me…" Impossible to explain to the non-Wardens why I couldn't leave Abernathy's for a week. Never mind not being there for the auguries; the mail-in ones would pile up alarmingly.

"Well, *I'd* threaten to quit," Betsey said.

"I think I'd have to threaten that too, if Helena made a stink," Judy said. "But now it's time for the party to start. Everyone find a car—we're going to the Lloyd Center."

"The party is at the mall?" I exclaimed. "We're not all getting matching manicures, are we?"

"No, you said you wanted to do that with the bridal party next week," Viv said. "Just get in Cynthia's car and stop asking questions. Live in the now, Helena."

I shut my mouth and obediently got into Cynthia's car, a late-model BMW that in the winter darkness looked black instead of midnight blue. "Meet at the ice rink," Viv called out, and our little caravan rolled out, down the long, sloping gravel driveway to Patton Road. Even in winter, it was over-grown, the dark needles of the evergreens warring with the bare branches of the maples and oaks. She and Jeremiah had chosen the house for that reason, Jeremiah, a wood magus, wanting to surround himself with potential weapons in case the Mercy came after them. It felt foreboding to me, but Viv seemed to like it.

Cynthia and Viv sat in the front seat, Judy and I in the back. "You win," I said. "I'm officially excited about the surprise."

"Good, because we worked hard at it," Viv said. "What time is it?"

Judy indicated the dashboard clock. "7:28. We should have plenty of time."

"The mall closes at nine," I said. "Is an hour and, what, fifteen minutes enough time?"

"Sure. If you don't dawdle." Viv closed her mouth and wouldn't say anything more.

Cynthia struck up a conversation about wedding plans, and I realized everyone in the car was part of the bridal party. I hadn't wanted very many attendants, and once you got past my sister and my two best friends, the number of people I might have asked increased alarmingly. So I'd stuck with three, which helped Malcolm narrow *his* list down to his brother and two closest friends as well. I listened to the three of them discuss the nail salon Judy had found that was open late on Wednesday and felt so content I didn't much care what plans Viv and Judy had made that required me not to dawdle at the mall.

Despite its being Saturday night, the mall parking lot wasn't very crowded for once, probably because the storm clouds were rolling in and I could smell rain in the air. We met

Poppy, Linda, Betsey, and Ruth at the ice rink, with the others trotting up moments later. I eyed Pen, a Nicollien glass magus, and Allie and Juliet, Ambrosite steel and stone magi respectively, but while they weren't acting like friends, they also hadn't come to blows. With luck, that state of affairs would continue. I wished I could get Pen alone to ask her if she felt safe, what with so many glass magi being abducted, but she seemed calm and not at all twitchy the way I'd probably be. Maybe she had Warden bodyguards who were discreet.

"Okay, you'll be divided into two teams," Viv said. "Betsey, Ruth, Cynthia, Juliet, and Pen, you're team A. Sue, Sheridan, Poppy, Linda, and Allie, you're team B. Helena, you'll go with…maybe we should flip a coin."

Judy rummaged through her purse and produced a quarter, which she handed to Viv. "Heads A, tails B," Viv said, and flipped the coin into the air and expertly caught it and slapped it on her wrist. "Looks like Helena will join team A."

We did some shuffling around until we were standing with our assigned groups. Viv grinned at us. "Welcome," she said, "to Quest for the Gold."

We all blinked at her. "I was going to do a photo scavenger hunt," she went on, "but that's boring. So we're doing a treasure hunt instead. Each of you has a different set of clues that will lead you to a treasure. You have—" she ostentatiously looked at her watch, which was a clunky plastic thing in bright blue and pink— "one hour and sixteen minutes to find your treasure. You might have to spend a little money and do some hunting, but none of the clues are hard to find. The first ones back at the front doors with the treasure are the winners."

Judy handed me a white envelope marked A and gave one marked B to Poppy. "Any questions?" Viv said. "Good. Happy hunting, ladies!"

It took me a moment to realize that was the signal to begin, by which time Poppy had already torn open her envelope. Quickly I did the same and extracted a half sheet of white paper. *A Journey of a thousand miles begins with a single step.*

"Journeys!" Pen shouted. "Where is it?"

Betsey was already at the nearest directory kiosk. "That way," she said, and we took off, not quite running—I thought we all felt awkward about running through the mall, even if it wasn't terribly crowded—but at a faster than walking pace.

The trendy little store, overflowing with trendy shoes, looked huge when I thought about all the places a clue might be. We hesitated before the entrance. "Should we…I don't know…search around?" Juliet said.

"Too time consuming," Cynthia said, and marched up to the counter. I followed her, feeling nervous. Cynthia was capable of anything.

The young man behind the counter looked up as she approached. His eyes widened. Cynthia was dressed down tonight, in jeans and a form-fitting sweater, but the form that sweater fit was gorgeous and curved in all the right places. Motherhood had only made those curves more voluptuous. Cynthia either didn't notice or didn't care about the young man's reaction. She smiled sweetly at him and said, "I don't suppose you have a clue for me?"

The young man cast his eye over six women all looking expectantly at him. "Is one of you the bride?" he said.

"Me," I said, raising my hand as if I were in school, then snatching it back in embarrassment.

He grinned and held up a white envelope. "It says," he said, "if the bride is here, I should give her the clue."

I held out my hand. He extended the envelope toward me,

then drew back. "After she sings 'I'm a Little Teapot,'" he added. "With all the actions."

"What?" I exclaimed. I looked around swiftly. There were five other people in the store, three of them watching us. "You made that up."

The man turned the envelope over and displayed the back, on which was written, in Viv's distinctive handwriting, the information he'd just given me. "I can't—"

"Then no clue," he said.

"Don't be a baby, Helena," Cynthia said. "We're wasting time."

My face flaming, I arranged my arms and began, "I'm a little teapot, short and stout—"

Muffled laughter ran through the store. Pen was grinning. Betsey and Ruth had their arms around each other, struggling not to laugh. Cynthia didn't even bother to pretend this wasn't the funniest thing she'd seen all day. "Louder," the man said.

I raised my voice and started to get into the groove, though my face hurt from blushing so hard. When I finished, "—and pour me out!" the store burst into applause. I bowed, telling myself not to be so stuffy, and the man handed me the envelope.

"Too bad you're getting married, or I'd have asked for your number," he said with a smile. I laughed, finally, at the amusement on his face, and tore open the envelope.

Too many Spaces, too many options, but the one you want is the smallest of all.

"I don't get it," Ruth said. "Spaces is capitalized, so it must be important, but the smallest of all? The smallest space?"

"Maybe the smallest store?" Cynthia suggested.

"Directory," I said, and trotted back to the one we'd used

before, trailing the others in my wake. Spaces...spaces... "Oh, Spaces, *Gap*," I said. "That's upstairs."

The nearest escalator was just around the corner, but crowded enough we couldn't race up it the way we wanted. I fretted and jigged in place until the thing deposited me at the top, then we speed walked down the central aisle to the store. "Gap, or Gap Kids?" Pen said, a trifle out of breath.

"'Smallest of all'...that sounds like Gap Kids," Juliet said.

A woman moved to intercept us as we entered. "Can I help you find something?"

"We're looking for a clue," Cynthia said.

The woman's brow furrowed. "A clue about what?"

"Um," Ruth said, "maybe we should ask at the desk?"

I glanced around the store. Mannequins modeling clothing, and doing it very well, stood in the display windows. Some of them were child-sized. "The smallest of all," I breathed, and turned to inspect the littlest mannequins.

"I really don't know what you're talking about," the woman said. "If you're not going to buy anything—"

"Do you have baby sweaters?" Cynthia broke in. "I need a sweater for my little girl."

The woman brightened. "Over this way," she said, steering Cynthia away from the display windows. I crouched beside the nearest mannequin and examined it thoroughly. Nothing. I squatted back on my haunches, discouraged.

Beside me, Juliet exclaimed, "I found it!" She withdrew an envelope from beneath the foot of another child-size mannequin and tore it open. "It says, *Buy a gift for the bride at Gimbels. Pay for it on the third floor, last register on the right.* Gimbels? I've never heard of it."

"I have," I said. "Cynthia?"

Cynthia was admiring a little pink sweater and chatting

amiably with the clerk. "I'll think about it," she said, setting the sweater down and hurrying over to us. "You found it?" she said in a low voice.

"Outside, and back the way we came," I said.

"But what's Gimbels?" Ruth said.

"It's Macy's," I said. "I mean, Macy's and Gimbels were huge department store rivals in New York City, decades ago— that was a really obscure reference for anyone but me, probably—"

"Let's just be grateful you're on our team," Cynthia said. "Now, what would you like? Something cheap."

We trotted through the store, past the expensive jewelry department, into fashion accessories. "Um…a scarf?" I said. "I feel weird asking you to buy me stuff."

"I'm determined to win this treasure hunt," Betsey declared. "I don't like the way Poppy looked like they'd already won. If buying you a scarf will defeat her, I consider it a small price to pay."

I snatched up the first scarf I saw, then said, "Wait. Not this one."

"Helena," Cynthia said, "this is not the time to get picky. We don't know how many other clues are left."

"I need to pee," Pen said.

Cynthia groaned. "Now, Pen?"

"It's getting urgent. I'll hurry."

"I need to pee too," said Ruth.

Betsey slugged her lightly on the shoulder. "What, should we all go to the bathroom together?"

"We'll hurry," Pen said, grabbing Ruth's arm. "You go pay for the scarf, and we'll meet at the second floor entrance. Hold my purse." She thrust it at Juliet, who took it, her mouth open to object, but the two were already gone.

"This one," I said, choosing a black scarf shot with blue that would go nicely with my good winter coat. "Hurry."

We ran up the escalator to the third floor, wove through the kids' department, and found a bank of registers. The one farthest to the right wasn't open. Betsey didn't hesitate. At the register next to it, she said, "We were supposed to pick something up here? A white envelope?"

The clerk accepted the scarf and began ringing it up. "I don't know anything about a white envelope, but I can ask." To the woman at the far end of the counter, she said, "Gwennie, is there a white envelope somewhere?"

The woman, middle-aged and stern-faced, looked us over with a narrowed eye. "Are they buying something?" The younger clerk waved the scarf at her. "Hmm. That's not much of a bridal gift."

"I chose it myself," I said.

"You're the bride?" The stern look disappeared, making the woman seem ten years younger. "Congratulations." She walked over to the end register and pulled out a white envelope from somewhere beneath the counter. I accepted it with a smile and a thank-you.

With the little bag containing my scarf tucked under my arm, I opened the envelope. *Time for a juice break.* "That's easy," Juliet said. "Maybe too easy. I wonder what kind of surprise is waiting for us at Jamba Juice."

"Let's meet Pen and Ruth and find out," Cynthia said.

"*Help!*"

Ruth's frightened voice stopped us all. Betsey said, "Ruth! What—you're bleeding!"

Blood trickled down Ruth's left temple. She staggered toward us, unable to keep a straight line. Betsey ran to her and held her up. "What happened?"

"Someone attacked us on the way out of the bathroom," Ruth gasped. "They hit me—I fell down—I heard Pen fighting them, and when I could see again, Pen was gone."

"What?"

"Oh, no," Juliet murmured, for my ears only. "No. Pen's a glass magus."

It still didn't make sense at first. Then I remembered. "A glass magus," I repeated. "Pen's been kidnapped."

8

"What do we do?" I said. "It's only been a few minutes. They might still be close by."

"Distract the mundanes," Juliet said, turning her back on me and opening Pen's purse. "And call Campbell."

Cynthia was saying, "We need to alert someone, and get first aid. Wait here." She strode off in the direction of the registers. Betsey helped Ruth sit on the floor. I pulled the scarf out of the bag and offered it to Betsey, who took it without making any stupid protests about it being new and a gift and used it to blot the blood on Ruth's head. She looked sufficiently distracted that I got out my phone and called Malcolm. He picked up almost immediately. "Bored with your party already?" he said. In the background, I heard music and the sound of conversation.

"Malcolm, Penelope Wadsworth's been kidnapped," I said.

"What? Hang on, Helena, it's too loud in here." I heard him murmur something, then a few seconds later the music died away, and Malcolm said, "Did you say someone was *kidnapped?*"

"Penelope Wadsworth. She's a glass magus, Malcolm, we're at the mall and she went to the bathroom and someone took her."

"Which mall?"

"Lloyd Center."

"How long ago?"

"Maybe a minute. Juliet is doing something to…I don't know. I hope to locate her."

"We'll be there as fast as we can. Is everyone else all right?"

"They hurt one of my friends, but she seems okay, just a bit bloody."

"Try to keep everyone together." He hung up.

I walked over to Juliet just as Cynthia came running up with the middle-aged clerk behind her. The woman dropped to her knees beside Ruth and said, "Are you all right? I can't believe you were attacked in the middle of the store!"

"I'll be fine. My head hurts," Ruth said.

"Well, I've called mall security and they're searching for your friend," the woman said. It sent a chill through me. Those people, whoever they were, who'd kidnapped Pen were almost certainly magi, and I had no doubt they'd be willing to use force against anyone who got in their way.

Juliet had dropped Pen's purse on the ground and was holding a compact mirror in her left hand. She breathed on it, and the surface misted over, but didn't clear as the condensation evaporated. I was afraid to interrupt her, but I couldn't look away. "It's all right, Helena," Juliet said. "This is a simple synchronicity magic. Like a one-way ansible. I'm trying to establish—oh, good, it took. I was afraid this didn't have a strong enough resonance with Pen."

The mist cleared, revealing not the reflection of Juliet's dark face but a shifting, bobbing hallway, like the view from a camera held by someone running. The plain, unadorned hallway was lit by fluorescent bulbs which gave the scene a green-tinged glow. "Looks like a back way through the mall," Juliet murmured.

More motion, this from beside me, distracted me from the vision. A man in a mall security uniform jogged up to us and, like the clerk, went to his knees beside Ruth. "Someone's called 9-1-1," he said, "and we'll get that seen to."

"It's not that bad," Ruth protested.

"No sense taking chances," the mall cop said, "and we're concerned about finding your friend, too. Where did the attack take place?"

"Near the bathrooms on the second floor," Ruth said. "I didn't see anything, just that Pen was gone when I came to."

Juliet cursed under her breath. "Outer door," she said to me. "They're getting away."

"Which door?"

"I don't—it's the parking lot. Must be Multnomah Street side."

I turned and ran. "Helena!" Juliet exclaimed, coming after me. "We can't do anything."

"We can't just let them take Pen," I said, running for the escalator. Behind me, the mall cop shouted something, but I ignored him. It wasn't as if he could do anything to stop us.

We pelted down to the ground floor, Juliet carrying on a running commentary. "They haven't gotten in a car yet," she said. "I don't know why—oh, I think Pen's fighting them. I got a good look at one guy's face."

I called Malcolm as we ran for the exit. "Multnomah

Street parking lot," I gasped when he answered. "How far are you?"

"Helena, you had better not be chasing them," Malcolm said. "It's far too dangerous."

"We're just—going to keep an eye on them, in case they drive away—"

"We can track them. Stay *back*."

I disconnected without responding. We wouldn't do anything crazy like get into a car chase. If they got away, we'd let them go. But I couldn't bear the thought of one of my friends being abducted like I was sure the Kellers had been.

We burst out of the doors into the chilly drizzle that had begun falling while we were inside. Breathing heavily, I scanned the parking lot. Even with all the lights, it was too dim to see much. Juliet said, "I think they knocked her out. I can't believe they did this in public! And no one tried to stop them!"

"As far as we know," I said. "Didn't you see any landmarks?"

"Just this old beater truck painted canary yellow," she said. "Unmistakable in daylight, but at night…"

"We have to try." I ran toward the parked cars. It was about twenty 'til nine and the lot looked sparser than when we'd entered. My phone rang. "I'm not chasing them, Malcolm."

"Do you have some way of finding them?" Malcolm asked.

"Juliet did something she called synchronicity."

"Good. Wait for us at the entrance." He hung up. I went back to scanning the parking lot. Ahead of me, a large, blocky dark shape moved down the aisle toward us. I had just enough time to think *It ought to have its lights on* before it was on us. I leaped to one side to avoid getting hit by the yellow truck.

"It's them!" I screamed.

"Stay back," Juliet said. She planted herself with her legs wide apart and her fists clenched close to her chest, facing the retreating truck. She bowed her head, and a deep rumble came from her throat, building gradually to a scream, the sound of someone pushed to the limits of physical endurance. The truck stopped as if it had smashed into a wall, rebounding off nothing. Then, to my astonishment, it rolled backward, gathering momentum as if the smooth asphalt were sloped instead of level. Cries of horror came from the cab of the truck, and the doors flew open. Two men jumped out and ran.

The truck came to a stop. "Oh, you are *not* getting away that easily," Juliet growled, and raised one hand with the fingers extended. One of the men kept running, but the other stumbled and fell. Then he flickered, like a bad TV image, distorted, and vanished.

"Damn it," Juliet said, then, "*Watch out!*" and shoved me to one side. Something flew past my head, right where my chest would have been, something that screamed like fireworks. I landed hard on my hands and knees and rolled to one side, my heart beating hummingbird-fast. Juliet ran past me, but I heard her footsteps slow and then stop. "Call Campbell," she said. "Tell him they're looking for a bone magus. If they can throw up a perimeter around this place, they might be able to catch him."

I got to my feet and brushed myself off, then remembered Pen and ran for the truck. The engine was still running, and the truck was still rolling backwards, so I had to hop to get into the cab and put it in Park. To my relief, Pen was in the back of the cab, stirring out of unconsciousness. "Pen," I said, "are you all right?"

"I'm going to throw up," she muttered, and did. I tried to help her, but the seat backs were in the way. All I could do was murmur comforting reassurances until she got herself under control and sat up, wiping her mouth.

Juliet appeared beside the truck. "Did you call him?"

"Not yet." I exchanged places with Juliet, who helped Pen out while avoiding the pool of vomit, and called Malcolm.

"We're almost there," he said. "You're not following him, I can tell." We each had apps on our phones that let us track each other's location, something I'd suggested when Malcolm had come home very late from the hunt one night and I'd freaked out a little.

"No, but Juliet stopped their car. I've never seen anyone lift a truck with magic before."

"Stone magi are powerful telekinetics," Malcolm said. "Did she capture any of them?"

"Thanks for not yelling at us for engaging with the kidnappers."

"I reserve the right to do so later."

I smiled. "No, they ran. One of them ward-stepped out, and I didn't see what happened to the other, but Juliet says he's a bone magus and if you set up a perimeter, you might catch him."

"We'll do that. Did they take Wadsworth with them?"

"They left her. She's okay."

"Thank God for that," Malcolm said. "Take her inside and make sure she's all right. I'll call you when I have more news."

I put my phone in my pocket and went back to where Juliet and Pen stood. Pen looked ghastly in the light from the street lamps, but she didn't look injured. "What are we going to tell everyone about Pen's escape?" I said.

"That I fought my way free in the parking lot and made an unholy racket, and they ran," Pen said. "And that I don't know why they took me or what they wanted."

"Glass magus," Juliet said. "That was incredibly lucky."

"Thank you," Pen said, hugging Juliet, who after a stunned moment hugged her back. Ambrosite and Nicollien…maybe all we needed was for the two factions to start rescuing each other from the Mercy.

I shivered. "Let's get inside, and I'll call Viv and tell her what happened."

"Damned jerks ruined our chances at winning," Pen said. "I hope I get a crack at them just for that."

An ambulance pulled up just as we were entering the mall, and a couple of paramedics rushed past us. We followed them, not as rapidly because Pen had started complaining of a headache. Back in Macy's, Betsey saw us and shrieked, startling everyone but the paramedics. I supposed they had to work under all sorts of conditions, and shrieking women weren't even near the top of the list. I left Pen and Juliet to talk to the mall cop, who'd been joined by a female comrade, and called Viv.

"Where are you?" she demanded. "You're going to lose."

"Viv, something's happened," I said, and filled her in on the details. *All* the details, in a very low voice. "Malcolm and… I don't know who's with him…anyway, he's hunting for the kidnapper."

Viv swore. "Is everyone all right?"

"I think Ruth is going to be fine. Pen's head hurts from whatever they did to keep her unconscious. But we're all right."

"Those bastards ruined your party. I'm so pissed off right now."

"Viv, it's not ruined. Okay, yes, it's a little…askew…at the moment, but just think what an exciting story I'll have to tell my children someday."

"Do you want us to come back? We're all outside at the rendezvous."

"I don't think they'll let you in." I glanced over my shoulder at where Ruth was being bandaged. "Where can we meet you? Back at your house?"

"It was supposed to be Voodoo Donuts for dessert. We'll go there and pick up a couple dozen donuts, and meet back at my place. Get there when you can, and don't worry about the rest, okay?"

"All right. See you soon."

"What was that about?" Cynthia said, startling me. I hadn't seen her approach.

"Just telling Viv what happened. Is Ruth okay?"

"Yes. She's about got the EMTs convinced she doesn't need a ride to the hospital. The mall cops are taking Pen's statement. Funny, they don't seem as concerned as I thought they should be. Pen's more persuasive even than I am."

Cynthia, while in on Abernathy's secret, didn't know anything about the Long War, or magic, and I intended to keep it that way. If Pen were using some kind of magic to persuade mall security this was nothing to worry about, I didn't want Cynthia to know. "Let's just all get out of here and back to Viv's place. I'm suddenly very tired."

It took another half hour to straighten everything out. Pen and Juliet together managed to convince mall security that there was nothing they could do, that the would-be kidnappers had fled and would not be coming back. Ruth's lack of a concussion convinced the paramedics she didn't need any more medical attention, though I could tell they wanted to press the issue. That really would ruin the evening, if one of us had to take an ambulance ride to the hospital. Eventually, we were allowed to go to our cars and leave. This time, I rode with Pen, watching her carefully for signs of further injury, but she drove carefully and didn't look as if she were in pain at all.

Our group was first back to Viv's house, and Jeremiah let us in. "I didn't know you were here," I said.

"I was banished to the bedroom, where I've been watching *Stranger Things*," he said. "Is Viv not with you?"

With Betsey and Ruth there, I couldn't tell him what had happened. "They all went to get donuts," I said. "Why does it feel so much later than 9:45?"

"If you were on that treasure hunt Viv and Judy planned, you're probably exhausted. She had everything ready for coffee and hot chocolate—why don't we get that started?"

So when Viv and the others rolled in fifteen minutes later, the house smelled deliciously of chocolate and coffee. "Oh, perfect," Viv said. The tip of her nose was pink from cold. "Everyone have a seat, and a donut."

"Forget donuts," Poppy said. "Pen was actually *kidnapped?*"

"You hear about these things happening, but it's always an urban legend," Linda said. "Were they white slavers? Pen, you were so lucky!"

Pen, shorter than me, doll-like and blonde, shook her head. "I don't know what they wanted. It all seems so surreal. I mean, they might have sold me to some foreign brothel—no, that's just absurd."

"You're not a wealthy heiress, are you?" Betsey said, laughing a little shakily.

"Not me. Poor as dirt."

"Maybe it was revenge. Did you piss off a crime lord?" said Cynthia.

"I hope not." Pen's laugh sounded less forced than Betsey's, but her hands were shaking enough that her coffee slopped up the sides of her mug. Having been kidnapped once before, I knew how it felt once the adrenaline high had passed.

"Well, I'm glad you fought them off. I don't know if I could have done it," Poppy said.

Sue put down her donut and put a professional hand to Pen's forehead. "I think you need to lie down," she said. "You're in shock."

Amid exclamations, we cleared the couch and urged a protesting Pen to lie on it. "I'm fine, really," she said. "I just—" She closed her eyes and breathed out. "I'm fine. It's just hitting me now what happened."

The rest of us stood awkwardly watching her. I had a feeling she needed to talk about it, but with Poppy, Linda, Betsey, and Ruth there, not to mention Cynthia, there was so much she couldn't say. Then Pen said, "So, we lost, right? What was the prize?"

That gave us permission to laugh. "A bag of gold-wrapped truffles," Linda said. "I think we ought to break them out and share. Everyone could use some chocolate."

We sat on the living room floor and ate truffles. Jeremiah had disappeared again, but I'd heard the front door open and shut and guessed he'd gone out. Maybe Viv had told him what had happened, and he'd gone to join Malcolm and the other searchers. As a wood magus, Jeremiah was attuned to the natural world in a way that made him gifted at hunting invaders—and people—down. I hoped they'd find the kidnapper. I wondered where the other one had ward-stepped to.

Pen recovered enough to sit up and eat a truffle. "I feel so stupid," she said. "All this fuss."

"It's a big deal, Pen, and you need to take it easy," Sue said.

"I will. And I think—sorry to break the party up, but I need to go home. Sue, will you drive my car? I still feel shaky."

"Sure." Sue helped Pen up. "Thanks for the fun, Viv. Congratulations, Helena."

It was the signal for everyone else to gather coats and purses and make their goodbyes. I noticed Juliet and Allie hanging back, angling to be the last to depart. When, finally, Cynthia hugged me and said, "Dinner at home tomorrow. I'll see you then, right?" Viv shut the door on her and sagged against it.

"I can't believe someone tried to kidnap her," she said. "Was it really because she's a glass magus?"

"One of the best, even if she is a Nicollien," Juliet said. "I hope she's all right."

"Her boyfriend is a steel magus. He can protect her," Allie said. "Where did Washburn go?"

"To join Malcolm," Viv said. "Though he didn't look hopeful. He said there was a chance the kidnapper wouldn't let himself be taken alive."

"I can't blame him," Judy said, flopping down on the couch. "His life would be forfeit anyway, if he is one of the Mercy."

The door opened. A moment later, Jeremiah entered, trailed by Malcolm, Mike, and Derrick Tinsley, bone magus of Malcolm's invader fighting team. Malcolm advanced on me, glowering. "You should not have followed them," he said. "That was incredibly reckless and dangerous."

"We were careful," I said, choosing not to mention nearly being run over and whatever the bone magus had shot at me. "And Juliet stopped the truck, so we saved Pen from being kidnapped."

"Nevertheless," he said, folding me in his arms and kissing the top of my head.

"You let her go home?" Jeremiah said.

"She's an adult, Washburn, we could hardly stop her," Juliet said. "She had Sue drive her home."

"Did you find the kidnapper?" I demanded.

"Yes. He committed suicide when he knew capture was inevitable," Malcolm said. "I wish I understood the hold the Mercy has on its operatives. We have no idea if the suicide was a conscious choice, or an implanted condition."

"They both sound awful," I said, giving Malcolm a final hug and stepping away, though keeping hold of his hand. "Is there anything you can learn from...the body?"

"Canales took it back to the Gunther Node for examination," Derrick said. "With luck, some analyst will identify his clothing or dental work or something, and we'll get an ID. Anything will help at this point."

"And we are still no closer to finding the missing magi," Malcolm said.

"Have some coffee, or hot chocolate," Viv said. "You all look half frozen."

"It's raining harder now," Mike said. "Not at all like home. Chicago is caked in ice and snow right now."

I had just accepted a mug of coffee from Judy, so I caught the look of suspicion she directed at Mike. I glared at her. She raised her eyebrows and shook her head. Now wasn't the time for me to call her on her hostility, but I hoped she had the sense to keep her mouth shut.

I handed the mug to Mike and said, "So, is it better here, or worse?"

A guarded look passed over his features. "Different."

"Better," Malcolm said. "As I keep telling him."

"I told you I'd keep an open mind." He glanced at me. "You might as well know," he told me, "Malcolm wants me to fill the open position on his team."

I gasped. "Take Olivia's—I mean, I guess he does need a paper magus." Olivia Quincy, killed six months ago by the Mercy in the assault on the Krebbitz Node, had been a good friend to me and to Malcolm. They hadn't replaced her in all that time, and it felt instinctively wrong that anyone could take her place. But that was stupid, sentimental thinking. "Will you do it?"

"I'm...thinking about it."

"That's a big decision," Judy said. "Definitely something to be careful about."

Her tone of voice verged on derisive. Mike said, "What's that supposed to mean?"

"It means," said Judy, "be careful."

Confused, I looked at Mike. He'd gone impassive, as if he and Judy were having a conversation only they understood. "You don't know a damn thing about it," he said. "Mal, I'm gone. See you back at your house." He left the room, and soon the front door slammed behind him.

"That was completely out of line," Malcolm snarled. "How dare you insult him?"

"He's going to get you killed," Judy replied, not at all afraid of Malcolm's looming bulk. "Do you know about Sharon Stewart? Ronnie Wessler? Or—"

"More than you, clearly," Malcolm said. "You should watch how you throw those names around. And never repeat them in Mike's hearing, do you understand?" His grip on my hand was growing painful. "Helena, let's go home."

"I—" One look at his face was enough to convince me we needed to leave. "Thanks, Viv, Judy. It was...memorable."

Then I realized I was Judy's ride. "Um, Malcolm, I need to take Judy home."

Malcolm released me, opened the door, and strode to his car. "Drive safely," was all he said before getting in and driving away. The rain was falling harder now, and Judy and I sat in my car for a moment, waiting for it to warm up. Judy looked like a marble statue, her damp, short hair falling forward over her face. I was afraid to say anything, though I was desperate to know what she'd meant.

Finally, I put the car in gear and backed down the long drive. We drove in silence for a few minutes, until Judy said, "Two years ago Mike Conti's entire team, all but him, was slaughtered by invaders. He was charged with negligence and sentenced to a year's probation. It's why he hasn't had a team since then."

"Judy, that can't possibly be the whole story! I told you, Nicolliens—"

"I didn't hear it from friends. It's in the official records. Malcolm's a fool if he thinks Conti is anything but a liability."

I didn't know what to say. Judy added, "If Conti joins Malcolm's team, they're all in danger. You have to convince Malcolm not to take him on."

"*I* do? What makes you think Malcolm wants my opinion? He's been fighting the Long War for years, certainly longer than I've been a Warden. I don't know anything about it."

"He trusts you. If you tell him—"

"I can't tell him that. He trusts Mike, and he's known him longer than we have. I'm sure there's an explanation."

"Helena, if he gets Malcolm killed, is that going to be a comfort?" Judy said. "Conti's illusions failed the team at a crucial moment because he got cocky. Who says he's learned from that?"

I pulled into the parking lot behind Abernathy's. "Who says he hasn't?"

Judy shook her head and flung open her door. "Don't say I didn't warn you." She slammed the door behind her and ran for the back door, disappearing inside.

I swore violently and smacked the steering wheel. Judy had to be wrong. Malcolm wouldn't want anyone so careless to be on his team. And yet…visions of Malcolm and Derrick and Hector torn apart by invaders tormented me. Mike's team killed. Probation. It didn't sound like the antagonism of an opposing faction.

I put the car in gear and headed for home. It couldn't be later than eleven, but I felt as weary as if I hadn't slept in days. Maybe I needed to talk to Malcolm, after all. If his life was in danger, I couldn't let his oldest friendship stand in the way of warning him.

9

B y Sunday night I still hadn't found a way to ask Malcolm about Mike. We had dinner with my family that evening, and Mike was his usual cheerful, engaging self. He really hit it off with my niece Isabella, playing a game with brightly colored lights on his phone and making her laugh. I watched him, and wondered about Sharon Stewart and Ronnie Wessler. Teammates? *Dead* teammates?

That night, as we were getting ready for bed, I said, "What kind of trouble did Mike have in Chicago?"

"I told you, that's not my story to tell," Malcolm said.

"Does it have something to do with Sharon Stewart and Ronnie Wessler?"

Malcolm paused in brushing his teeth. "If you're so curious," he said, "why don't you ask Mike?"

"Oh, I don't want—you implied it would upset him—"

"Then you shouldn't ask me, if it's something Mike would be upset by." Malcolm rinsed and put his toothbrush away.

"I'm worried for your safety. Judy said he was put on probation back in Chicago."

"Judy," Malcolm said darkly, "has it in for Mike. I don't know why she's suddenly exhibiting Nicollien sympathies—"

"It's not Nicolliens. It's in the public record. Malcolm, is it really a good idea to have Mike on your team, if he's dangerous?"

"He's not dangerous," Malcolm said, an edge coming into his voice. "And you shouldn't talk about things you don't understand."

I lost my temper. "And whose fault is that? If it's so bad you won't tell me, and Mike won't talk about it, don't you think that means it's a serious problem?"

"Ask Mike," Malcolm said. "I'm done discussing this." He turned his back on me and sat on the bed, taking off his watch and putting it on the bedside table. I stared at him, angry tears filling my eyes. I hated it when we fought, hated more when I wasn't sure I was in the right. All I wanted was to keep him safe, as far as that was possible with the line of work he was in. Fine. If he was going to be stubborn, I could be just as stubborn as he. I climbed into bed and lay with my back to him, arms crossed over my breasts. *Be that way. I don't care.*

Malcolm turned off his bedside lamp and lay down. I listened to his breathing, waiting for it to slow into sleep. Was he lying there awake, replaying our argument? He'd been in the wrong, too. We were married—almost married, I reminded myself—and that meant we needed to be open with each other, not keep secrets. *It's not his secret he's keeping*, I thought, perversely.

"I'm sorry," Malcolm said, not moving. "I understand you were only trying to protect me. You have to trust me, Helena."

"And you can't trust me?"

"I told you, it's not my story to tell. But I'll ask Mike to talk to you. If he does move here and take the position with my team, his actions will affect you as much as they do Tinsley's wife and daughters."

I rolled over and snuggled up against his back. "I'm sorry I pushed. You're right, you shouldn't betray a friend's trust. I just...worry."

Malcolm rolled over to take me in his arms and stroke my hair. "Just think," he said, "next week this time, we'll be in the honeymoon suite, happily married."

"I'd almost forgotten. It seems like forever away."

"There's the rehearsal and dinner coming up fast. I hope Mike and Judy can keep from coming to blows."

"Me too. I think Judy can control herself, though."

"Mmm. You know, there are some other things we might rehearse."

"Really? Like what?"

Malcolm's hands strayed under my nightshirt. "I'm sure I can think of something."

Judy was in the office sorting augury requests from payments when I arrived the next morning. "Did you talk to him?" she asked, not looking at me.

"Did I—oh. I did. He's going to ask Mike if he's willing to tell me the gory details, whatever they are."

"Just don't be too quick to take Conti's word for it. He might try to spin things his way."

"Judy, do you have something against Mike? You're acting awfully antagonistic."

Judy slapped the pile of envelopes on the desk and looked

up at me. "I've known a lot of men like him," she said. "So confident it's almost arrogance. I hate it when they get away with what might as well be murder, with barely more than a slap on the wrist. And now he's in a position to let that spill over onto people I care about."

"Judy, you're jumping to conclusions. We don't know what happened in Chicago, not really. There are so many details that don't make it into the official record. And regardless of that, I simply can't believe Malcolm would defend someone who'd been careless enough to get people killed. I have to believe something else is going on."

Judy sighed. "All right. You have a point. Maybe I'm over-reacting because he was a jerk when he was in here before."

"He wasn't a jerk!"

Judy eyed me. "He was a typical Ambrosite snob about Nicolliens."

"You weren't exactly polite to him, either."

She sighed. "Yeah, I guess not." She stood and handed me the small stack of augury requests. "Bad first impressions, I guess. It's not like I know the man, and I trust Malcolm's judgment. I hope I'm wrong."

"Me too."

"Anyway. Has Ken Gibbons been in contact with you?"

"Not recently. I had an idea, though."

"What?"

"I'm going to enter the oracle without an augury request. I want to see if it still goes to the past."

A frown creased Judy's forehead. "There's no guarantee it will go anywhere other than the present, if it's inconsistent."

"I know, but if it does...actually, I don't know what that will prove, except that I don't have as much control over the oracle as I thought." Now that I'd said it out loud, it didn't sound like such a great idea, but it would give me something to do that wasn't passively waiting for the oracle to transport me.

Judy shrugged. "Better do it soon. Mondays are too busy for any extracurricular activities."

She followed me out to the front of the store, where I set the augury requests on the counter and drew a deep breath. "Here's hoping," I said, and willed the oracle to open for me.

When I walked into the stacks, I looked around, and my heart beat faster when I saw sturdy oak bookcases and the now-familiar pink linoleum. The stillness, not that of the oracle but of a store uninhabited, echoed in my ears. I stopped, listening for movement, but heard nothing but my own breathing. It took me a moment to realize what was different: today the past smelled of hot coffee. Where—or rather, *when*—was I?

I was seized with an urge to explore, find a way out, and never mind what Ken had said. Traveling through time…if my research was correct, I was the first person who'd ever done so. Think what it could mean to science, or magery, or both!

But a few long paces brought me to my senses. I couldn't guarantee, if I exited the oracle in this time, I'd be able to return to my own time, and I had no desire to be trapped in the past. Instead, I closed my eyes and focused my attention inward, feeling for my connection with the oracle. "Thank you," I whispered, "I'm done now."

The smell of coffee vanished as if it had never been, replaced with the scent of warm honey. I opened my eyes and saw the familiar yellow 2x8s. Sighing, I retraced my steps to the counter and picked up the first augury request. "It happened," I said to Judy, "and I was able to return myself the way I always do. I just don't know what it means."

"See if the augury takes you there," Judy suggested.

"It's never done it twice in a row."

"Not for two auguries in a row. But the first time was just you entering the oracle."

"That's true." I extracted the paper. *Where is Rosario Alvarez?* Another missing glass magus? I walked into the oracle and, to my surprise, found myself once more in the past. So Judy had been right, though I wasn't sure, again, what it meant.

I found the augury—*The All-True Travels and Adventures of Lidie Newton*, which looked like something I might want to read —and returned to the counter. "It happened again."

"I like being right, but I'd prefer knowing what I was right about," Judy said. "Try again."

But the next three auguries were normal. When I returned from the third, I said, "There's got to be some system to it. Something triggers the change."

Judy went to open the door for the Nicolliens. "Call Gibbons. Maybe he has an idea by now."

I didn't get a chance to call Ken; he called me around noon, after the morning rush had ebbed and I was finishing up the mail-in auguries. "Is this a bad time?" he said.

"No, it's fine. I was going to call you, in fact. I managed to go to the past twice in a row this morning, but I don't know if that's significant or not."

"It is, if my understanding is correct." He didn't sound happy. "It's not a good thing," he went on, confirming my impression.

My heart sank. "Do you think it will happen more frequently? Until…I don't know what might happen. Something bad, probably."

"You're not wrong." Ken cleared his throat. "I'm not entirely certain how it's happening, but my research tells me *what* is happening. Abernathy's contact with the past is…I suppose the best image is of a worn spot in fabric, like someone's knee wearing a hole in his pants over time. Every time you make contact with the past, you wear on the fabric of space-time a little more."

The image of a hole in space-time frightened me. "It's not —the invaders' dimension, is it? Are they going to come pouring through into our world through Abernathy's?"

"It's not the same thing. Wherever they come from is orthogonal to our reality, and they're no more capable of using this weak point than they are any other breach to our world. But it could mean a disruption to the linear flow of time. A place where time doesn't exist. And that could be catastrophic. Certainly will be catastrophic to Abernathy's, if it isn't stopped."

I gasped. "But I don't know what's causing it! I can't stop it if I don't know how it started."

"Don't worry, Helena, I have a theory." His mellow, unctuous voice soothed me for once. "I think what's happening is Abernathy's current configuration, the locations of the books, is identical to that of the earlier time you keep entering. Not all the books, of course, but enough of them that Abernathy's temporal signature—"

"I don't know what that is."

"It's a fancy term for a person or thing's unique identity at a particular place and time. At any rate, its temporal signature is currently enough like the earlier Abernathy's that when the oracle, which is unique and can be said to exist in all times at once—"

"Wait. Stop." I felt dizzy. "I'm sorry to keep interrupting you, but I don't understand what you mean. The oracle came into being in 1782, so it can't possibly exist in all times."

"It's not complicated." Now his tone of voice irritated me, as if he were talking to a dimwitted child. "Once the oracle came into being, it was as if it had always existed. I assure you I'm right about this. It's one of the things all the named Neutralities have in common. At any rate, it's not important to the point at hand. May I continue?"

"I—sure." I still felt confused, but it was the kind of confusion where I felt if I could overload myself with enough facts, it would start to make sense.

"What happens," Ken said, speaking a little more slowly, "is the oracle's presence—its alertness, so to speak—provides the magical force that allows the two times to slip over and into each other, and anyone within the oracle's field, for lack of a better word, is transported from one time to the next."

"So someone in the past might come into the future—our present?"

"Precisely!" Ken might as well have patted my head in approval. "The problem is, as I said, the gradual wearing away of time-space at the point where the times connect. But as you remove books for auguries, the matching temporal signatures will degrade, and it will stop happening."

"But not soon enough, it sounds like." I chewed my lip in thought. "If we rearrange the shelves thoroughly, that should alter the signature, right?"

"Possibly. It could be that the presence of those books, regardless of their physical location on the shelves, will continue to trigger the connection."

I swore, and apologized. "Then…we need some way to identify what books are doing it, and pull those."

"I'm sure a glass magus could devise a ritual that would do that," Ken said. "Though it would take time."

"And it sounds like time is something we don't have," I

said. Another idea niggled at me, an idea so awful I couldn't bear to give it space in my head. "There's another solution, but it would be drastic."

"What's that?"

I let out a deep breath. "We could remove *all* the books and replace the store's contents entirely."

Ken whistled. "That *is* drastic. I'm not sure the situation calls for any action so dramatic."

"There's no way to know how many more times the store can connect with the past before it ruptures, or whatever it is that happens. I'm not sure we have time for anything less dramatic."

"It's up to you, my dear. I'll continue my research, and perhaps I can come up with a better solution."

"Thanks, but I think I have to move ahead on this."

After I disconnected, I sat at my desk and closed my eyes. In my imagination, I saw hundreds of cartons of books loaded onto trucks, hundreds of other cartons spilling out onto the shelves. This wasn't just drastic, it was catastrophic. Moving Abernathy's from England to the United States was nothing compared to what I proposed to embark upon. I knew from reading about that transfer how small a volume of books the oracle needed to survive, and I could think of ways to ensure it wasn't damaged. But this was going to cost a *lot* of money. If it was less than a million dollars, between the new books and the cost of the labor, I'd be very surprised. And the oracle would have to accept or reject every book we proposed to add to it, just the way it did when people brought in books for trade. It was going to take forever.

Maybe I was wrong. Maybe I needed a glass magus— something in short supply at the moment. Pen would be willing, I was sure. I should talk to her before I took any drastic measures. I dialed her number and got her voice mail. "Pen, how are you?" I began, remembering in time that she'd undergone a horrific experience just days before. "I hope everything's all right. There's something I need to talk to you about, if you'll call me when you get a chance." I hoped that wasn't too abrupt. Sometimes my concern for my oracular charge made me forget other people had problems, too.

Pen called back around five. "I'm fine," she said when I asked how she was doing. "Still a little shaky. It was just so sudden, I can't quite believe it happened. I'm afraid I'm sort of a coward now. Jethro goes everywhere with me." She laughed. "He's more upset about it even than I am. I don't suppose you have any news about the kidnappings? Like, the bastards have been caught and all the missing magi returned?"

"No, sorry," I said. "I wish I did. I'm so worried about Harry and Harriet."

"They're survivors. They're probably giving their captors hell."

"I hope so. No, I had a different question in mind. It's about Abernathy's. I don't suppose you could do magic that would identify particular books? Like…some kind of mystical search engine?"

"Sure. What kind of books?"

Now that it came to it, I felt stupid explaining. "It seems Abernathy's is…sort of traveling in time. Or connecting to an earlier time. I need to figure out which books are causing it."

"Wow. I didn't think time travel was possible."

"Neither did I. Ken Gibbons at Meryford University has been looking into it for me, and he thinks Abernathy's is resonating with an earlier version of itself. If I can identify the books that are identical in both places, and get rid of them, the problem should stop."

"Wow," Pen said again. "That's...not small. Is that the only solution?"

"No, but it's better than the alternative. But if it's not possible, I need to know."

"It's *possible*. In the sense that theoretically I should be able to devise any search magic you care to name. But... Helena, I don't know about this. It may take several magi, and it's going to be nearly a week before I can promise any results."

"That's okay. Are you willing to do it, then?"

"Sure. It would be a tremendous challenge, but I like that. I'll talk to the magi at the Gunther Node and see if they're willing to help. We might be able to shorten the time—I take it this is time-sensitive?"

"It is. Supposedly the problem's getting worse."

"Then we'll move as quickly as we can. I'll come down tomorrow morning and see if I can't assess whether it's possible at all, give you some better estimate. Don't worry, Helena, we'll figure it out."

"Thanks. And I'll let you know if I learn anything about the kidnappers."

I hung up to discover Judy standing in the office doorway, hands on hips. "Were you going to explain any of this to me?"

"Come on, Judy, there hasn't been time. I swear half those Ambrosites just wanted someplace warm to chat with their friends. I told you about Ken's theory."

"But not that the need for a solution was so dire. How much time do we have?"

"I have no idea. Which means sooner is better." I explained the solutions I'd come up with and watched her expression go from unhappy to stunned to horrified when I mentioned replacing the entire stock.

"That's insane," she said. "We'd never make it work. Do you have any idea how many books are in this store?"

"No," I said, "and neither do you, but we both have a good guess. I'm not saying it wouldn't be fiendishly difficult, but if Pen and the other glass magi can't figure it out, it may be our only option."

Judy grimaced. "You'll need to talk to the Board," she said. "We can't pay for something like that out of petty cash."

"I'm not looking forward to it. You know Mr. Ragsdale is going to use this as an excuse to criticize my custodianship."

"He can hardly argue with an expert like Gibbons." Judy checked her phone display. "It's 5:14. I don't think anyone else is coming in today. Let's get cleaned up and ready to go."

Armed with a bottle of Windex and a squeegee, I washed the glass countertop until I could see my reflection in it. "Maybe Pen can use you," I told the sheet of glass. "You've certainly seen plenty in the last year." I wiped down the keys of the ancient cash register, which didn't need it, but I was right there and it was something to do.

Judy walked past carrying the broom. "You and your obsession with glass," she said. "You're practically a glass magus yourself, the way you get excited over a streak-free surface."

"There's nothing wrong with that," I protested.

My phone rang. It was Malcolm. "This isn't to tell me you're going out with Mike again, is it? Because I like him, but I want to spend time with you."

"It's not," Malcolm said, and the grimness in his voice killed my teasing mood dead. "We've just heard from the Silvestres Node about Rudy Galli, their missing glass magus. He turned up dead just outside Washington, D.C. about four hours ago."

10

My throat began to close up. "Not Harry and Harriet?"

"No. As far as we know, Galli is the first to be found, living or dead. This doesn't mean they're in any more danger than they were before, Helena."

"Still..." I sank onto the tall stool behind the counter. "What else do they know?"

"He was shot at long range, in the middle of a crowd, which suggests he had escaped and the Mercy was desperate to keep him from returning to us and revealing their location or plans."

"How does that mean he escaped?"

Malcolm sounded more grim than I'd ever heard him. "Had the Mercy executed him, they would have buried him where no one would ever find him. This speaks to them slipping up, which gives me hope."

"I see." It was hard to see a death as anything positive, but if it meant finding the other missing magi, we could at least make the best of it.

"The Silvestres Node is trying to figure out how he got to where he was killed. They're hoping to be able to trace his movements and possibly identify where he'd been held for the last ten days since he was reported missing."

"That's so awful. Did he have a family?"

"I don't know. We've been told very little, it not being in our jurisdiction, but Lucia is even more determined to find our missing magi before—" He went abruptly silent. I didn't need him to finish that thought. "At any rate," he finally continued, "Lucia has some work for me, but it will be later. I'll have dinner ready by the time you get home."

"Thanks. You'll tell me what you learn, right?"

"Of course." He hung up. I closed my eyes and breathed in the smell of roasted apples and, more faintly, the acrid smell of Windex. Part of me wished Malcolm didn't have to spend so much time on Lucia's chores, but it was outvoted strongly by the rest of me, which hoped Malcolm's work would lead to finding the Kellers. I said a silent prayer for their safety, then went to the basement to put away the cleaning supplies.

Cleaning hadn't taken very long; I still had about half an hour before I could lock up and go home. I sat at my desk and leaned back until the two front legs of my chair left the floor and my head rested against the wall. No sense putting off this unpleasant task any longer. I flicked through my contacts list until I came to Ragsdale's office number. He'd probably already gone home for the night, but there was no way I was calling him there.

"Mr. Ragsdale," I said to his voice mail, "this is Helena Davies. I have an urgent matter regarding Abernathy's I need to present to the Board as soon as possible. Please call me as soon as you get this. I promise it's not a frivolous request." I hung up and looked at Judy, who was standing in the office doorway still holding the broom. "What do you want to bet he ignores me?"

"No bet," Judy said. "Maybe you should call another Board member."

"In the morning. I have to give Mr. Ragsdale time to be a jerk so I don't look like I'm going over his head. I might call Ms. Stirlaugson herself, since this is fairly important."

"Good luck." Judy disappeared in the direction of the basement. I sighed and rocked forward in my chair, then propped my elbows on the desk and rested my chin in my hands. Ragsdale believed I'd betrayed him—him personally—in having a relationship with Malcolm and had made it his mission in life to prove I was unworthy of being custodian. I was so tired of him being rude and dismissive of me, even more tired of having to respond with politeness to every attack he brought against me. But he was my overseer, and if I wanted to stay custodian, I had to prove myself to him time and again. Three more months. I could handle three more months.

To MY SURPRISE, Ragsdale called first thing in the morning, just after I finished breakfast. "You have a problem?" he said.

His anticipatory tone of voice told me he hoped it was the kind of problem that would prove I was an unworthy custodian. "Abernathy's has a problem," I said. "I have a couple of solutions, but I need authorization from the Board to implement them."

Ragsdale was silent. Probably he was assessing my words for weaknesses. "What problem?" he finally said.

It was my turn to go silent. I wanted to wait to tell the

whole Board what was going on, but Ragsdale probably wasn't willing to be put off. "Abernathy's is making contact with an earlier version of itself. My expert tells me it's wearing a hole in the fabric of space-time. I know that sounds like science fiction—"

"You expect me to believe this?"

"Mr. Ragsdale," I said wearily, "what possible reason could I have for making this up? It sounds impossible, but I've visited that other time, and I assure you it's true. I need the Board's authorization to implement a drastic solution to the problem, and I need it soon."

"Ms. Davies, you had better not be wasting the Board's time."

"How soon can the Board meet with me?"

He went silent again. "In four days," he said. "I hope you appreciate that we're rearranging our schedules for this. I'm taking a lot on faith."

"Thank you, Mr. Ragsdale, I do appreciate it." I didn't say *I hope it will be soon enough.* No sense antagonizing him further. "Will you let me know where and when to go?"

"Monique will call you." He hung up without saying good-bye. I let out a long, frustrated breath. I'd rather deal with his assistant Monique any day.

"You were talking to Ragsdale," Malcolm said. He walked past me to rinse his coffee mug and set it in the dishwasher.

"Was it obvious?"

"You did use his name. But you also get this funny, tense look on your face whenever you speak to him, like you're suppressing an urge to scream." He put his arms around me and rested his chin on my head. "You are remarkably patient."

"I don't feel patient. I feel I'm only barely in control of myself. Why does he have to be such a jerk?"

"People deal with disappointment in many ways." He leaned in for a kiss. "Have a nice day. I'll let you know if we learn anything about the Kellers."

"Thanks." I returned his kiss with interest.

Pen was waiting at the front door when I arrived at Abernathy's, huddled into her heavy coat against the chilly wind that felt as if it were blowing straight from the North Pole. Her boyfriend Jethro waited with her, hulking and broad where she was petite. "I'm sorry you had to wait," I said. "You should have called Judy to let you in."

"We only just got here," Pen said. "I don't have much time, so can I look around?"

"Please do."

I refrained from following her into the stacks, reasoning that it might distract her. Instead I hung my coat and purse in the break room and returned to where Jethro waited by the counter. "Is she all right?" I said in a low voice.

"Twitchy," Jethro said, his light tenor at odds with his heavyset frame. "She's had nightmares about it. I don't think she'll really be over it until the kidnappers are caught."

"That makes sense. I can't even imagine how horrifying it must have been, being carried away for who knows what purpose. And now that one of the missing magi has turned up dead—"

Jethro sucked in a breath. "Dead? I hadn't heard that. Don't tell Pen."

"I won't."

Pen emerged from between two bookcases. "So explain to me what's happening," she said. "There are certain books that are triggering this…jump…in time?"

"Sort of. I don't totally understand it myself. Ken—Dr. Gibbons—thinks there are books in the store now that are identical with ones in an earlier time, and when the oracle becomes active, they connect both times."

"When is the earlier time? What year?"

"I don't know."

Pen wrinkled her nose and shook her head. "That's hard. If you knew the year, or better, the month and year, we could do magic to reveal the contents of the store at that time and compare it to the contents now. But that's not the problem."

"It isn't? It sounds like more than enough problem for me."

"The problem," Pen said, "is that magic of that kind will reveal the full contents of the bookstore, or it couldn't compare the two inventories to see which books are identical. It would void the indeterminacy principle and kill the oracle."

"Oh." A chill went through me. "And if you don't know the year?"

"Same problem applies. It would just take a lot longer. Like, it could take most of seven months to compare Abernathy's contents now with its contents then, even if we limited the search to the time it's been here in Portland. But it would still kill the oracle."

I swore under my breath. "So the drastic solution is the only solution," I said.

"What's the drastic solution?" Jethro asked.

"Replacing the entire contents of the store."

Pen's mouth fell open. Jethro whistled. "That's drastic," he said.

"I'm sorry I couldn't be more help," Pen said.

"You were a lot of help. You kept me from going off on an impossible tangent." I let out a deep breath. "I...don't think I can wait on the Board's approval to start this process going."

"Let us know if there's anything we can do to help," Pen said, and the two waved goodbye.

I left the store front and ascended the stairs to the apartment above the store. Judy, coffee mug in one hand, let me in. "Helena! Did something happen?"

I must have looked awful. I felt awful. "Pen can't identify the key books without destroying the oracle. It's going to have to be the drastic solution."

Judy swore as I had done. "Did Ragsdale call yet?"

"I'm meeting with the Board on Friday. Maybe we can get the process started before then." I swore again. "The rehearsal dinner is on Saturday. I get to face the Board and then deal with my soon-to-be mother-in-law."

"I thought Madeleine was persona non grata. You're letting her into the wedding party?"

"She's Malcolm's *mother*. And she's been less antagonistic the last few months, after I pointed out to her that her continued nastiness was going to ensure she never saw her grandkids. It's worse, though. Malcolm's grand-mère is coming down from Vancouver on Friday and she'll be at the dinner, too."

"You mean Madeleine's mother?"

"Yes. Her French-Canadian mother, who might be even worse than Madeleine. Malcolm says she's not at all like her, but she likely treats *him* just fine, oldest grandson and all that." I sighed. "I'm starting to feel tense. The oracle misbehaving, Madeleine, the dinner. Wanna bet it's going to snow?"

As if the universe felt I didn't have enough on my plate, the day was the busiest we'd had all month. Rudy Galli's death was the only thing anyone could talk about, not that there was much to tell. Dave Henry came in around 11:30 with an augury request from Lucia, and he had more information. "A couple of magi were able to infiltrate themselves into the investigation of Galli's death," he said while Judy wrote up his receipt. "They found he'd left magical traces all along his path and were able to backtrack it to D.C. The trail went cold there."

"Isn't that helpful?" I asked.

"Sort of. The traces were deliberately obliterated, so we're pretty sure wherever Galli was held wasn't where the trail ended. But between the auguries we received for our missing magi, and the ones Lucia was able to wrangle out of some of the other nodes that've had disappearances, we've narrowed down the search to somewhere within a very large circle centered on D.C."

"That's still a pretty big place," Judy said. She handed Dave his receipt, which he took with an abstracted air.

"Yeah," Dave said, "it is."

He turned to go, and I said, "Wait—Dave, is Lucia free this evening? I need to talk to her about Abernathy's problem."

"Maybe around eight. She's very busy."

"It won't take long, I promise."

"I'll let her know you're coming." He waved and left the store, crowding past a couple of Wardens clutching augury requests like lottery tickets.

It was four o'clock before I realized the nagging feeling in my stomach was hunger. I hadn't even had time to eat. Grousing, I took five minutes to grab the tuna fish sandwich I'd made that morning and a Diet Coke. The sandwich was mushy and damp, reminding me that the last time I'd had a mushy, damp tuna fish sandwich I'd sworn never to make it in the morning again. I really needed a vacation. Which I wasn't going to get. I suppressed feelings of self-pity and returned to the waiting Wardens.

At ten 'til six, I saw the last Warden out of the store and sagged into the counter. "We've never had a busier day."

"And there are still mail-in auguries," Judy said. "Sorry, that sounded like a criticism," she added when I raised my head and gave her a pained look.

"They can wait until morning." I straightened and popped the joints in my neck, which made me feel slightly better. "I'm going to visit the oracle and see if I can't relax. You can lock up if you want."

"Ten minutes early?"

"At this point I don't give a damn what Mr. Ragsdale thinks." I focused my attention on the oracle and walked between the bookcases.

It hadn't occurred to me that I might also walk back in time. But there was the pink linoleum, and the oak shelves. I stopped where I was and closed my eyes. The smell of dust and old leather soothed my spirits somewhat, despite my knowledge that this moment brought the oracle one step closer to disaster. "I'll figure this out, I swear," I whispered, though I still had no sense that the oracle was present. I didn't know why I couldn't feel it in the past, and that unnerved me. "It's going to be hard, but I'll do it."

The shelves shuddered, and I was back in the present. The oracle's awareness pressed down on me gently, like a feather bed—soft, but would grow heavier over time. "I wish I understood any of this," I said, walking toward the heart of the oracle. "Why it happens sometimes and not always. How much longer we have before destruction. Maybe we need to shut down the oracle for a while. That would keep the disaster from happening."

I rounded a corner and stood in the center of the oracle, where four tall bookcases stood sentinel around a small open space. "So what do you think?" I asked. "If we stop using you until we can reorganize the store——"

Light flared, bright enough that I flung up an arm to shield my eyes. Squinting through tears, I saw familiar golden letters spring up along the spines and covers of the books, flowing like liquid gold from one to the next. "I'm listening," I said. "Tell me what to do!"

But the letters, forming words I felt on the brink of understanding, didn't do anything but move. I waited, hoping they might spell out something useful, like *Remove all the books with titles beginning with 'The'*. That would be nightmarish, but at least it would be direction.

Golden letters twirled into a spiral that became a tight coil, like the cord of the ancient telephone in the office. The coil bent, curved, and formed a circle in midair, at head height to me. The air in the center of the circle shimmered like heat haze, and a blurry image formed. It was——me. But not a reflection of me. My hair lay loose around my shoulders, not pulled back in a ponytail the way it was now, and I was wearing a different shirt. "Is that...the future?" I asked, awed. "Or the past?"

The image wavered, then shrank...no, it was like a camera was pulling back to show more of the scene. I was walking through the stacks, but I was in the past——I recognized the oak bookcases. I rounded a corner, and light grew, natural sunlight. I stepped out from between two bookcases into an open space, and the vision popped like a soap bubble. The golden letters faded and disappeared. I calmed my too-rapid breathing and said, "I hope that means guidance of some kind. Explore the past? Ken said that could be dangerous, but I've never known

you to be wrong before, not when you were in your right...
whatever it is you use for consciousness."

The oracle's attention shifted. I could never explain to
anyone how I could tell when it was focused on me, but I knew
the difference. It wanted me to move on.

I left the oracle and discovered it was 6:03. Time to go
home for dinner and then to the Gunther Node. Maybe Lucia
would have an idea I'd missed.

"YOU DON'T HAVE to come with me," I said. "Not that I don't
want to spend time with you. But it's likely to be boring."

"I feel as if I haven't seen you for a week, what with all the
extra work I've had," Malcolm said. "And I know you don't
like driving at night during the winter."

That was true. "I'm not going to argue you out of it. Does
Mike want to join us?"

"Mike is following up on a lead with Tinsley and Canales.
I suggested he spend some time with them to get a feel for how
well they work together. They will need to forge their own
bonds, without my presence, if he is to join our team."

"Did you...talk to him?"

"I did. Mike is a very private person, Helena, and it's hard
for him to open up. I think he saw the need for it, though, and
I imagine he will want to talk to you soon."

"I feel almost guilty about making him talk about something that obviously disturbs him."

"I hate to make decisions for other people, but I've known
Mike for nearly fifteen years, and I judge it will be better for
him not to keep his pain bottled up. Think of it as catharsis for
him, and a relief from worry for you."

That helped a little. "I hope you're right."

We talked wedding plans on the drive to the node, not that there was much left for us to do. Aside from my concerns about the rehearsal dinner, I was a little worried that I wasn't *more* worried about the big day. But Deanna was so competent, and sent me a daily email reassuring me that things were going smoothly, that worry was pointless. I smiled, thinking of my beautiful dress, and Malcolm said, "That smile is filled with a world of secrets. Care to share?"

"You're going to love my dress. I only wish there were some socially acceptable way for me to wear it more than once."

"I have to remember to pick up the tuxes Thursday morning."

"We're going to be the best-looking couple that ever got married in Portland."

Malcolm pulled off the road and parked next to the airplane hangar that was the entrance to the Gunther Node. "I'm sorry we can't have a honeymoon. I promise to make our wedding night memorable."

I got out of the car and hugged him. "I don't mind. Much."

"You need some kind of vacation, love. You look so tired at night."

"Not haggard, right? I don't want to look haggard for my wedding."

"No, just tired." Malcolm tucked me under his arm and steered me toward the white painted circle, like a crown of thorny leaves, that allowed us to enter the Gunther Node, wherever it really was. He left me there and walked to the telephone on the far wall, speaking our names, then returning to me. "Tired, as if—"

The world blinked, and we were elsewhere. "—you ran a marathon every day," Malcolm said.

"It will be easier once this problem is solved," I said. "I hope Lucia can help."

The giant concrete chamber that was the Gunther Node's transfer hub smelled faintly of gardenias, and despite its chilly appearance, it was always comfortably warm—a constant 73 degrees Fahrenheit, Lucia had once told me. Colored lines like tangled string wove across the floor, directing visitors to wherever their business lay. I started toward the long, curving hallway that led to Lucia's office, remembered what Dave had said about how busy she was, and thought better of it. "Excuse me," I said, stopping a black-clad tech, "do you know where Lucia is?"

"Brown 32," the woman said. "Down the elevator to the second floor, then follow the line."

"Thanks." I found the brown line after a moment's search, and Malcolm and I set off.

Eight o'clock was apparently the node's quiet time. I'd been there several times, and this was the least busy I'd ever seen it. A couple of techs strolled past, pushing a mining cart full of glowing purple ore, *sanguinis sapiens* in its unprocessed form. Some Wardens in black fatigues hailed Malcolm with a wave. I reflected on the first time I'd been here, terrified and bleeding and in pain, with Malcolm a captive, and even then I'd been struck by how strange and yet familiar it all was.

The elevator took a long time coming. When it arrived, we stood aside to let some people off, then entered and Malcolm pushed the button for the second floor. We were the only ones in the elevator, and I thought about grabbing Malcolm and kissing him, but I wasn't sure there weren't hidden cameras and I didn't want to give Lucia something to be satirical about later.

The doors began to slide shut. "*Hold the elevator!*" someone shouted, and Malcolm stuck his arm out, making the doors open again. "Thanks," the man said, darting through. It was Darius Wallach, carrying a cardboard filing box with its lid fitted securely on. A bunch of holes were punched in the lid and sides that looked uncomfortably like air holes. Wallach smiled at us. He usually wore his snowy white hair pulled back from his lined, dark face, but today it was loose and surrounded his head like a frizzy halo. "Could you push the first floor button?"

I pushed it. "Thanks," he repeated. "What brings you here so late?" The box shuddered, and I heard a chittering sound, a high-pitched *yipyipyip* that sent a chill up my spine. Surely Wallach wasn't walking around with an invader, or a familiar, in such an insecure container?

"I'm here to talk to Lucia about Abernathy's problem," I said. I edged away from the box, trying to put Malcolm between me and it.

"Oh? What problem?"

"Abernathy's is resonating with an earlier version of itself. The oracle is traveling back in time."

Wallach set the box on the floor and put one foot on it. The lid bumped against him, but he pressed down harder. "Say again?"

"Well, actually it's sending me back in time, not traveling itself."

Wallach's puzzled expression became one of amusement. "Of course it's not," he said. "Time travel is impossible."

"But it's happening," I said, stammering. The humor in his eyes disconcerted me more than dismissal would have. "I've seen it."

"You've seen something, but I'm sure it wasn't the past." Wallach leaned down to thump the side of the box, stilling its contents. "I promise you, I know what I'm talking about. Time travel to the future, maybe, but definitely not to the past."

The elevator dinged, and the doors slid open. I didn't move. "How can you be so sure?"

"Lots of theory, lots of math," Wallach said. "And enough experimentation to prove the theory and math. Who told you you were traveling in time?"

"Dr. Gibbons at Meryford University."

"Huh. I don't know him. Doctor of math, or science?"

"Neither. He's a historian. Ph.D."

Wallach snorted. "And you believed him?"

"I didn't have any reason not to," I retorted, stung.

"It sounds as if you know things about this Helena needs

to understand," Malcolm said as the doors slid shut again. "Do you have a few minutes?"

"It will take far more than a few minutes to teach you everything I know about how time travel doesn't work." Wallach bent and hoisted the box, then shook his head at Malcolm when Malcolm offered to carry it for him. "Tell me what's been happening with Abernathy's."

The story, beginning with the first event and continuing through everything Ken had told me, including my near-encounter with someone in the other space, took us from the elevator to Wallach's lab—one of them, anyway; I'd learned he had several scattered throughout the node. It was warmly lit with dozens of old-fashioned incandescent bulbs I thought were illegal now, the walls painted creamy white and the floor black granite tiles. Two lab tables, each equipped with a sink and rows of test tubes, faced each other across the room.

Wallach listened intently, not interrupting. As I wound down, he carried the box to a door in the far side of the room that turned out to be a closet. Unlike the lab, it was lit by a single bulb that dangled loose from the ceiling. Wallach deftly upended the box into a Plexiglas cage and a chitinous form, glistening like an oil slick, swarmed out. He slapped a lid atop the cage and snapped closed the several latches holding it on. It stank of rotten eggs, the smell of an unharnessed invader, and I covered my mouth to hold back a shriek. Invaders were attracted to custodians, and I'd been attacked often enough that I had a healthy fear of them.

"Don't worry, Ms. Davies, that cage is magically secured," Wallach said. "So. If I understand you correctly, the oracle has been making a connection with some other place, one in which you can't sense the oracle's presence even though you are still able to retrieve an augury."

"Yes. Ken said it was resonating with—with some other time," I said defiantly.

Wallach grimaced. "This is what happens when amateurs get hold of *A Brief History of Time*," he said. "It's plausible, I'll give you that. You're not at fault for believing it. But it's impossible."

"You keep saying that. How can you be so sure? I mean, what did your experiments show that proves you're right?"

"That really would take too long." Wallach indicated a couple of tall stools and sat on one himself. His white hair looked ivory in the warm light. "The short answer is that the human body isn't made to run counter to entropy. Nothing is. To travel back in time, you have to pass through it in the opposite direction to what matter is intended to do. The few times we managed it, it...unraveled is probably the nicest term for what happened to the subjects. Thank God we figured it out before we tried it on a living creature."

"But I've read about Einstein-Rosen bridges. Wouldn't that make time travel instantaneous? You'd just move from one point to another. That's what I thought was happening with Abernathy's."

"An Einstein-Rosen bridge is still just theoretical, but from what we know, it doesn't work in reverse either. You might be able to use one to send you into the future, but it would be a one-way trip. Billings thinks she's done it, but so far she hasn't devised an experiment that would prove her test subject items are traveling into the future and not just disintegrating."

I felt frustrated and a little embarrassed. "So what *is* happening?"

Wallach shook his head. "Probably someone's created another oracle somewhere."

I gasped. "But I—that was my first thought, and Ken said

it was unlikely. He knows all about the named Neutralities, and he said Elizabeth Abernathy was incredibly lucky to have succeeded. That nobody else knows how."

"That doesn't mean it couldn't happen again." Wallach drummed his fingers on the tabletop. "I don't know much about how the oracle works, but I know everything there is to know about ansibles, and this sounds almost like how an ansible works."

"Almost?" Malcolm said.

Wallach's brow furrowed. "Ansibles are for data, not for physical objects. No one's ever made an ansible that could teleport things or people."

"But we teleport into the Gunther Node every time we come here," I said.

"That's magic, not technology. Yes, an ansible has a magical component, but it's still tech. Science."

"I don't understand the difference."

"An ansible sets up a resonance between two particles at a distance. Tricks them into believing they're the same particle. What happens to one happens to the other. The distance is irrelevant—could be across this room, could be the span of a galaxy. But it's always been thought that moving a physical object between the points of an ansible was impossible. It ought to destroy the object. Even so…everything you've told me suggests that's what's happening."

"But *why* is it happening? Do we still have to remove all the books?"

"I don't know," Wallach said. "I'd have to do more research. You want to remove all the books?"

"Ken said, if it's resonating, it's because the configuration of the store now is—well, obviously if it's not time travel, that's not true."

"No, that part could be true. If someone's built another oracle, they almost certainly modeled it on Abernathy's, which could mean the configuration of the two is close enough to set up a resonance. But I wouldn't take drastic measures yet. Let me take a look. There might be something I can suggest."

"I think we have a bigger problem," Malcolm said.

"What's that?" I asked. My head already ached, and his tone of voice, deep and troubled, made it worse.

"If someone's built another oracle," he said, "we might want to ask ourselves who that would be."

I swore. "The Mercy."

"It might explain the missing glass magi," Malcolm went on. "Glass magic is meant to reveal what is hidden, and that certainly applies to the secret knowledge the oracle disperses."

"As if we didn't have enough problems," I said.

"One thing at a time," Wallach said. "I'll examine the oracle tomorrow and see what else I can tell you. You talk to Lucia about whatever you were here for—"

"It sounds like it might be irrelevant now." I rubbed my aching forehead. "But she needs to know the Mercy may have built their own oracle."

"So tell her that," Wallach said. "Then get some sleep. You look exhausted."

I nodded. "Thanks, Mr. Wallach."

"It's fortunate I ran into you, no?" Wallach opened the door for us. "When should I come by?"

"Tomorrow at nine? Before the Wardens start lining up?"

"I'll see you then. Don't worry, Ms. Davies, we'll figure this out."

It should have been comforting, but all I could think of was how embarrassed I was at having been wrong. It was stupid, because how could I have known Ken was wrong, when he sounded so certain? "I wonder," I said, biting my lip.

"Wonder what?" Malcolm asked.

"Nothing. It's stupid." The passing thought that Ken might have deliberately misled me wasn't worth entertaining. He wasn't one of the Mercy, or he'd be in hiding with the rest of them. No, he'd just been wrong, and I should have realized that him knowing about the named Neutralities didn't translate to him being an expert on time travel. Well, we'd both been mostly wrong. I should call him in the morning and let him know about this new development.

We tracked Lucia down in Brown 32, which was a cavernous space that echoed with our footsteps—my footsteps, anyway; Malcolm always moved like a cat. "Make it quick," Lucia said when she saw us. "I haven't had dinner yet and my blood sugar is flatlining."

"I thought I was traveling in time, but it turns out the Mercy may have built a second oracle," I said.

Lucia blinked. "That's remarkably concise for you. Walk with me and give me the details."

We walked back toward her office and I explained what I remembered of Wallach's words, wishing I understood it better. Lucia said nothing until we reached her office door, then said, "So that's why they're kidnapping glass magi."

"We think so, yes," Malcolm said.

Lucia made a *hrmpf* sound and pursed her lips in thought. "You talked to Ken Gibbons?"

"Yes. I plan to let him know what we've learned tomorrow."

"Keep me informed. And if you think of any way to use this resonance to locate the second oracle, I want to know about it." She went into her office and shut the door, not inviting us in. Malcolm shrugged.

"Home," he said simply, and we walked back the way we'd come and found a tech to send us back to the airplane hangar. I felt so tired, as if I'd walked from our house to the Gunther Node instead of driving. Malcolm turned up the heat in the car, and I leaned my aching head against the car window, which was chilly and soothed the pain somewhat. The next thing I knew, Malcolm was shaking my shoulder and saying my name. "We're home."

I wiped a bit of drool off my cheek and let him lead me inside and put me to bed. My last thought, on drifting off, was *I'd better not be coming down with something five days before my wedding. Deanna would kill me.*

But I woke refreshed and, if not relaxed, at least feeling competent to handle whatever Abernathy's might throw at me. I showered, brushed out my hair, then went to my closet to find something to wear. My eye fell on a sage green blouse with three-quarter length sleeves and very wide cuffs. I hesitated. It was the shirt I'd seen myself wearing in the oracle's vision. I fingered the stiff cotton of the collar, then slipped it off the hangar and put it on. Maybe it would come to nothing, but if I didn't make an effort, nothing would change.

I arrived at the store just after 8:30 and found Judy already up and working at the computer. "Finances," she said curtly. "There's not enough coffee in the world to make this better."

I tactfully didn't say anything, just gathered what was left of yesterday's mail-in auguries and escaped.

No time travel—all right, it wasn't time travel, but what else could I call it?—happened for any of the four auguries I completed before Darius Wallach knocked on the front door. I let him in, wincing at the frigid breeze that came with him. "So what can you show me?" he said without preamble.

"I'm...not sure. It happens irregularly, and I can't take you with me into the oracle unless it's a dire emergency. The oracle doesn't seem to think it's that."

Wallach set his battered leather briefcase on the counter and took out a construction of wires and slim metal rods. He set it beside the briefcase and twisted and pulled on bits of it until it looked like a spider that had exploded. "This will tell us whether an ansible has been active in the area recently. It can't tell what the ansible is connected to, but it's a start."

He twisted a segment of the spider, and it began emitting a hum that made the roots of my hair tingle. The many spiky tendrils of wire and metal quivered, then shook fiercely, rocking the thing on its unstable base. Wallach grabbed it to keep it from falling. It looked like he was having trouble holding onto it, and I thought about helping, then decided it was stupid for me to interfere when I had no idea what was going on.

The tendrils whipped around, one scoring a hit on Wallach's forehead and making him hiss in pain. He set the thing down and stepped away from it. "Won't be long now," he said. A second later, the movement stopped, and the thing fell over, clattering against the glass countertop.

"So what does it mean?" I asked.

"Be patient. Give it a minute." Wallach shoved his hands into his coat pocket and tapped his toe in an irregular rhythm. I watched the spider, waiting for it to explode further or begin moving again. Nothing happened for longer than the minute Wallach had mentioned. My eyes watered, and I squinted, then blinked. It wasn't my eyes. Greenish-blue light gathered along the thing's tendrils like water droplets, flowing and combining and then coming apart again. The light grew brighter as I watched, but instead of growing paler with the increased brightness, the color deepened to a rich neon turquoise, like nothing I'd ever seen before.

"Huh," Wallach said, picking the thing up. Turquoise light bled down his fingers and made his dark skin look nearly ebony. "Never saw that before."

"What—" I began, then shut my mouth on my impatience. Wallach looked at me and grinned, an expression that transformed him from a dignified old scientist to a mischievous boy.

"You're not good with waiting, are you?" he said. "Never mind, I like that quality in others. Patience may be a virtue, but waiting for things to come to you is the slow road to senescence. It's definitely an ansible, and the biggest one I've ever seen. I'd bet hard cash it's the biggest ansible ever created."

"But how is that even possible?"

"The oracle is a strange creation. Maybe your Dr. Gibbons understands it, but even he can't know everything about it. My hypothesis is that someone has built a second oracle and managed to make it work, and the two are similar enough that occasionally they build up resonance and more or less turn on the ansible. How it's capable of transporting objects, I have no idea, unless the size makes a difference." He scratched his head. "Did I hear a rumor you think the oracle is a living creature, and not a magical field?"

"Yes. I've communicated with it, and it seems to have… personality, I guess."

"I might be able to work with that." He gathered up the spider and, with some effort, made it collapse into the briefcase. "I'll be back later. I need some tools and a couple of magi assistants. You don't mind me taking up space up front here?"

"If you can solve my problem, you can take up as much space as you like. The Wardens will just have to deal with it."

Wallach chuckled. "I never knew you were so fierce. I'll see you later, Ms. Davies."

I leaned against the corner when he was gone and watched the bookcases as if I expected something to come leaping out of them. Why hadn't I ever seen anyone else in the other place? Aside from that one near-encounter, it had always been empty, but if it was another oracle, presumably there was another custodian, one who would have just as much access to the oracle's space as I did. Was it just dumb luck that the Mercy hadn't used their oracle to attack me?

My eye fell on the remaining augury requests, but a thought occurred to me. Should I tell Ken what I'd learned now, or wait for Wallach to experiment further? I took out my phone and sat on the stool behind the counter. Ken should probably know as soon as possible, so his research didn't go down any other false paths.

Movement caught my eye, a ripple like flowing water. I glanced at the countertop, which shone like an imperfect mirror in the indirect light from the window. Whatever reflection it had caught was gone now. I looked toward the street, but saw nothing moving but tree limbs, bare and skeletal, shaking in the wind, and an old Ford truck that ambled past slower than the speed limit. The countertop rippled again, and I looked down in time to see the glass move, flowing in rings as if an invisible stream of water was pouring into it.

I hopped off the stool and screamed, "*Judy!*" The rippling continued, and the sharp scent of ozone filled the air, the smell of a lot of magic in one place. I felt rooted to the spot, unable to look away or run, caught both by fear and my desire to know what was happening.

Judy came pelting through the stacks. "What—what is *that?*" she exclaimed, halting a few feet away from the counter.

"I don't know. Don't get any closer."

"Helena, get away from it."

I edged a few steps back. "I can't—"

The rippling glass spun like a whirlpool, the edges pulling away from the plywood top of the counter until it was a deep funnel with a top higher than my head. Then it collapsed on itself, forming a head-sized sphere that hovered six inches above the countertop, rippling with wavelets all across its surface. It bulged, here and there, irregular bumps covering its surface until—"It's a face," I whispered, backing away farther.

The thing's mouth flexed, opened once or twice. "I hope someone can hear this," it said, and Judy and I both gasped, because it was Harriet Keller's voice.

"Harriet!" I exclaimed. "Where are—"

"I can't hear you, if there's someone there," Harriet went on, "and I have no way of knowing whether there *is* someone there. But I'm taking a chance that someone is in Abernathy's at this hour. Helena, Judy, we were ward-stepped here, wherever here is, and I wish I could be more help in locating us. There are more magi here than just I, but they keep us isolated. I haven't seen Harry since they brought us to this place, and I do hope he's all right. I have no idea what use they have for him."

The face smoothed out and vanished. Judy and I both cried out in dismay. Seconds later the face reappeared, more quickly this time, and Harriet said, "They have me working on what is clearly part of something bigger. I think the isolation is to prevent us from colluding in an escape, but they can't prevent me drawing conclusions about the work. I think it's another oracle. I've done what I can to sabotage the process, but I'm afraid of making myself look so incompetent they'll dispose of me."

Again, the face disappeared and reappeared. "I don't dare keep this up for long," Harriet said. "Here's what I know. By the amount of sickness from the ward-stepping, we're still in the United States. The air is damp and humid. There's no heating nor air conditioning, but the ambient temperature isn't much cooler than sixty degrees, which tells me we're some-where south and east. Harry and I were transported to this building from another location by van, and when they brought us in, I saw an evergreen forest. I don't know what kind of trees they are. I know it's not much, but maybe it will help. I—"

The face vanished. This time, it didn't reappear. The sphere hovered for a few more seconds, then dropped, landing on the counter and shattering like thin ice. Judy and I shrieked and covered our faces, but the shards didn't travel very far. The sound of the crash lingered in the air, then was gone, leaving a silence that echoed with the memory of glass breaking.

I lowered my arms and said, "She has to be all right."

"Or they caught her talking to us," Judy said.

"Can we please be optimistic?"

"I'll call Lucia, you call Malcolm." Judy ran for the office and, presumably, her phone. I dug mine out with shaking hands and called Malcolm. My feet crunched on broken glass as I paced, waiting for him to pick up, but I was too rattled to care.

"Malcolm, Harriet contacted us," I said when he picked up. "She's alive."

"Did she tell you where she is?" Malcolm said.

"She didn't know more than the generalities." I repeated as

much as I could remember from Harriet's "conversation" and added, "Is that helpful?"

"The part about the forest is very helpful. The rest confirms that we're looking in the right general place—somewhere in the southeast."

"Do you suppose she's all right?"

"Harriet Keller has more experience with front-line fighting than I do. I am certain she's all right." Malcolm let out a breath. "I need to take this to the rest of the searchers. Let me know if you hear anything else."

I put my phone in my pocket, kicked glass shards off my shoes, and went to the basement to get the broom and dustpan. This was progress. Harriet was alive, and Harry probably was too. I was sure there were things he knew about glass magic that the Mercy could use even if he wasn't a magus any longer. So they were still building the oracle. Was that why the ansible connection wasn't always there? I wished I'd been able to ask Harriet questions. There was so much I didn't know, and I felt the lack keenly.

It took some time to sweep up all the glass from the floor and counter. By the time I was finished, it was after ten o'clock, but I judged it better not to have a bunch of Wardens tromping around in broken glass. I returned the broom to the basement, put away the mail-in auguries for later, and unlocked the front door. "Welcome to Abernathy's," I said. "Please form an orderly line."

"Nice day," the first man in line said when I accepted his augury slip. "Hope it doesn't rain later."

I cast an eye at the street outside, which did look warmer and drier than it had all week. "I need nice weather for this weekend."

"The big day is coming up soon, isn't it? Congratulations."

He sounded sincere, not like some of the Nicolliens who were still upset that I was marrying an Ambrosite.

"Thanks. I'm excited." I took his augury request into the oracle.

The cool, dry air comforted my still-frazzled soul. Malcolm was right. Harriet's information was helpful. The searchers would find the missing magi, and everything would—

The bookcases shuddered, and the smell of roses vanished, replaced by the scent of old leather and dust. Reflexively I looked at the augury slip, but it hadn't changed, and up ahead I could still see the blue light of the augury. My shoes tapping across the pink linoleum, I followed the twisty path to where the book lay, flat on its face with its spine pointing inward. I reached out to take it, then stopped. I didn't think I was in exactly the place the oracle had shown me in vision, but I was wearing the right shirt, my hair hung loose around my shoulders…this was as close to the vision as I was likely to get.

I backed away from the augury and tucked the slip into my pants pocket. The oracle had given me direction, and I ought not to ignore that. I turned and began searching for a way out.

The bookcases loomed over me, ominous in a way they'd never been before. Probably that was my imagination talking, or it might be that the light, never very bright, felt dimmer now, casting shadows that seemed to whisper to each other as I passed. I held my head high and ignored them. I was the custodian of Abernathy's, damn it, and this upstart oracle the Mercy was trying to build could hold no horrors for me.

I passed through an intersection, then backed up. Was it my imagination, or was the light brighter off to the right? I turned and headed in that direction. Yes, the light was growing brighter, a pale natural light unlike the bluish-tinted air of the oracle. My steps slowed. I had no idea what I would find outside the stacks, and though I no longer feared being lost outside my own time, it was certainly reasonable I might be lost many miles from home. And suppose there were people outside the second oracle? People who would likely not be friendly to me?

I stopped around the corner from what I judged to be the exit, squared my shoulders, and walked forward into the light.

12

I stood at the end of a corridor formed by four bookcases facing each other, mismatched but still far more elegant than Abernathy's. The sounds of passing traffic came to my ears, similar to what I heard every day in Abernathy's, but subtly different. It took me a moment to realize the hissing noise of cars on wet pavement was missing. The smell of leather and dust still filled the air, but I was still surrounded by bookshelves filled with old books, so that probably accounted for it.

I stood, listening for nearby movement, for a full minute. The corridor seemed to open up into a larger space, but all I could see of it was a distant wall, paneled in wood stained a medium brown shade, like dirt. All I could hear was still the rush of traffic, not very loud and not very much of it. Swallowing my nervousness, I walked forward and rounded the corner into the open space.

It was a store front, complete with counter and cash register, though where Abernathy's cash register was antique gold, this one looked like a relic of the '80s, with a pebbly beige case and a LCD display. Large windows, streaky from improper cleaning, let in diffuse light from an overcast sky. The pale pink linoleum floor, in this context, reminded me of an old K-Mart I'd shopped at with my mother when I was little. The store had the same run-down, dispirited feeling as that one.

"Where did you come from?" a man exclaimed. Startled, I whipped around to see a young man with spotty cheeks and an AC/DC T-shirt standing in a doorway that led deeper into the store. He held a paper coffee cup that emitted a delicious aroma overriding the smell of dust, and looked stunned, as if customers weren't part of his daily experience.

"I—just walked in," I said, taking hold of my startled fear and bottling it for later. "I thought no one was here."

"I didn't hear the door." He gestured, and I looked over my shoulder at the front door, which was solid, unlike Abernathy's with its glass window, but had identical bells over it.

"I was looking for something by John Grisham," I improvised, hoping to distract him. "But it's hard to find anything in here."

"It's not well organized," the young man said. He made no move to come forward, but I could see the hand holding the coffee cup shaking and realized he was afraid. Of me, or of what I represented? He couldn't possibly know who I was. And if I stood here much longer, he'd become suspicious.

"That's all right," I heard myself say, "I'll keep looking." I turned, took two steps toward the bookcases, and stopped as the door swung open, setting the bells to jingling. A tall, solidly built woman wearing a hoodie and workout pants entered, carrying a plastic bag which smelled richly of barbecue. She startled when she saw me, her eyes going wide for the briefest moment.

"Where did she come from?" she said, addressing the young man.

"She just walked in off the street," the young man said.

"I don't think so." The woman switched the bag to her left hand and reached behind her to flip the deadbolt. It shot home with a small click that sent a thrill of fear through me. "You don't recognize her?"

"Should I?"

"That's Helena Davies."

I bolted for the aisle between the bookcases. The bag hit the ground with a squishy thump, and the woman grabbed me by the wrist and swung me around into the nearest shelves. Books fell, and I cried out in pain. "I don't think so," the woman repeated, this time sounding menacing. "Elliot, search her."

I struggled to free myself, but the woman had a grip like a vise and I only succeeded in hurting my wrist. Elliot, his eyes wide and panicked, patted me down awkwardly and relieved me of my phone. The woman grunted approval. "Wait here," she told him, and dragged me toward the doorway Elliot had come through. I kicked her, making her grunt again, this time in pain, but it didn't slow her down at all.

The hall was dark, lit only by the light coming from the store front, and I could just make out posters lining the walls before the woman pushed open another door and shoved me inside. I stumbled, caught myself on a shelf, and turned in time to see her slam the door shut on me, leaving me in blackness. I felt for the knob and rattled it; locked. I pounded on the door and shouted, "Hey! Let me out!" That made me feel stupid, but I pounded a bit more before giving up. It wasn't like my demands meant anything to my captors.

Breathing heavily in fear and anger, I felt around for a light switch, but found nothing. The room felt small, like a closet, and smelled of chemicals and cleaning solution. I turned in a slow circle and shrieked as something light brushed my face. An instant later I recognized it as a string, not a spider web, and flailed around until I caught hold of it and tugged. Light, wan and dim like sunlight through a grimy window, cast shadows over my surroundings. It was, in fact, a large closet, with a couple of metal shelf units opposite the door and a white wooden cupboard with only two doors next to them. To the right, a broom and a mop leaned against the wall.

I leaned back against the door and tried to calm myself. Eventually Judy would realize I was taking an awfully long time in the oracle and draw the right conclusion. She'd tell Malcolm, who would use the locator app to find my phone, and he and the Wardens would descend upon this place. But that might not happen immediately. If there weren't any Wardens nearby, they'd have to ward-step to get here, and that assumed there were wards close enough to make a difference. I couldn't wait for rescue. I had to get out of here, now.

I assessed my surroundings, starting with the cupboard. It contained some bottles of drain cleaner, the crystal kind, and a stack of folded rags. There was a toolbox on the lowest shelf, but it was locked. Why would anyone lock a toolbox kept securely in a closet? The shelves also held spray bottles of various cleaners, a bucket containing two worn sponges, and a squeegee with a threaded handle that would screw onto a pole for cleaning tall windows. I tested the spray bottles and found one that had a nozzle with three settings, one of which was a steady stream. I twisted the nozzle to that setting and practiced squirting the door. Maybe I could shoot someone in the eyes with the nasty-smelling chemical when they came for me.

I hefted the broom, which had a heavy metal head and

nylon bristles, but regretfully laid it aside. There wasn't enough room in here to swing it hard enough to hurt someone. The mop had a shorter handle, but a light head—not a good weapon. That left me with chemical warfare. I put the bottle where I could reach it readily and settled in to wait.

I checked my watch. 10:22. When had I entered the oracle? It was at least ten minutes ago. How long would Judy wait before concluding something had gone wrong? I eyed the toolbox. If I had a couple of paperclips, I could try picking the lock. Unfortunately, I didn't have any paperclips. I didn't have anything useful on me. I grabbed the toolbox and pried at the lid anyway. It was a cheap lock, but proof against my efforts. Finally I gave up and shoved the box away. It struck the wall with a thump and a rattle. Probably it held any number of tools I might use as weapons. Even a hammer would be useful, to break the doorknob off and reveal the locking mechanism.

I eyed the toolbox again. Then I picked it up and turned it to hold it by the sides instead of the handle. It was reasonably heavy. I raised it as high as I could manage and slammed it down on the doorknob. It made an almighty crash, but the doorknob didn't move. I did it again. This time, the knob jerked and pulled away from the door a fraction of an inch. Heartened, I raised the toolbox once more.

The door opened in my face. "Cut it out," the woman said. I slammed the toolbox toward her head. She ducked, cursing, and its weight caught her on the shoulder instead of the face. She swore again and punched me in the stomach. All the air left my lungs in an explosive *pah*, and I staggered back-ward into the shelf. The woman wrenched the toolbox out of my hands, threw it on the ground behind her, and got one hand around my throat, choking me. I clawed at her hand, desperate for air. "No more resisting, if you want to live," the woman said, then released me. I sagged to the floor, coughing and trying to suck in air at the same time.

The woman grabbed my wrist and hauled me upright. "You going to give me any more trouble? Because you can either walk, or you can be carried."

I shook my head. The woman pulled me out of the closet and dragged me farther down the hall, past the dim outline of another door next to the closet and on to a third door at the end of the hall. This one was metal and had a bar across it, like a security door. The woman shoved it open, and I blinked in pain at the sudden bright light of outdoors. My eyes hadn't yet adjusted when she pushed me into the back of a cargo van. It had no windows and was stripped bare, with no seats but the two up front. The woman climbed in after me and shut the doors. "Drive," she said, and I saw Elliot in the driver's seat, his head silhouetted against the sunlight.

The van rattled its way along bumpy streets, though I didn't think they were unpaved or it would have been an even rockier ride. The woman sat on the floor facing me, her eyes hard. I shivered. Wherever I was, it wasn't as cold as Portland, but the van was unheated and I was still just in my shirtsleeves.

"Where are you taking me?" I asked. My throat hurt from where she'd choked me. The woman smiled and said nothing. "They'll know I'm missing," I said. "It's only a matter of time before they find me."

"We've taken care of that," the woman said. I felt cold from more than the chilly air. Her demeanor was casually competent, the attitude of someone who never failed to get what she wanted. She reminded me of Judy that way, though she was about ten inches taller than Judy, darkly tanned even in winter, and built like a wrestler.

I thought about arguing with her, decided it was pointless,

and scooted around until I was sitting with my back against the van's cold side. That made my bones ache with cold, so I sat up and wrapped my arms around my knees to stop my shivering. The woman didn't seem to care about my comfort, but why would she?

I glanced at my watch. 10:40. It was a mistake. The woman noticed and grabbed my wrist, immobilized my arm, and unfastened the watch band. I fought her, slapping and kicking, and she smacked me so hard across my left temple my vision went blurry. I slumped to the floor, breathing heavily and trying not to pass out. When I could see again, my watch was gone, and the woman's little smile was wider. "Give it back," I said.

"Make me," the woman said. I pushed myself back into a sitting position and glared at her. That watch had been a gift from my parents and I loved it. I hated that woman so much.

We drove for what felt like forever. At some point the road became truly rough, bouncing me around and forcing me to throw out my hands to keep my balance. The stink of exhaust grew steadily until between that and the pummeling I'd taken and the jostling ride, I wanted to throw up. If I could have managed to throw up on my captor, I'd have done it happily, but she would just have hit me again. She, damn her, didn't seem at all put out by the bouncing. I wondered if she was a magus. She had to be one of the Mercy, she and Elliot both, but not everyone who'd disappeared when the Mercy was exposed had been a magus. Not that it mattered. The woman could probably snap my spine without resorting to magic.

The van slowed, gave one last bump that made my butt leave the floor, and came to a halt. The woman uncurled herself, stood slowly, and opened the van door. I couldn't help it. I bolted—and came up short. Three men and two women stood in a semicircle behind the van. Two of the men held nasty-looking guns, one of them big enough to be a hand cannon. I wasn't so stupid as to believe the others weren't armed as well, though with magic instead of weapons. I held my hands up to show they were empty, not that it mattered, and swallowed the knot of fear in my throat.

We were somewhere in an evergreen forest, not the tall evergreens of my home state but conifers that grew horizontally, spreading their canopies to interlock with one another. A faint smell, unpleasantly bitter, filled the air. Snow still gathered on the lower limbs of the trees, though the ground was clear but damp. Behind my captors stood a two-story wooden house, too big to be a cabin despite being made of logs. A faint plume of smoke issued from its chimney. The windows were all shuttered, giving the place a dreary, unwelcoming look.

One of the men, the one with the hand cannon, gestured with it. "This way."

I walked toward the house as he directed. One of the women preceded me and opened the door with a gesture that would have been courteous if she hadn't worn such a mocking expression. The door opened on a hallway that looked like it might run the width of the house. A rustic living room, complete with furniture made from pale logs with dark knots, lay to one side. Inside, the air was warmer, but not by much, and scented with the rich smell of beef stew. My stomach rumbled. It must be past noon.

The woman who'd opened the door laughed derisively. "I suppose you want us to feed you."

"As if I'd trust any food you gave me," I said.

She laughed again and pointed down the hall to where I could just see a staircase going up. "That way," she said, and I wished I could claw her eyes out. But I was very aware of the gun pointed at my back, so I did as she said and mounted the stairs, looking about covertly for a way out of this mess.

At the top of the stairs, a hallway extended in both directions, lined with old-fashioned sepia-toned portraits of unsmiling people. The woman opened a door and gave me a little shove. I turned on her, snarling, and she laughed again. "Don't think I won't use magic on you if you try anything," she said. "Inside."

I entered the room, and the door shut behind me, the lock clicking shut. As if escaping would do me any good. I had no idea where I was, I was inadequately dressed for the weather, and I had no way of contacting anyone. I sank down to sit against the door and buried my face in my hands. *Look on the bright side*, I told myself. *If this goes on long enough, you won't have to endure the rehearsal dinner.* That only made me more miserable. What lie would the Wardens have to tell my parents about where I was? No one would believe I'd missed the dinner for fun.

I scrubbed a couple of stupid tears out of my eyes and looked around. I was in a tiny bedroom, done in the same rustic décor as the living room downstairs. The bed was covered by a patchwork quilt with a starburst pattern of blue and purple. I got up and dragged it off the bed and wrapped it around myself, and felt better immediately. A dresser beneath the window proved to be empty of anything but dust. I pried at the window, but it gave not even a millimeter, and I suspected it of being magically sealed. The shutters covering the window were on the outside, so I couldn't even open them to look out.

I clutched the blanket tighter around me and sat on the bed. The mattress was too firm, almost rock-hard, but it was still softer than the hardwood floor. I couldn't think of anything else to do. Scream? Break the window? Which was probably magically proofed against breakage, too. I felt so helpless I wanted to kick something.

I closed my eyes and focused on my breathing until I was calmer. Malcolm could still trace my phone, I just wouldn't be anywhere near it. And from what the woman had implied, they'd taken steps to make sure I couldn't be traced magically either, just as they had the kidnapped magi. So I couldn't count on anyone finding me. If I was going to escape, I could only count on myself.

I opened my eyes and stared at my hands. The question was, what was I escaping from? The Mercy didn't need me, since I'd refused to give them auguries and fought their elite magi warriors called weavers when they tried to force the issue. So why keep me captive instead of just killing me when I showed up in their oracle? I wasn't under any illusions about their fundamental nature or the goodness of their collective hearts. They wanted something from me. I wished I had a clue as to what.

Something hummed against the window glass, a buzzing noise like a bee. Nothing was visible, though, and as the hum grew louder, I thought *That would have to be an enormous bee.* I stood and walked to the window, laying my palm against it. The window vibrated rapidly enough to tickle my hand. I listened for the sound of big equipment, or maybe a helicopter, anything that might shake the windows, but heard nothing but the low, insistent hum.

Then a voice spoke. "Welcome to the resistance," it said. Startled, I yanked my hand back as if it had been burned. I didn't recognize the voice, couldn't tell if it was male or female. "This communication is one-way, so don't bother talking. The Mercy has us all working on some large project that we think is a second oracle. You'll be assigned a piece that won't make sense to you, but that's normal. Do your best to work slowly and sabotage it any chance you get, but don't take unnecessary risks. They've already killed a couple of us. We know this because one of them is a talker. If you can get her going, she reveals way more than she ought."

"Which—" I began, then reminded myself this person couldn't hear me.

"We're planning a breakout, but communication is hard. One of us will speak to you again this evening. Don't try this magic yourself until you know which windows are ours. If you give us away, it could be fatal. Good luck." The vibration slowed until the window was still and the room was silent. I pressed my fingertips to it, but felt only cold.

So someone knew I was here, even if he or she did think I was a glass magus. Too bad I wasn't, or I could do as they suggested and communicate with my fellow captives. With the dark brown shutters closed over the window, I could see my reflection in the glass, wavery and dim. It reminded me of seeing myself in the oracle's vision the day before. Why had the oracle given me that guidance if this was the result? It couldn't have wanted me to be captured, could it? I returned to my seat on the bed and drew my legs up to sit cross-legged. The oracle wasn't human and it didn't think like people did. It might have a purpose in letting me get captured, but I had no way to know what that was.

The speaker had been awfully confident about their ability to use the window to communicate. How would a glass magus find out which window to use? They could probably see into any place there was glass, or a mirror. So...maybe they could see me! Which, unless it was Harriet, would be no extra help, as there was no reason to expect the captured magi to recognize me.

That made me wonder how the woman who'd stolen my watch had known my face. I felt uncomfortable about that, as if she'd watched me while I slept. It was possible the custodians, for lack of a better word, of the second oracle knew me on the grounds that they should know their enemy, but it still felt wrong.

I got up and paced in a tight circle in front of the window. There was nothing I could do but wait, and hope the next person through the door didn't have orders to shoot me dead.

13

H ours passed. The light that filtered through the shutters gradually dimmed as the day wore on toward evening. I tried the light switch, but nothing happened. A glance at the ceiling told me why. The light socket was empty, the glass shade missing. They weren't taking any chances on leaving me with even the flimsiest of weapons. I retreated to the bed and sat with the blanket huddled around me. My stomach ached with hunger to the point that I might even have accepted food from my captors. If they weren't going to shoot me, they probably wouldn't bother poisoning me, but the food might be drugged to ensure my compliance with whatever they had in mind.

Just as I was thinking this, the door opened. I shot to my feet. It was the woman from the store, a malicious smile on her face. She carried a plastic bowl that smelled deliciously of stew and a bottle of water. "Dinner," she said. "It's not drugged."

"Like I believe you." She was wearing my watch on her left wrist, which infuriated me. I took the bowl roughly from her, making the stew slop up the sides. "What do you want with me?"

"You'll find out soon enough." She shut the door behind her. I sat on the bed and wolfed the stew. It tasted canned, not homemade, but I was so hungry I didn't care. The bottle of water was still sealed, so at least that hadn't been tampered with. Finally full, I set the bowl on the dresser and stretched. I didn't feel lightheaded or sick, so maybe she was telling the truth. It still didn't answer the pressing question of what they intended to do with me.

Night fell, and no one came for me. I lay on the bed and stared at the bar of light beneath the door, which was all the illumination my room had. I'd never wished so much to be a magus, if only because I likely wouldn't be in this position if I were. My helplessness infuriated me. I couldn't even fight my way out. All I could do was lie here and wait.

The glass buzzed again. I jumped up and hurried to the window, pressing my fingers against it as if that would help me communicate. The voice—the same voice, or someone else? I couldn't tell—spoke. "Helena, it's Harriet. Rest your cheek against the glass and breathe normally."

Harriet! I leaned awkwardly over the dresser, pressed my cheek to the glass, and tried to calm my breathing. The glass was cold, but not icy, and it would be comfortable for a minute or so before starting to hurt. In this position, the buzzing rattled my skull, but pleasantly, like a massage. "All right," Harriet said, "I can hear you. Say something—speak slowly, though."

"How did you know it's me?" I asked.

"Not that slowly. One of our jailers is a talker. Everett is good at goading her into giving things away. She couldn't resist bragging that they'd captured Abernathy's custodian. Are you well? They shouldn't have hurt you, but some of them enjoy inflicting pain even when it's against orders." It didn't sound anything like Harriet, but I clung to the knowledge that I had someone familiar nearby.

"They haven't hurt me. I don't know what they want." My breathing sped up, and I made myself calm down.

Harriet's bland voice didn't change. "You're safe for now. With you captive, the Wardens are denied the benefit of Abernathy's. If they kill you, the custodianship will go to Judy, so it's in their best interests to keep you alive. I hope that's comforting."

"A little. Are you all right? Is Harry all right?"

"We're all well enough. They keep us busy with this new oracle they intend to construct. Apparently none of the Mercy's own glass magi are competent enough to perform the magic necessary, which is why they kidnapped the rest of us. I don't know why they didn't take Penelope Wadsworth—"

I remembered that awful night with a shudder. "They tried. She escaped."

The pane rattled as if Harriet had breathed out a sigh. "Oh, that is good news. We have so little of it. When Rudy Galli escaped, we hoped—but they told us they'd killed him."

"The Wardens found his body. It helped them narrow the search. Do you know where we are?"

"Not at all. Somewhere well east of Portland, that's all."

"They'll find us. I know they will."

"Have faith, dear." Harriet's voice grew faint for a moment. "How did they capture you?"

"I...sort of captured myself. The two oracles are connected, and I walked from one into the other. One of the Mercy's people recognized me."

"Oh, my." The buzzing stopped. I stood bent over, my

cheek still pressed to the glass, for a few seconds, and was about to move away when it started up again. "Terence believed such a connection might be possible, from what we were doing, but we had no idea…we're so sorry, dear."

"It's not your fault." I chose not to mention the oracle's vision, since I had no idea what it meant. "I don't suppose you know why it only happens sometimes?"

"The second oracle is erratic," Harriet said. "Some of that is our doing, but we can't stop it working entirely. We have no idea why it chooses to become active, or even if there's an 'it' that can make choices. But it's likely that the connection occurs when both oracles are active."

"That makes sense." At least as much as any of this made sense. "So you're sabotaging the Mercy's oracle?"

"We walk a fine line. We can't allow it to be functional, because that would mean our deaths. But we can't appear to be too incompetent, or they'll kill us. We do what we can. But I'm afraid for you."

"Why? You said they can't kill me."

"No, but if they believe you have knowledge that might help them, they won't be gentle with you."

Fear shot through me, a sharp electric jolt. "You mean torture."

Harriet's response was slow in coming. "I don't know what to tell you. If you cooperate——"

"But I can't let the Mercy have a working oracle. Who knows what they might do with it?"

"It's your choice, dear. You said the Wardens are close to finding us?"

I didn't think I'd been that optimistic. "I think so."

"Then we'll pray for a miracle. Try to get some sleep. You'll be better able to resist, if…"

"I feel better knowing I'm not alone here. Thank you." It was true, I did feel better than I had ten minutes ago.

"I wish I could do more. I'll talk to you again tomorrow night." The buzzing faded, then stopped, and I stood and stretched my back, which ached from being bent over the dresser.

I wasn't alone. Harriet's words had calmed me more than frightened me, though the idea of torture made my hands shake. Surely even the Mercy was more sophisticated than that? I'd seen a bone magus make someone pliable, more ready to talk, without causing any pain, and didn't that make more sense than torturing someone into saying whatever the torturer wanted to hear to get him to stop? I clutched that somewhat reassuring thought to my heart and lay on the bed again. There was no way I could sleep after all this, but I might as well try.

I woke later to sunlight slipping through the cracks around the shutters. I missed my own comfortable bed, missed even more my usual companion. Malcolm would find me, I was sure of it. I sat up and finger-combed the tangles out of my hair. My mouth felt fuzzy and my eyes gritty, I longed for a shower, and my stomach was complaining of hunger again.

The door opened. This time, it was a stranger, a dark-skinned man with a shaved head and hard brown eyes. "Out," he said, jerking a thumb for emphasis.

I left my quilt on the bed, not wanting to look like a help-less refugee, and did as I was told. He wrapped one meaty hand around my upper arm and tugged me along like a disobedient child, down the hall to the stairs and then to what I thought was the back door. The yard behind the house was small, with the forest growing nearly to the back door. A shed large enough to count as a tiny house nestled between the trees, whose low spreading branches brushed its roof and put it in permanent shadow. My captor hustled me along to the shed, flung open the door, and shoved me inside.

Before I could make use of my temporary freedom, two more people grabbed my arms. I fought back. I was so tired of being manhandled and dragged everywhere I didn't care if it got me punched again. But it didn't matter. The two didn't hit me, just forced me over to a table with restraints dangling from it. Panicked, I fought harder, and that was when they hit me, making me double up with pain. One man picked me up and set me on the table, the other grabbed my shoulders and forced me down. I struggled feebly against their hands. Straps went across my shoulders and waist, my hips and my shins, pinning my arms to my side and making it impossible for me to kick them, much as I wanted to.

All this happened in silence, my grunting and gasping being the only sounds. I might as well have been a mannequin, for all the men reacted to my thrashing. When I was completely strapped down, the men retreated, shutting the front door behind them. I panted, trying to regain my composure, then said, "Is anyone there?"

Silence. I turned my head from left to right, but saw nothing but blank white walls. I made myself breathe normally, closed my eyes, and listened. There was no one else in the room. The ceiling was unexpectedly high and held up by beams painted black. Against the white ceiling, they looked like abstract art, and I traced their lines with my eyes until they made my vision blurry. "Hello!" I shouted when I couldn't take the silence any longer. "Anyone!"

The door opened. "—have to see about that," a woman said. She had a slight Southern accent. "Let's see what she has to say first."

That chilled me. "I'm not telling you anything," I said, sounding braver than I felt.

"That's what they all say," a man said. His voice was gravelly, the voice of a man with a cigarette habit of long standing. "Personally, I think defiance makes breaking them so much sweeter."

"You can't trust anything I'll say under torture." I raised my head, but couldn't see either of the speakers.

"Who said anything about torture?" the woman said. I heard footsteps, then she loomed over me so I had a clear view of her chin and nostrils. She had auburn hair pulled back from her face and wore, as best I could tell, a white lab coat that had a sinister air under these circumstances. "You might even enjoy this."

She laid a cool hand against my left temple. I flinched away, and she grabbed my head with her other hand and pressed harder. A stinging pain, like a hypodermic needle, twinged through my scalp, and I gasped. The pain vanished almost immediately, before I could protest. All my muscles began to relax the way they did in a really hot bath. In fact, I felt as if I were floating in my bath at home, and closed my eyes against the sensation.

This was how they made it work, by relaxing me until I didn't care what I said. I gritted my teeth and closed my hand tight, making my nails cut into my palms. The tiny pain kept me anchored to reality. *How long can you keep that up, though?* I thought. Maybe it was futile, but I wasn't going to give in without a fight.

"There," the woman said, "that's not so bad, is it? Tell me your name."

"Daffy Duck," I said.

The woman laughed, sounding genuinely amused. "Not

quite ready, are we?" The lassitude increased. My body felt heavy and warm, limp as cooked pasta and as able to resist. "Now. Tell me your name."

"Helena Davies." It was a small thing, not a betrayal.

"Helena, you're the custodian of Abernathy's, aren't you? Tell me what that's like."

Words spilled out of me. "Like having a best friend. It's comfortable, you wouldn't understand because you're not a custodian, but it feels like——" I clenched my teeth. All of this sounded so innocuous, but who knew what this woman might make of it.

"Now, Helena, you know you want to explain it. It's hard, isn't it, being the only one like you? I bet you've been longing to tell someone. I'd love to listen."

"It's not a thing, it's a creature," I said helplessly. "It has desires. It wanted me to become it so it wouldn't be lonely, but that's impossible, no human could survive that. I wondered once if the oracle was made up of people, of custodians when they die, only they don't die, they become the oracle. But that's wrong. It's just itself."

"That's fascinating," the woman's soothing voice said. "So where do you think it came from?"

"I don't know. Elizabeth Abernathy didn't know the truth. I've read her diary and she thought it was a kind of predictive field, though she didn't call it that."

"Do you think she captured it?"

"It doesn't act captured. It seems to like being the oracle, except that it's lonely." Tears ran down the sides of my face and pooled in my ears. Underneath the pathetically helpful person I had become, I felt humiliated.

"So you don't know where we'd find another one."

"No."

"Unfortunate," the gravelly-voiced man said. "So it's hopeless."

"No, I don't think so." The woman stroked my hair, and I didn't jerk away, and hated myself for it. "Could it be something that became self-aware over time? Something that grew out of Elizabeth Abernathy's predictive field?"

"I suppose so. I don't know," I said through my tears.

"It makes sense," the woman said. Her voice was sharper, and I sensed she wasn't addressing me. "Like an artificial intelligence. Enough information, enough neural processors, accrete over time, and it…wakes up."

"You have no proof of that," the man said.

"It makes more sense than the idea of a captured, non-human entity." The woman stroked my hair again. "Return her to her room and feed her. I will have more questions later."

The two men who'd subdued me appeared at my sides—they'd been so silent I hadn't realized they'd come in with my interrogators—and unfastened the straps, hauling me to my feet. I was too heavy to move my legs, far too heavy for them to lift, but one of them did so anyway, hoisting me over his shoulder and carrying me back to my room. He laid me down not very gently on the bed, and the second man set a tray on the floor. Then they left, closing and locking the door behind them. I lay boneless on the bed and wept in humiliation and fury. All my resolve hadn't mattered a bit, in the end.

When I ran out of tears, I tested my limbs and found I could move, at least a little. I rolled off the bed and crawled to the tray. There was a stack of pancakes, not very warm, a plastic cup of orange juice, and a little pot of maple syrup. The syrup made me cry again, though I wasn't sure why—maybe because it seemed a genteel touch, so out of character for my captors. There was a plastic fork and no knife. I sat on the floor and ate, scraping the last drips of maple syrup with the fork so nothing went to waste. The orange juice was from concentrate and too pulpy to be enjoyable, but I drank it down anyway. I had no idea when they'd think to feed me again.

When I was done, I lay on the bed again and closed my eyes. I didn't think I'd ever felt so low as I did at that moment. Malcolm must be going crazy by now, not knowing where I was. *I* was going crazy not knowing where I was. I also hated not knowing what help my babbling words might be to the Mercy. It sounded like they hadn't known about the oracle being a creature, which made sense; most of the Wardens didn't know that information. So what were they trying to do with the glass magi to make their oracle work?

I lay there, my thoughts going round in circles from wondering about the Mercy's oracle to worrying about Malcolm to trying not to panic about missing my own wedding, for about an hour, at which point the door opened. I sat up, my heart pounding. Another interrogation?

"Don't worry, we're just going for a walk." It was the gravelly-voiced man from the shed. He was in his late forties, I guessed, shorter than average and with a truly amazing head of graying black hair that looked shellacked into place. He wore a gray suit with a red shirt and no tie and looked rumpled, like he'd slept in his clothes. He gestured to me to stand.

"Just us? Aren't you afraid I'll run?" My legs were shaking too badly to support me.

"Where would you run to? Come, I want to show you something." He came into the room and took hold of my arm, helping me stand. It was gentle, not at all like the other men, but I shied away from him. He smiled, a little sadly, and let me go. "I realize we haven't given you much reason to trust us," he said, "but I promise I mean you no harm."

I held still, afraid I might fall if I tried to walk. "Then let me go."

This time, his smile was amused, as if I'd said something mildly funny and he was giving me a pity laugh. "You know I can't do that. Please, come with me. I think what I have to show you will change your mind about a number of things."

I stretched one leg, then the other. If I went with him, I'd be out of this room and maybe find a chance to escape. "All right," I said. "But you're not going to change my mind."

I followed him down the stairs and into the living room. The big, bulky furniture made of sanded logs made me think of Vikings, the honey-colored wood warmed to gold by the sunlight streaming through the big front window. A doorway opposite the window led to a very modern kitchen, far more modern than the rest of the house appeared. The man gestured for me to sit at the island in the center of the tiled floor and went to the stainless steel refrigerator, removing a plastic box of deli meat, some sliced cheese, and a jar of sliced pickles. He brought that and a loaf of bread to the island and took a seat on a stool opposite me.

"I know you've been told a lot about the Mercy," he began. "That we're evil, that we want the invaders to win. That's not at all what we're about." He assembled a roast beef sandwich and handed it to me.

"I heard all about you from one of your masters," I said, ignoring the sandwich, though my stomach liked the smell of it. "And from someone who came to his senses. You're collaborators and you're going to get yourselves killed when the invaders no longer have a use for you."

"Jeremiah Washburn is a confused young man." He put

together his own sandwich and took a large bite. "Go ahead, it won't poison you."

I thought about refusing again just to annoy him, but he didn't seem to care one way or the other whether I starved. So I bit into the sandwich and waited for him to continue.

"We are the ones fighting the Long War properly, not the misguided Wardens," he said. "How better to defeat the invaders than by keeping them close at hand? We let them believe we share their vision, and when the time is right, we will strike."

"And I suppose that's why you killed all those steel magi? Part of your cunning plan?"

"Some sacrifices must be made for the sake of the future. And you can't say good didn't come of it. That new alloy aegis, for example."

"That's a logical fallacy. I can't remember what it's called, but you can't prove the alloy aegis wouldn't have been developed if you hadn't killed all those people."

"Perhaps." He took another bite, chewed and swallowed. "But you can see why we need an oracle, since we don't have access to Abernathy's."

"I don't see why not. It's not as if I know who the mail-in auguries are from. You could send in requests just like anyone else. The oracle gave auguries to Rafael Santiago—you must know that." The sandwich was delicious, which annoyed me that I might get any pleasure out of this ordeal.

"We have done so," the man said. "Every one of our requests in the last six months has resulted in no augury. Your oracle may or may not be a thinking entity, but it certainly is opposed to us."

"Then you can't believe I'll help you, if the oracle thinks it's a bad idea."

He shrugged. "We believe you're a reasonable woman. Are you finished eating? Then let's look at what we've developed."

I stuffed the last bite of my sandwich into my mouth and followed him, hoping we were going outside again and I might run away. But we went back through the living room and across the entry to another door, which the man opened. The room beyond looked like a nineteenth century gentleman's study, complete with oversized desk and leather armchair. Built-in bookcases lined one wall, loaded with books whose spines all matched. Judy hated libraries like that, because Abernathy's tended to reject them and then we were left with stacks of heavy books to get rid of. An antique globe on a wooden stand stood in the corner next to an umbrella holder made of—I swallowed in disgust—an elephant's foot.

The man went around to the other side of the desk and sat in the armchair. He indicated another, smaller chair as if suggesting I sit. I thought briefly about running, realized I wouldn't get very far, and sat. The man opened a drawer and pulled something out of it. "This is part of our oracle," he said.

I leaned forward to look at it. It was maybe a foot tall and half that in diameter, made of translucent blue glass rectangles. It looked like a Jenga set halfway through a game, if the blocks were glass and glued together. I lifted one hand to touch it, then thought better of it and folded my hands in my lap.

"You can touch it. It's inert," the man said. "When it's active, it creates a field through which the oracle can work."

"That's what you needed the glass magi for."

The man nodded. "It was unfortunate we had to stoop to kidnapping, but our own glass magi didn't have the skills necessary." He ran a finger across the top of the structure as if wiping away dust. "And they ought to be pleased to be involved in something so momentous. No one's created an oracle in over two hundred and thirty years."

"Yeah, I'm sure they're thrilled about being under threat of death if they don't help their enemy."

"We'll send them home when it's finished."

I laughed. "That is such a lie. Are we done? Because I'm in the mood to go back to my cell."

"You don't have to be locked up."

"I know you feel certain I won't run because we're in the middle of nowhere, but you can't be that foolish."

The man leaned forward, his blue eyes intense. "You could help us."

"That is *so* not going to happen."

"Think about it, Helena. We *will* build this oracle and we *will* use it to fight the Long War. You know more about Abernathy's than anyone else. I have no doubt that your knowledge will be key to figuring out why our oracle works sporadically. Two oracles, Helena! What could we not accomplish if we worked together! Not to mention the way the two are physically linked. Who knows what else we might be able to make of that? We should be allies, you and I. You don't want Dr. Ellery rendering you…pliable…again, do you? I would much prefer it if you worked with me voluntarily."

For the briefest moment, I thought about playing along, pretending to agree with him. It would get me greater freedom and might even lead to me getting my phone back, calling Malcolm… I shook my head. I might convince this man, who did seem genuinely interested in my willing compliance, but those hard-eyed men who'd strapped me down would never believe it. "You killed people I cared about in the name of your supposed plan," I said. "You killed at least one of the glass magi you kidnapped. If the second oracle starts working properly, you can't afford to let me or the other glass magi live. Let your Dr. Ellery at me, because there's no way in hell I'm cooperating with you."

The man looked sad. "I hoped you were reasonable," he said.

An explosion rocked the building's foundations, making us both jump. The glass structure teetered, and I snatched it up and without thinking swung it hard at the man's head. It smashed his temple, and to my surprise and delight his eyes rolled up in his head and he sagged in his chair. I stood, clutching my impromptu weapon to my chest, and raced out the door.

14

I ran across the hall and ducked behind the staircase just as half a dozen men and women in heavy boots came down it. Another explosion, and then the sound of automatic weapon fire, shattered the forest's stillness. The men and women ran out the front door, leaving it swinging open behind them.

I crept to the door and peered around the edge. Half a dozen black SUVs blocked the narrow road away from the house, and men and women in black or white fatigues poured out of them, armed with guns, knives, or long wooden staffs. The Wardens! I almost ran out to greet them before realizing I'd just be cut down in the crossfire. I retreated to the stairs and looked around. There had to be something I could do.

I ran up the stairs, still clutching my glass weapon. The kidnapped magi had to be around here somewhere. If I could free them... I came to the first door off the second floor landing and tried the knob. Locked. I pounded on it. "Is someone in there?"

"Who are you?" came the muffled reply.

"Helena Davies. Are you a Warden?"

"Amber Mayfield of the Hermes Node. Do you have the keys?"

"No, but I—" I sized up the doorknob, which looked fragile against the solid oak door, then looked at the structure in my hands. It had almost worked with the toolbox. At worst, I'd shatter the glass and slice the hell out of my hands. "Stand back." I raised the glass as high as I could, then brought it down sharply on the doorknob.

It worked better than I'd dreamed. The blue glass flashed white, and with a cracking sound the knob sheared off completely, leaving a round hole containing the latch mechanism. Fingers came through from the other side and wiggled it, making the door pop open. A plump older woman with silvering blonde hair stared at me. "Wow," she said. "What was that?" She noticed the glass structure in my hands and one hand went up to cover her mouth. "Did you...you didn't just use that as a battering ram, did you?"

"More like a sledgehammer. Come on, we have to free the others!"

Amber shook her head. "We have to disable the oracle—the second oracle. The Mercy can't be allowed to have the use of it." She pushed past me and ran down the stairs without waiting for me. I hesitated, torn between following her and continuing along the hallway. The knowledge that I knew nothing about glass magic or what the magi had been working on decided my path for me.

I ran to the next door, discovered it was locked, and slammed my makeshift sledgehammer down on the doorknob without knocking. Again, white light flashed, and for a moment I wondered if it was really such a smart idea to use something with who knew what kind of power as a blunt instrument. Then the door popped open, and Harriet flew out, shoving me hard against the wall. "Oh!" she exclaimed, and converted her grip to a hug. "I'm so glad to see you, dear."

"We need to free everyone so we can escape," I said. "Do you know where they're being held?"

"The locks are stone-sealed," Harriet said. "Did you—" She covered her mouth with one hand, just as Amber had done. "Don't tell me you used *that* to smash the doorknob off?"

"I did. I'm starting to worry about that decision."

"It just hadn't occurred to me that it would work, but of course…" She lowered her hand and touched the thing gingerly. "Let's see how many more people we can free before the magic runs out."

"Is it giving off magic?" I suddenly had the image of myself glowing with radioactive contamination.

"Not the way you're thinking. It's safe. Mostly. Safer than leaving our people in the hands of the Mercy, anyway."

We opened four more doors before the glass took on a dull sheen, and smashing it against a doorknob resulted in a *thunk* and a crack running across the glass before the knob fell off. I shifted it to the crook of my left arm and opened the door. Harry stood by the window, which was missing its glass. One shutter had fallen to the ground, and the other hung at an angle, swaying slightly in the wind. "Thank God," he said with feeling when he saw us. Harriet flung herself at him, and they held each other tightly. "I was afraid I might have to climb down the face of this building. I'm not sixty anymore, you know."

"What about the others?" I said.

"Gloria, Peter, and Amber are still missing," Harriet said, surveying the little crowd around us. "But we think Gloria made an escape. None of us have heard from her in two days. I do hope she's safe."

"Amber went to do something about the oracle." I looked out the window at the back yard. Figures sheltered behind trees, taking shots at the house though not, fortunately, at us on the second floor. "What do we do now? We can't get out without being shot at."

"Miranda, you and Butch search for keys and find Peter," Harriet said. "The rest of us will search for the oracle. Hurry. If the Wardens don't prevail here, all our lives are forfeit." She turned and ran for the stairs.

"What do you mean, if the Wardens don't prevail?" I said, hurrying down the hall after her.

"The Mercy may be many things, but weak isn't one of them," Harriet said. "They are well-armed and well-trained, just as the Wardens are—they used to be Wardens, remember?"

"That's true, but there's no tactical advantage to them holding this position," Harry said. He stumbled as he ran, but seemed to have no trouble keeping up thanks to his long legs. "If they can ward-step away with the oracle—"

"But the oracle's not here," I said. "It's in that store, wherever it is."

"The effect is manifesting there, true, but the oracle's...I suppose its body...is here," Harriet said, pounding down the stairs with all of us trailing in her wake. "We don't know why they did it that way. There's a lot we don't understand, and won't until we have time to compare notes. If we survive this, we should be able to work out how their oracle works."

She made a sharp gesture with her left hand that looked to me like some kind of commando signal, and I was reminded that Harriet had fought for years in the Long War—unusual for a glass magus to do so, but she never talked about those days and I'd never pressed her for details. We all came to a stop at the bottom of the stairs, and Harriet gestured again, this time for us to follow her and stay quiet.

We went toward the back door, but turned left before reaching it at a narrow, flimsy door that opened into blackness. Stairs leading downward creaked under even Harriet's slight weight. When she flipped a switch, fluorescent bulbs attached to the wall near the ceiling shed a cold, brilliant light over the passage, which was bare concrete with just a slim wooden pole for a railing. I didn't need to be told to keep quiet. It was the kind of place that encouraged stillness. Even our feet seemed to get the message, making barely any sound.

At the bottom, Harriet glided forward silently. I followed immediately behind her, wishing I dared clutch her hand, but I didn't want to impede her movement, if she needed to work magic. She flipped another switch, and more bulbs flickered into life, revealing a long corridor that disappeared out of sight. It was much longer than the house, and with its curving roof felt more like a tunnel than a hallway. Harriet swore, startling me. "Harry, get behind me," she said. "Helena, go to the rear of the line. If anything happens, run for it."

"Run for it? What might—"

"Don't argue, dear, we don't have time. Just do as I say."

I obediently shuffled past the other magi to the end of the line, inwardly seething, not at Harriet but at my own inadequacy. If I were a magus...I wouldn't be Abernathy's custodian, and I wouldn't be in this position. Of course, being at the rear was no guarantee of safety if the Mercy operatives came down the stairs after us. I shrugged my shoulders against the nervous chill I felt between my shoulder blades and followed Terence, a short brown-skinned man with

Indian features who smiled worriedly at me before moving forward.

We walked for several minutes. The place stank of wet concrete and the sharp smell of magic. I wondered if we were below the water line here, if the Mercy had dug this tunnel out by magic and only magic was keeping it from flooding. The farther we went, the more nervous I became. I couldn't help being aware of all the wet earth above me, pressing down on me... I shook the image away. There was nothing I could do if the tunnel collapsed, which it certainly wasn't going to do.

Terence stopped, and I nearly plowed into him. I looked past him at where the tunnel had opened up into a concrete bunker filled with wooden trestle tables. Chairs were scattered throughout the room, some of them knocked over as if their occupants had left in a hurry. Harriet knelt next to a huddled form on the floor. It was Amber Mayfield, lying in a pool of blood with her chest a mass of knife wounds. "She must have surprised them," Harriet said, her voice tight with anger. "There's nothing left. We're too late."

"What was here?" I asked.

"We've never been here," Harriet said, "but we guessed its existence. The magic they had us working on had to be assembled to be effective. This is where the oracle was, until they took it away. Ward-stepped it somewhere else. We are *never* going to find them now."

"There's still a chance. If they use the oracle, it will open a portal—" My throat closed up involuntarily. "They can enter Abernathy's if the resonance creates an ansible."

"An ansible?" Harry dismissed this as incomprehensible and said, "We thought there might be a resonance. From what I've learned, any oracle must...tap into, I suppose...the same oracular space. Like zebras drinking from the same watering hole. There was always a chance they would start to overlap. It's why we were so concerned about not letting the Mercy have a working oracle."

"Yes, because they could attack Abernathy's directly."

"That too," Harry said, "but worse is the possibility that the overlap would grow so huge it would destroy both oracles."

He said it so casually I didn't understand him at first. "Destroy?"

"We can talk about this later," Harriet said. "Let's get out of here and see if we can't help the Wardens."

We ran back down the tunnel this time, me in the lead, and pounded up the stairs to a world strangely free of noise. No gunshots, no shouting, nothing but the rising wind that promised a storm was on its way. I was halfway down the hall to the front door when I heard running footsteps on the stairs. I froze, and Terence bumped into me, but before I could hustle everyone back to the dubious safety of the basement stairwell, a woman in white hunter's fatigues came down the stairs and rounded the corner. "I found them," she shouted. Moments later, more footsteps pounded down the stairs, and Malcolm, his hair in disarray and a bruise beginning high on one cheek, came into view.

"*Oh,*" I said, rushing forward for him to snatch me up in his arms and crush me tightly to him. It hurt, but I didn't care, I was so relieved to see him safe.

"You're not hurt?" he murmured into my hair. I shook my head. "I have never been so terrified in my life as when I received Judy's call telling me you'd gone into the oracle and hadn't come back out."

"I knew you would worry, and I'm so sorry, it was an accident. Sort of." I buried my face in his chest and breathed in the smell of him, his woody aftershave and the smell of sweat and, more faintly, blood. "Is everyone—did we win?"

"They ran, so I guess so," the woman said.

Mike appeared in the doorway, looking dangerously competent in his fighter's fatigues. "Mal, we still have to clear out the woods."

"Approach that shed with caution," Malcolm said. "There might still be people there."

Mike nodded and ran out the door, followed by the woman. Malcolm relaxed his grip on me and said, "Are all the glass magi accounted for?"

"Assuming Peter was rescued, yes," Harriet said. "Amber Mayfield is dead, and Gloria Slocum disappeared two days ago."

"We have not seen Ms. Slocum," Malcolm said. "I think we should assume she was killed by the Mercy. If she had escaped, we would have heard from her by now."

Harriet looked grim. "The Mercy escaped with the second oracle. They could be anywhere by now."

"Oh, but the store—we could find that!" I exclaimed.

"The store?" Malcolm said.

"Harriet told me the oracle was here, but it was manifesting at a distance. They have a store like Abernathy's— that's what I went through to." My heart sank. "But I don't know where it is. I was stuck in a windowless van when they brought me here, and they drove for at least two hours to reach this place."

"That still gives us an area in which to search," Malcolm said. "It puts us within range of several cities and towns. They could not easily uproot a store of even a very small size."

That cheered me. "So long as we deprive them of an oracle, I'll be happy." Then I remembered what Harry had said, and my cheerful mood vanished. "Were you serious about the oracles being destroyed?"

"It's a possibility, yes," Harry said, "but I think we ought to get out of this place. Though I doubt the Mercy is coming back."

"They evacuated quickly," Malcolm said, "which makes sense, if they were guarding the second oracle. They could not afford to let it be taken." He tucked me under his arm and gave me a squeeze. "You should all wait here while we ensure the perimeter is secure. Then we will go to a safe location and ward-step everyone back to the Gunther Node."

"But—" I began when he released me, feeling bereft. Then I mentally slapped myself for being needy and said, "We'll wait."

Malcolm kissed me, so sweetly, then ran out the door. I rounded on Harry. "All right, no more waiting," I said. "Explain how the oracles might destroy each other."

"They had me working on improving the form that holds the oracle, since I'm no use as a magus," Harry said, as matter-of-fact as if it didn't bother him that he'd lost his magic. "Building new structures for them to test, like that one you're carrying. That meant they had to give me information about the oracle itself, how it works. Had me quaking in my boots, I can tell you that, since it was the kind of information they'd eventually kill to protect. At any rate, I worked out that the second oracle, when it's active—awake, maybe—exists in a parallel space to ours. Not like the universe the invaders come from, which is orthogonal to us—"

"What does orthogonal mean?" Ken had used that word too.

"At right angles. Which is inaccurate, because their reality is a non-Euclidean space—oh, never mind," Harry said quickly, seeing my expression grow more confused. "At any rate, it's enough to know the second oracle inhabits a place separated from ours by the thinnest of membranes. And one of the things I discovered is that *any* oracle will inhabit that same space. Which means that's where Abernathy's oracle exists."

"That makes sense." It certainly fit what I'd learned over the two years of my custodianship. "But I don't see how that means mutual destruction."

"It's not a given. I'm not sure myself about the details. It wasn't like they gave me time for my own research." Harry grimaced. "But the structure of that parallel space suggests that the two oracles can overlap each other, and since they're essentially identical, there's a chance they can become… confused about which of them is which. Leading to mutual annihilation."

"Wait—what do you mean, identical?"

Malcolm came back to the door. "Time to go."

Burning with impatience, I followed him to one of the black SUVs and got into the back compartment. Malcolm followed me, sitting beside me and tucking me under his arm once again. Harry and Harriet followed us, Harriet sitting in the front seat next to the white-clad woman we'd seen before, Harry sitting next to Malcolm. Moments later, Mike squeezed in next to Harriet. The SUV rumbled into life and took off down the bumpy road. I was grateful for Malcolm's steadying arm around my shoulders.

"I mean," Harry went on as if we hadn't been interrupted, "there are different ways to construct an oracle, but they all produce the same results. Elizabeth Abernathy didn't have glass magi at her disposal, back in 1782. The Mercy took advantage of the new magic and improved on her design, I'm not ashamed to admit. It's only a matter of time before they make it work consistently."

"But that can't be true," I said. "The oracle is a creature. What you're talking about sounds more like a…a field, like what everyone believed Abernathy's was until I learned differently."

"No one knows at what point the oracle became conscious," Harriet said. "I've read Elizabeth Abernathy's diary. Horrible handwriting that woman had. She didn't believe it was a creature, and she was as close to it as anyone. So it's possible it started out as a field and gained consciousness later."

I took Malcolm's hand and held it so I wouldn't twist my blouse into knots with anxiety. "So they still have the oracle, but they no longer have their glass magi. Doesn't that mean the end of it? Since it's not complete, I mean."

Harry and Harriet exchanged glances. "They were awfully close to the solution," Harriet said. "It's possible they don't need us anymore."

"I need to talk to Ken," I said. "Once he learns it's not time travel, he can start focusing on how to stop the Mercy taking over the oracle's space."

"Ken Gibbons?" Mike said. "Is he helping you? Of course. He's a natural choice. And it's just the thing to make him feel needed, after his trouble."

"What trouble?"

"He has the neurological marker," Mike said, "but his node didn't have the advanced testing techniques Lucia's people devised. His testing was brutal, I've heard, and he was ill for some time afterward. Glad to hear he's back to work. His contributions to Warden knowledge are unsurpassed."

"I didn't know about the testing. How awful!" I had the

marker—what the Board of Neutralities chairwoman Laverne Stirlaugson persisted in calling the "traitor's mark"—but I'd proved my loyalties decisively in front of the Board and had never had to undergo the testing that would have shown whether or not I was one of the Mercy. I had extreme sympathy for those who had.

"The Raffles Node has a reputation for being hard on potential traitors," Malcolm said. "I don't approve of their methods, but this is a hard war, and hard choices must be made."

"I don't like it either." I snuggled more closely into his embrace. "I was afraid I would miss the rehearsal dinner."

"Afraid, or hopeful?" Malcolm teased.

"Well, what would you have told my parents and Deanna about why the bride didn't show up?"

"You have a point. I had to lie to your mother and Cynthia about your being too ill for the planned manicure activity. Judy, ever hopeful, rescheduled it for tonight."

"How did you find us?"

"At first, I used the locator on your phone, but you had been missing for nearly half an hour by the time I learned about it, and I judged that was enough time for someone to throw me off the scent by ward-stepping your phone somewhere far away. Which turned out to be true. Your phone, which we will not attempt to retrieve because it is almost certainly the focus of a trap, is somewhere in Saskatchewan. I'll supply you with a new one tomorrow."

"So where are we now?"

"Virginia. In the George Washington National Forest."

"*Virginia?* So poor Mr. Galli made it a long way."

"Yes, and his murder was key to helping us find this place. The Mercy couldn't make his body disappear, not with how his killing happened in a public place, and we assumed he couldn't have gone far before being killed. Though we were wrong about that. The house where you were kept was on the edge of our search perimeter."

"I'm so glad you found us."

"The Mercy is full of talented magi and ex-Wardens, but it is not infallible. They made a couple of key mistakes, one of which involved taking Harry." Malcolm nodded at him. "The loss of his aegis distorted his magical…I hesitate to call it an aura, which gives the wrong impression, but that's essentially what it is—the part of a human that responds to magic and is constantly replenishing itself. It's impossible to hide that aura, but individual humans all appear the same to someone searching for those auras. All except those rare individuals, like Harry, who've survived losing their aegis or have otherwise nearly been drained of their magic."

Harriet took her husband's hand and squeezed it. "I always said you were unique. You wouldn't really have tried to climb down the face of the building, would you?"

"I was almost desperate enough to try it. I don't think the rest of you were privy to what I heard. Our deaths were imminent."

Harriet closed her eyes and shuddered. "What a night-mare. I'm glad it's over."

"Except it won't really be over until the second oracle is destroyed," I said. "Not that I want to depress anyone. Least of all myself." How could I possibly focus on wedding things if I was worrying about Abernathy's being destroyed?

15

M alcolm's safe location turned out to be an ordinary-looking house in a town about an hour's drive from the forest. A pleasant woman in a flowered dress opened the door for us without saying anything, nodding at Malcolm. The house smelled of macaroni and cheese, which made my stomach rumble. That roast beef sandwich hadn't been nearly enough to satisfy me. But no food was forthcoming. Malcolm led us through the house as quickly as if he knew it well, stopping in a back bedroom as flowery as the woman's dress. "Hold tight," he told me. The woman in white hunter's fatigues came forward and put one arm around my waist.

Something wrenched at my stomach, making it want to turn inside out, and the smell of hot gunmetal filled the—air? There was no air, and I gasped, instinctively trying to fill my lungs. My eyes felt dry and aching, and I could see nothing but blank grayness. Then there was solid ground under my feet, and I coughed out the emptiness and drew in a deep, gardenia-scented breath. The woman's arm kept me upright as I swallowed hard to keep the sandwich down. Good thing I hadn't had any of the macaroni and cheese, or I would have decorated the concrete floor with it. Between the floor, the gardenias, and the not-too-cool air, I could guess, even blind as I was, that we were at the Gunther Node.

"I can stand," I told the woman, blinking away gray mist. As my vision cleared, I saw Harriet twist into existence beside me. I staggered away from the stone magus and bent over, hands on knees, while my vision finally cleared. Behind me, someone threw up. Good thing the floor was concrete and easily cleaned.

I stood and looked around. The node was as busy as it ever was, but it was easy to see Lucia headed this way, striding rapidly and never stopping or moving out of someone's way. They all got out of hers. "Is anyone hurt?" she asked me as soon as she was near enough.

"I don't think so," I said. "A few were killed. The Mercy escaped with the oracle."

"I don't want to hear that story until everyone's back," Lucia said. She eyed the cracked glass sculpture I held, and without looking reached out and grabbed the arm of a black-clad tech who had the misfortune to pass too near. "Get Wallach up here, to my office," she said. "I want him there yesterday." The tech said nothing, just bolted off in a new direction and was swallowed up by the crowd.

"Abernathy's has been shut down since yesterday noon," Lucia said. "I sent word to the Board. I'm sure you can guess what Ragsdale's reaction was."

"What is his problem?" I shouted. "I was *kidnapped* and he wants to blame me for that?"

"Calm down, Davies, everything's fine. Stirlaugson was frosty with him. I think he may have gone too far—though just between the two of us, there are Board members who were already getting fed up with his antagonism toward you. Your forbearance is legendary. I'd have punched him in the face three months ago."

"I'm starting to wish I had. He's developed this attitude that he can treat me like crap and I have to take it or risk the Board's censure. I don't think they wanted me to be servile."

"No. Something you might want to bring up when you speak with them tomorrow. They sent a messenger who came here looking for you when it turned out Abernathy's was closed. Your appointment is at seven o'clock tomorrow evening."

"I'm pretty sure that was supposed to be confidential, Lucia."

"I'm persuasive." She grinned at me, a wolfish look, then glanced past me. "Is that everyone, Campbell?"

"It is," Malcolm said, coming forward to put his arm around me. "It took some argument to convince the other glass magi to come here rather than returning to their homes, but they saw the value in sharing their knowledge. They are all rather adamant about not allowing the Mercy to have a working oracle."

"Good. My office, then." She cast an eye over the gathering. "Maybe somewhere larger."

We did go to her office first, where we found Wallach sitting at Lucia's desk, doodling on a scrap of paper. "You'd better—oh," he said, seeing the crowd of people. "Ms. Davies. Harriet. I take it the rescue was successful."

"Is your Brown 28 lab cleared?" Lucia asked.

"Better make it Red 36," Wallach said, rising. "Brown 28 is still being cleaned after the incident."

I wanted to ask what the incident was, but Wallach was

already following Lucia out the door and Malcolm steered me after them. Wallach hadn't said anything about the glass sculpture, but I was sure he'd noticed it. Probably he was biding his time.

It turned out I'd been to Red 36 before. It was the room where Malcolm had undergone the Damerel rites a second time. It was brightly lit by LEDs that made the room gleam with a cheery whiteness. Cabinets with doors set with frosted glass stood against the far wall, and the long padded table I remembered too well still sat in the center of the room. Its leather straps still gave the room an ominous feel, like the set of a horror movie featuring a mad doctor and surgical torture. Wallach gestured all of us inside, then sat casually on the table, flicking one of the straps so it swung slowly into another one and made them both sway. "Sorry about the lack of seating," he said.

"We'll make this quick," Lucia said. "Davies says the Mercy escaped with the oracle. Somebody explain that for me."

Harriet said, "Without going into irrelevant detail, the Mercy created an artificial body, so to speak, for a second oracle. They were able to carry almost all of it away, except for what Helena stole—how did you get that, dear? Surely they didn't just give it to you."

"I took it from a man who wanted me to change sides," I said. I offered the glass sculpture to Wallach, who took it with a bemused expression and turned it over in his hands. "I hit him with it and ran away when the Wardens showed up."

"So this is part of it?" Wallach said. "Interesting. How many did they need to make it active?"

"The number varied," Harry said. "Between twenty and thirty."

"They must have poured gallons of *sanguinis sapiens* into these things," Wallach said, idly raising the thing to eye level and looking through one of the square holes. "I bet the oracle sucked them dry."

"They were learning to make it use less," said the glass magus called Terence. "But it's almost certainly why they needed all that *sanguinis sapiens* they stole from the South American nodes six months ago."

"So do they have a working oracle, or not?" Lucia said.

Harry and Harriet exchanged glances. "They were close to figuring out the secret," Harriet said. "We did what we could to slow them down, but it's now only a matter of time. The only advantage we have that I can think of is that their oracle has to manifest at a distance, unlike Abernathy's. It will take time for them to set up properly again."

"The store I walked into—the one connected to Abernathy's when both oracles are active—was about two hours' drive from where the oracle's body was," I said.

"They'll probably abandon that store. Too risky," Lucia said. "Which means they could be anywhere now."

"Having one of their foci will let us track them, though they'll certainly try to obscure their magic," Wallach said. "It would be faster to wait for them to fire up the oracle again and let it connect to Abernathy's."

Malcolm's arm went around my shoulders again. "Out of the question," he said. "Only Helena can pass between them, and she is not trained to face down magi fighters."

"But what if one of them enters Abernathy's?" I exclaimed. "We have to take the fight to them."

"*You* are not part of that *we*," Malcolm said.

"Why not? I'm a Warden. And it's my Neutrality that's under attack. There has to be *something* I can do."

"Abernathy's oracle isn't active all the time, is it?" Wallach said.

I shook my head. "It's there all the time, but it's only active when I make it so."

"That might not be good enough," Wallach said, tapping the glass sculpture with his thumb and forefinger. "I'll need more time to learn the details, but I can tell right now they're trying to create an oracle that's always on, so to speak. If that happens, it's likely when Abernathy's becomes active, it won't be able to help getting tangled up in the second oracle. That could mean its destruction—mutual destruction, but that's small comfort."

"I can't let that happen," I said. "Malcolm, you know that."

"What can you do to prevent it?" he said.

"I don't know, but Ken Gibbons will. I need to tell him what we've learned. There may be something about the nature of the oracle we can turn against the Mercy."

"I want you to promise me you won't cross over again," Malcolm said. "If they capture you again, there is no guarantee we'll be able to find you."

"I won't do anything reckless. I don't want to be captured."

"We should close Abernathy's doors for the duration," Lucia said. "If it's not active, the Mercy can't do what you did."

"The Board will never go for it," I said.

"They will if they're sensible. I'll add my recommendation to yours." Lucia walked over to where Wallach was absorbed in his study of the glass sculpture. "Any ideas how to disable the second oracle?"

"You're unexpectedly optimistic," Wallach said. "I'll need a vat of *sanguinis sapiens* to see if I can't get this thing running again, and you glass magi can show me what you've learned. Between us, we should be able to figure this thing out. But we can't shut down Abernathy's. If we're going to learn anything about the ansible, we have to be able to turn it on. If that's what you call it."

Malcolm's arm tightened around my shoulders. I said, "We have to stop the Mercy from destroying the oracle. That can't be without risk."

Lucia turned her attention on me. "It's your life you'll be risking."

"The store is always full of Wardens, many of them front-line fighters. If I find myself in the second oracle, I'll back out immediately."

Now Lucia looked at Malcolm. "I'll send a team of enforcers," she said. "Don't get killed."

"I don't plan on it."

"Nobody ever does, Davies." Lucia sighed. "I'll order the *sanguinis sapiens*. Where do you want it, Wallach?"

"Purple 8," Wallach said, standing. "Ms. Davies, I suggest you keep Abernathy's open and make a record of the times the ansible opens."

"I can do that." Malcolm was so still beside me he might as well have been a statue. "And I'll call Ken and tell him what's happened."

"Don't worry, Mr. Campbell," Wallach said. "I doubt the Mercy will be able to restore their oracle today. It maybe more than a week, if they have to find a new storefront. I doubt Ms. Davies will be in any danger."

"She is a Warden," Malcolm said quietly. "It's what we do."

My heart broke at the resignation in his voice. I wished I could reassure him that I would be safe, but he knew that was a lie. And yet it comforted me to know he wouldn't try to over-protect me or keep me from doing my job.

"Then let's get moving," Lucia said.

"KEN, IT'S HELENA," I said to Ken's voice mail. "Again. I have some important information about Abernathy's and I really need to talk to you. Please call me—I know you're probably busy, but…anyway, I'll talk to you soon." I hung up and let out a deep sigh. "He's probably teaching a class or something."

"I'm sure he will call you back soon," Malcolm said.

Judy poked her head in the doorway. "It's almost two."

I hugged Malcolm. "I shouldn't have let you stay during Nicollien time."

"I find I don't give a damn what the Board thinks. Helena…" His voice trailed off.

"If you're about to tell me how dangerous this is, I already know."

"It's not that. I am having difficulty not carrying you off to some safe location and keeping you there until the problem is resolved. Knowing you were in their hands—my instinct is to protect you, love."

"I know. But if we're going to save the oracle, it will be because I'm out there doing my job."

His arms tightened around me. "I've told the office not to expect me for the next few days. I plan to stay here to keep an eye on things. If you disappear again…" He sighed. "I realize there's nothing I can do if that happens. It's not as if the oracle will open for me."

"No, but it makes me feel better having you here." I kissed him and had to resist the urge to make it longer. "And Mr.

Wallach is right. If they did have to abandon that storefront, it will take them some time to find a new place. It will give *us* time to find a solution."

The Ambrosites were lined up when we returned from the office. Malcolm took up a position near the front door. In his stained, scruffy fatigues, with the bruise he hadn't yet had healed, he looked menacing, which reassured me. If the Mercy sent its weavers pouring through the ansible, they would be in for a nasty surprise.

I accepted the first augury slip—*What treatment should we pursue?*—and entered the oracle, comforted to see its usual bluish light and the rows of yellow bookcases, piled haphazardly with books. "Do you know the danger you're in?" I asked. "You haven't behaved as if you were worried about anything, not like when the Mercy kept trying to get an augury. Do you even know about the other oracle?"

I rounded a corner, still looking for the blue glow of the augury. It was only two o'clock and already I felt so tired I thought if I stopped moving, I might fall asleep on my feet. "I could really use a vacation," I said. "I don't know if that's something you understand. I'm getting married on Sunday and it would be so nice to have a honeymoon. Warm beaches, the ocean air...so different from Portland. Not that I resent this job at all. But it's been over two years and that's a long time to work six days a week, eight or nine hours a day. Though you don't get vacations either, so I guess we're in this together."

The augury was so small I almost missed it, a tiny spark of blue nearly buried in a pile of larger books. It was slim, no bigger than my hand, and had a drawing of a ring of children dressed in native costumes from a dozen lands on the cover. *Peace is a Circle of Love*, the title read. Somehow it was cute and not saccharine. "Thanks," I said, and the oracle's presence faded.

When I handed it over to the woman at the front of the line, she took one look at it and burst into tears. Shocked, I dithered about what to do and ended up patting her shoulder awkwardly and saying, "Is it not what you expected? We can… you don't have to pay for it if it's not—"

"My mother had this book," the woman said, accepting the Kleenex Judy handed her and wiping her eyes. "It was lost in the move to the assisted living center. She…her memory isn't good, and she keeps asking for it. I can't wait to be able to give it to her."

"Wow. I hope it helps."

"It would be worth it even if we never deciphered the augury," the woman said, drawing vials of *sanguinis sapiens* from her expensive purse. "She's already lost so much."

When she was gone, the next man in line said, "I didn't know Abernathy's could do that sort of thing. It can't possibly be a coincidence."

"Abernathy's understands more than we realize," I said, accepting his augury request. I'd seen the oracle give out auguries for free when a child's life was at stake, had seen it move books to spell out, literally, answers to questions, had even seen it work magic I couldn't have imagined. That it might know the secret needs of the human heart did not surprise me at all.

The oracle remained quiet all afternoon, the ansible dormant. Around four, Darius Wallach and a handful of the glass magi, including Harry and Harriet, trooped in. Wallach had the glass structure, which still had a great crack through it, but once again glowed translucent blue. "Carry on, Ms. Davies, don't pay any attention to us," Wallach said. Harry and Terence carried oversized shoeboxes filled with glassware of all shapes and colors. They set them down on the counter, which was still bare plywood. There hadn't been time to replace the glass Harriet's communication had destroyed.

When I came out of the oracle, Wallach and the glass magi were fiddling with the strangest contraption I'd ever seen. It looked like something a baby might build in learning how to stack objects, a pyramid that rose three feet into the air with the Mercy's glass sculpture at its center. "What *is* that?" I asked.

"I *hope* it's another ansible," Wallach said. "A much smaller one than the oracle has become. The idea is to make it resonate with its fellows so it lights up when the second oracle is active. That should give us warning without you having to find out the hard way. Unfortunately, we can't tell if it's working until it lights up. A more active probe would alert the Mercy."

"That makes sense." The thing glowed already, but with the same kind of ambient light that filled the oracle. I started to check my phone, then remembered it was in Saskatchewan. Now that I was free, I could be annoyed at how the Mercy had inconvenienced me. Stole my phone, stole my watch... I resisted the urge to call Ken again on the office phone. If he'd called, Judy would have taken a message. He was probably busy, but surely he was finished with teaching and office hours by now? Maybe I could find his home number, assuming he had one. So many people had given up land lines these days.

Though the store was full, there didn't seem to be any people waiting for auguries. A team of three enforcers took positions around the store front, frighteningly alert. The glass magi surrounded their ansible, murmuring in low voices and occasionally shifting pieces of it. Malcolm lounged by the front door, apparently asleep, which I knew was false. Mike had come in at some point and he and Judy were ignoring each other like a couple of cats claiming the same stretch of alley. I stretched my back, and Malcolm opened his eyes. "Tired?" he said.

"A little. I didn't sleep well last night."

Malcolm's lips compressed in anger, and I remembered where I'd spent the night. I crossed the room to put my arms around him. "You came for me," I pointed out.

"I will always come for you." He held me close, and I closed my eyes and felt the last of my tension dissipate. We had a plan, we knew what the Mercy was up to, and I was safe, if only for now. Ken's silence aside, I felt more optimistic than I had in days.

Something rattled, the clatter of glass on wood, and I opened my eyes to see Wallach setting out a pile of what looked like glass clamshells on the counter. Harriet picked one up and tapped it against the glass sculpture. Blue color bled across the clamshell's surface, as if it were paper dipped in colored water. When the color had spread, streaky and faint, over the whole clamshell, she handed it to Wallach. "There's one for each of us, and Lucia," she said. "If the ansible lights up, so will these. Since we can't afford to sit around Abernathy's staring at it."

"You're leaving?" I said, feeling unexpectedly nervous.

"The information we need will be available via the comm immediately, and it's not as if any of us are equipped to fight," Wallach said. "That's what your enforcers are for. But we're within ward-stepping distance, if that makes you feel better."

"That's all right. It's a good plan." I hugged Harry and Harriet as they prepared to leave. "I'm so glad you're all right."

"So are we," Harry said with a smile and a wink.

The rest of the afternoon was uneventful. The enforcers didn't seem to mind that they had nothing to do. Having them lurking in the corners made me feel awkward, like they were a bunch of guests who'd overstayed their welcome. But I couldn't ask them to leave, feeling superstitiously that the second they drove away would be the moment the Mercy came pouring into the store.

Mike hovered behind the counter, staring at the floor. Judy came and went, once carrying the broom, and while she never went near Mike, she couldn't stop staring at him. Finally, I cornered her in the office and said, "Should I ask Mike to leave?"

"You could ask him to stop messing around," Judy said irritably.

"What messing around? He's just standing there."

Judy waved a hand like brushing away a fly. "He's—you can't see it. He's creating illusions. It's distracting."

"You're not doing anything that important. I thought you were going to stop with the antagonism."

"I don't think it's antagonistic to worry that the enforcers won't be alert."

"They didn't seem to be paying any attention to him."

"Helena." Judy and I both startled. It was Mike. "You got a minute?"

"I...sure. Do you need something?"

"Mal said you wanted to know what happened in Chicago."

"I'll leave," Judy said, but Mike shook his head.

"If it will get you to stop looking at me like I'm going to open fire on a kennel of puppies, I want you to hear this too," he said, though he didn't look at Judy when he spoke. Judy hesitated, then crossed her arms over her chest and leaned against the desk.

"Mike, you don't—" I began.

"It's not a secret. *She* already knows most of it, apparently," Mike said, nodding in Judy's direction. Judy's lips thinned. "Two years ago there was a major incursion in Chicago. We were busy for days, never got much rest. By the end we were all pretty sleep-deprived." He smiled, a wry, mirthless expression. "It's why I wasn't executed."

My mouth hung open. "Executed?"

"Gross negligence in the field that results in Warden deaths can get you executed, yes. And I was grossly negligent." Mike's voice was flat and unemotional. "My team was following an invader, a big one. It escaped containment and took off downtown. Middle of the afternoon, lots of traffic, lots of pedestrians. It was my job to keep up several complicated illusions, the least of which was to conceal the fact that we were armed with some decidedly nasty-looking weapons. Not actually illegal, but only because no mundane law enforcement has ever heard of them to make them illegal. The point is, I let the illusions slip. All of them."

My phone rang. Without looking, I swiped at the screen and the sound cut off. "Sorry," I said.

Mike shook his head. "People saw the guns and freaked out. The invader had made itself look like a woman. We went after it, and the cops showed up and drew the wrong conclusion about four heavily armed people pointing guns at a civilian." He swallowed hard. "Stewart went down first. Single shot to the head. I think the cop got lucky. Wessler took three bullets and I don't know which one killed him. By that time I was on the ground face down, so I only heard Wu scream, didn't see the shot that took her out. The invader escaped, as if it weren't enough of a debacle already.

"I was arrested, but the Wardens prefer to punish their own, so after a massive expenditure of magic covering up the truth, I was free to face the tribunal. They were merciful, by their standards. For a long time I wished they'd killed me."

I gasped. "Mike, you can't think that. It was hardly—" I shut up. It *was* his fault, and my saying otherwise was just stupid.

"No team wanted me after that, not on a permanent basis. And honestly, I didn't want another team." Mike drew in another shuddering breath. "That Mal wants me to join his team…he always was loyal beyond belief."

"So you think you're ready now?" Judy said. I turned on her, wanting to yell at her for still being so critical, but she sounded curious, not antagonistic.

"I've had two years to try to atone for that moment's lapse. On some level, I'm never going to be ready," Mike said. "But Mal and I have talked about it, and he made a good point that if I don't get back out there, it's a betrayal of my dead team-mates. Any of them might have been the ones to fail, and they wouldn't have given up. So…" He let his voice trail off, opening his hands in a gesture of submission.

Judy pushed off the desk. "That's not a history I'd want to live with," she said. "I know you don't care about my opinion, but I think two years is more than enough." She walked past him and left the office.

Mike remained silent for a long moment in which I struggled to think of something to say. Finally, he raised his head and fixed me with his eyes. "If you tell me to leave, I'll give Mal a reason and go back to Chicago."

"Me? Why me?"

"Because you're the one who'll mourn if I let him down. Because I...Helena, I don't know how to make this decision."

"You can't pass it off on me. You know that."

He sighed. "I know. But it was a pleasant idea."

I came forward and laid my hand on his shoulder. "I don't think you should let fear rule you," I said. "That's all."

"Huh." His eyes went distant, as if he were seeing something far outside this room. "Maybe that's enough."

"And, Mike...if Malcolm trusts you...you don't think he's stupid or reckless, right? I think you could do worse than to trust him in return."

That lopsided, mirthless smile returned. "That's exactly what he told me. The two of you are perfect for each other."

"I hope so." Three more days and Malcolm would be my husband for real, not just in my heart. "I'd like it if you stayed, Mike. And you're welcome to stay at our house for as long as you need."

The smile became genuine. "I promise not to abuse that invitation," he said.

16

Nothing changed on Friday except that I convinced Malcolm he shouldn't come to the store on Nicollien time. He wasn't happy about that. "If something happens," he said, "I should be there."

"I'm not going to tell you not to worry about me," I said, clearing our breakfast plates, "because this *is* dangerous. But we have Mr. Wallach's warning ansible, so I won't walk into the second oracle unexpectedly, and I promise not to do anything stupid. I'm more in danger from the Board if I violate the Accords again."

He scowled. "I know. It goes against my every instinct."

I kissed him, taking his face between my hands so he couldn't turn away. Not that I thought he wanted to. "I had to learn to let you go on the hunt. That went against my instincts, too. This is no different."

"It's different because you aren't trained to fight." He put his hands over mine and brought them to rest against his chest. "And I know that's not something you've ever wanted."

"Maybe it's something I should consider. I hate feeling helpless."

"We can discuss it further after the wedding. No sense giving you more to worry about beforehand. But, if you feel comfortable with it, I could teach you to shoot."

I leaned against him and sighed. "Owning a gun isn't something I've ever thought about. Not for myself. I don't have anything against them, you know. But I also never thought I'd be in a position where I'd be in personal danger. I don't know. I'll consider it."

"I can answer any questions you have. And I won't push." His arms went around me. "I love you."

"I love you."

But Malcolm's dire forebodings aside, the day was quiet. The enforcers continued to lurk, making my customers nervous. The ansible on the counter remained dormant. Around noon, a storm came up, a big thunderstorm that rattled the windows and poured rain in buckets into the street. Instead of making me gloomy, it cheered me. It felt as if the world weren't indifferent to the turmoil I felt. Ken still hadn't called, and I chose not to call him again. He knew I'd called, and if he was busy, which he probably was—wouldn't this be close to the start of a new semester?—he didn't need me harassing him. I tried not to worry that something had happened to him. He was the world's greatest expert on the named Neutralities, so if the Mercy hadn't gone after him back when they'd started building their oracle, they weren't likely to suddenly snatch him off the street.

Malcolm was at the door precisely at two o'clock, with a bag of cheeseburgers and a couple of bottled Cokes. "I guessed you hadn't eaten," he said.

"You guessed correctly. You all don't mind waiting a few

minutes so I can eat, do you?" I asked the line of Ambrosites, and retreated to the break room before they had a chance to do more than shake their heads. Malcolm followed me with the delicious-smelling bag, and we sat at the chilly little table and ate. Malcolm was once again dressed in fatigues and a fitted sweater, over which he wore a heavy black duster that probably concealed a number of weapons.

"No problems?" he asked.

"None. I'm starting to get that feeling you have when you've been waiting for something for so long you lose your edge."

"A dangerous feeling. It helps if you let go of the anticipation. Let the ansible do the worrying for you, by which I mean it will give you plenty of warning. And I think Wallach is correct that it will take some time for the Mercy to find a good location to reassemble their oracle."

"Do you know what the Wardens are doing to locate it?" I swigged down some Diet Coke and suppressed a burp.

Malcolm pretended not to notice. "I don't. But I know they aren't waiting passively for the ansible they created to light up."

"I wish—no, I don't. I was going to say, I wish there was something I could do to help, but—see, that's why I chose not to say it, because I didn't want you laughing at me."

"I'm not laughing at you. I'm laughing because you are delightful in your desire to be active in fighting evil. You are already doing something, love, in keeping Abernathy's open."

I sighed. "It's just so hard, watching that ansible and wondering if it will light up when I'm already inside the oracle."

"That's my fear as well. But the likelihood is small. How

many of the times previously did the connection occur after you'd entered?"

"Um...not many, I guess. I don't remember exactly. One or two? It's more common for the connection to fade around me."

"Then I think you have little to fear." He wiped his mouth and tossed his balled-up napkin into the air, making it catch fire and turn to ash just before falling neatly into the trash can.

"Show-off," I said.

"Practice." He smiled at me. "And speaking of practice, Mike has agreed to take the position with my team."

"Oh, that's wonderful! I'm so glad."

"I have a job for him with Campbell Security, for his mundane life, and he'll start a week from Monday. He needs some time to collect his things and settle his affairs in Chicago."

"I told him he could stay with us until he found a place. You know, if he decided to stay."

"You're very generous. Thank you for making him welcome."

"It was easy." I cleared away my trash the conventional way and drank the last of my Coke. "The Board meeting is at seven."

"I remember. We can stop for something to eat before-hand. I wish the Board were not quite so cavalier with your time."

"It could be worse, I guess. And you know you don't have to come with me."

"You know I could hardly do otherwise."

I'd half expected, with Malcolm there, that the ansible would burst into life, whatever that looked like, so I could attempt to drag him into the oracle with me. But it remained dormant, its pale blue glow steady and reflecting off the myriad glass pieces surrounding it. Some of them took on new and unusual colors when the blue glow struck them, ruby red becoming deep purple, emerald green turning a lovely shade of turquoise, my favorite color.

When the last Ambrosite left around 4:15, I spent a few minutes admiring the sculpture Wallach and the glass magi had made. I'd have called it modern art, but it made sense to my eye in ways most modern art didn't. But I wasn't very well educated about modern art, so that was natural.

Six o'clock rolled around, the enforcers left, and Malcolm and I drove to the building near the Morrison Bridge where the Board of Neutralities met. It was an undistinguished red brick building that rose several stories tall, and at this time of night, all its windows were dark. I'd never been there so late before, and wondered briefly if I'd gotten the time wrong—but no, there was light in the lobby, making the tall atrium glow against the darkness.

A man I didn't know waited alone at the curving desk. "Ms. Davies," he said, handing me a visitor's badge, "Last elevator on the left, press the B button. Mr. Campbell will have to wait here."

"Of course," Malcolm said, then kissed me lightly and said, "Good luck."

The last time I'd been here, I'd been on trial for, if not my literal life, at least for the part of my life that included Abernathy's. I couldn't help remembering that long walk from the reception desk to the elevators, stared at by dozens of people. I never had found out whether this building was reserved entirely for the use of the Wardens, or if they shared it with ordinary people and businesses. That didn't make sense to me, but I'd given up trying to figure out what the Board found sensible.

I pressed the B button as instructed and watched the doors close. This time, I was ready for it to hesitate three floors down and then move smoothly sideways. I hoped it wasn't taking me to the Blaze, which was a magical construct used to compel the truth out of witnesses. For one thing, this wasn't a trial—I hoped—and for another, the Blaze blinded me because I could see through the illusion put on it. I didn't need to be at any more of a disadvantage than I was.

The doors slid open on a hall of rough, black stone that swallowed the light from the elevator like a sponge soaking up ink. The damp air smelled loamy, much as the access chamber to the Athenaeum always did. A woman in dark blue robes stood opposite me, holding a lantern on a pole. The lantern's white light had a purplish tinge to it, tinting everything slightly blue. Maybe the woman's robes were black instead.

The woman peered at my name badge as if there could be any doubt about who I was. "Come with me, Ms. Davies." She turned and walked off down the hall. I hurried to catch up.

The hall felt more like a tunnel, though for the first time I wondered how the Wardens had carved it out of the earth under Portland. I'd completely lost my sense of direction, though I was sure we weren't deep enough to be going under the Willamette. Or maybe the elevator was a portal through space, like the Gunther Node's transportation hub, and we were somewhere else entirely.

At the end of the hall, the woman pushed on the stone wall, making it sink inward and then slide to one side. I followed the woman through the cathedral-like space that smelled like a day-old campfire and into a smaller, round room. By comparison to the cathedral, it was almost cozy, or would have been if I hadn't associated it so strongly with fear. The carpet was the same color as the woman's robes and soft underfoot. Several backless chairs stood around the walls of the chamber, none of them occupied; the five people in the room sat at the long judge's bench opposite the door.

Placed at intervals along the bench were four prisms of cloudy glass about two feet high that glowed with a dim golden light. So four of the Board members would be participating from a distance. That made sense, as not all of them were from the Americas.

A circle of stones about four feet across at the center of the room reminded me, with the smoky smell from the cathedral, of an unused fire pit. I breathed out in relief. The Blaze was inactive tonight.

My companion set her lantern against the wall by the door and picked up one of the chairs, setting it in front of the stone circle. At her gesture, I sat. It was a little too close to the judge's bench, forcing me to tilt my head back to see the Board members clearly. Laverne Stirlaugson, chairwoman of the Board, sat at the center, directly opposite me. To her left, past one of the cloudy prisms, sat Timothy Ragsdale, nasty smile on his face as usual. Probably he was hoping this meeting would uncover some flaw in my character or a hitherto undiscovered violation of the Accords. Two more cloudy prisms stood on the bench past Ragsdale, their golden light pulsing gently like quiet breathing.

On Stirlaugson's right sat Ariadne Duwelt, her short red hair caught back from her face with a couple of jeweled clips that caught the soft light from the prism next to her and flickered like tiny stars. Duwelt was, if not on my side, at least not antagonistic to me, and I hoped she might actually be friendly to my cause. Next to her, though, was someone definitely antagonistic to me, Erich Harrison. He'd wanted Abernathy's to move back to England because he was friends with the custodian of the major node in London, and I didn't think his attitude toward me had changed much in the year since his side had lost. I didn't know anything about the woman at the far end of the bench except that she was probably from some-where in South America. I felt so grateful that this time, at least, I wasn't in trouble.

Or so I thought. "Ms. Davies," Stirlaugson said, her voice icy. "Why didn't you inform the Board of what was happening in Abernathy's?"

"I—actually I did, Ms. Stirlaugson. I called Mr. Ragsdale as soon as I had a solution in mind, to get your approval to move forward."

"That was several days after the problem began," Ragsdale said. "You should have notified us immediately when you discovered you were slipping back in time."

"I didn't know I was moving—actually, it's not time travel —how do you know all of that?"

"So you admit you concealed things from us?"

I ignored Ragsdale and addressed Stirlaugson. "Ms. Stir-laugson, as custodian of Abernathy's it's my duty to handle the day to day matters of running the store. I can't afford to go running to the Board every time something strange happens. I judged it better to figure out what was happening before bringing the problem to your attention. I'm sorry if you think I should have done otherwise, but I acted in good faith. And I didn't conceal anything."

"You see the problem," Ragsdale said to Stirlaugson. "She claims it's time travel and then that it isn't. She's clearly not competent—"

"Oh, shut up, Timothy," Ariadne Duwelt said. "Your

antagonism is getting old. Ms. Davies has done nothing but serve Abernathy's without fear or favor for over two years. Ms. Davies, I understand you were held by the Mercy for over a day. Are you well?"

"I'm fine. They didn't hurt me. Thanks for asking."

Duwelt nodded. "I suggest we let Ms. Davies tell her side of the story," she said, "from the first incident to now."

Stirlaugson pursed her lips, then nodded agreement. I shifted my weight, wondering who they'd had the apparently garbled and incomplete version of the story from in the first place. "A week ago last Monday, I entered the oracle for a routine augury…"

I gave them as many details as I remembered, though I glossed over the bits of the bachelorette party that had nothing to do with Pen's abduction. I spoke until I was nearly hoarse, at which point the robed woman appeared at my side with a bottle of water I gratefully accepted. When I came to the end, describing what I remembered of Wallach's explanation of how the little ansible was supposed to work, no one spoke for several seconds. Then a metallic voice came from one of the prisms, saying, *"Despite Mr. Wallach's opinion, it may be too dangerous to keep Abernathy's open while the Mercy can potentially access it."*

"I agree with Ayodele," Harrison said. "If Wallach's ansible is set to give us warning of the Mercy activating their oracle, that should be more than enough. We needn't risk giving them an open passage into Abernathy's."

"No one ever came through in all the times I experienced the connection," I said.

"That's no guarantee it won't happen in the future," Stirlaugson said. "But I think we overrate the danger. Ms. Davies, are you capable of closing the ansible?"

It took me a moment to remember which ansible she was talking about. "I don't know," I said. "It didn't occur to me to try. Do *you* think it's possible?"

"The connection of a custodian to her Neutrality is complex and little understood," Stirlaugson said, leaning forward slightly. "Better to say such a thing is not impossible, at least in theory. If you can exert that kind of control over the oracle, the Mercy will be unable to take advantage of the connection."

"I…it's not like I'm not willing to try, but I'm not sure it's a good idea to hinge our defense on a possibility." I took another drink of water. "I've been trying to contact Ken Gibbons, to see if he has any ideas. He's the one who thought it was time travel, but Mr. Wallach says otherwise."

"Dr. Gibbons understands the named Neutralities as no one else does," Harrison said. "You say you've been in contact with him?"

"He hasn't called me back, but yes."

"Ms. Davies is right that it's not a good idea to risk Abernathy's on the possibility that she can shut down the ansible," Duwelt said. "I don't know, Laverne. We're talking about losing the oracle entirely."

"Yes, and that's another question," Stirlaugson said. "Does the Mercy know about the potential for mutual annihilation?"

"I don't know," I said. "Harry Keller didn't say if he'd shared his findings with them. But based on talking to one of the Mercy about the oracle, I'd say they don't. I think he would have asked different questions if he'd known."

"*But is that useful?*" another metallic voice said, this one with a broad Australian accent. "*It's unlikely they'll give up trying to build their oracle on those grounds. More likely they'd try to find a way to destroy Abernathy's to protect theirs.*"

"Or we can do the same to them," Stirlaugson mused. "Maybe it's time we enlisted Abernathy's help against our enemy again. Tomorrow we'll come for an augury, and to assess the situation."

"That's a good idea." I shut up before I sounded too syco-phantic. Stirlaugson made me nervous—well, she did hold my future in her hands.

"Timothy's reports have all been positive. Your probation is going well," Stirlaugson added. I managed not to grimace. Ragsdale looked like he'd swallowed something bitter. I guessed if he could have made me look bad to the Board, he would have. "Do you have any questions for us?"

"No, Ms. Stirlaugson. Everything's fine—I mean, aside from the obvious. We don't have to worry about investigation by the police, the finances are in order. The oracle seems content."

"How do you know?"

"Oh, I just…it's a feeling I have. And when it's dissatisfied, it has ways of communicating. Like refusing to give an augury."

"Then you're convinced it's a creature."

"I am. I don't know much about it, or what it wants, but that makes it even more important that we not allow it to be destroyed. It's the only one of its kind."

"Understood." Stirlaugson stood, prompting the others to rise as well. Belatedly I got to my feet. "Tomorrow morning, Ms. Davies," she said. "Until then, rest well. You look as if you need it."

I nodded my thanks and retreated across the room, not waiting for the lantern woman to precede me. But outside in the cathedral-like space, I had to stand patiently for her arrival because the chamber was too dark for me to see the exit. I was sure she didn't loiter on purpose, but as if Stirlaugson's words had been a trigger, I was suddenly very tired and ready for sleep.

So, an augury for the Board tomorrow, then the rehearsal and dinner. A jolt of panic shot through me. I was getting married in two days. *Two days.* Was I ready? Not to be married, of course—I was past ready to be Malcolm's wife—but for all the little details. I hadn't read Deanna's last two emails; what if some disaster had happened? Had Malcolm picked up the tuxes? Could Malcolm's mother Madeleine control her animosity long enough to make the event come off smoothly? What about his grand-mère? She was supposed to arrive today, but were we supposed to get her from the airport, or was Madeleine's maid doing that?

I realized I was breathing too heavily just as we reached the elevator. I hurried inside and mashed the button for the lobby, leaned against the brass wall, and made myself relax. Now was not the time for panic. If anything had gone seriously wrong, Deanna wouldn't have depended on an email notification. And I might have a hectic schedule, but Malcolm hadn't been in to work since Wednesday, and he no doubt had everything under control.

Even so, when I emerged from the elevator and crossed the lobby to Malcolm's side, I flung myself into his arms and said, "We're still getting married, right? Nothing's gone wrong? The hotel didn't burn down?"

Malcolm laughed and hugged me. "Panic finally setting in?"

"Little bit."

"Well, no fear. Everything is still on schedule. Including the dinner tomorrow."

I shuddered. "I can't wait until that's over. I have this

nagging dread that Madeleine will think of something horribly rude to say, and it will all end in a fight."

"I think she's finally resigned to this marriage. Or she took your threat to withhold her grandchildren seriously."

"I was serious. I don't want her influencing our children, when we have them."

"Which is why she took you seriously." He gave me a final squeeze, then released me to take my hand. "And I understand Andria is bringing a date. Which may only be her unsubtle way of proving how little she thinks of me, but will certainly spike Mother's plans if she harbors any secret ideas about the two of us breaking up at the altar."

I laughed. "I must be even more tired than I thought to find that funny."

"Home, and sleep. But I'm afraid I have to go out on the hunt tonight, since Saturday and Sunday are busy."

We crossed the plaza separating the Neutralities building from the parking structure, huddling into each other against the bitter wind that found its way through the seams of our coats. "Oh," I said, disappointed, "and here I was thinking we could take one last opportunity to have unmarried sex."

Malcolm drew me closer. "I'm never going to be too busy for that."

17

I woke early the next morning as if to some internal alarm, though I'd set mine for eight o'clock to give myself an extra hour's sleep. I lay in bed, listening to Malcolm's even breathing, for about ten minutes before realizing I was done sleeping. Sighing, I rolled out of bed carefully so as not to wake him, then shut the bathroom door and turned on the tap to fill the bathtub. I had a feeling I was going to need the inner peace a good hot bath always gave me.

By the time I'd bathed, relishing the heat, dressed, and completed all the little morning routines, it was still only 7:15. I collected my phone and went downstairs to the kitchen. Popping a couple of English muffins in the toaster, I started the coffee maker and checked my phone for messages. Ken still hadn't called. What time was it there? It was Saturday, so maybe he wasn't at his desk, but that also meant he wouldn't be busy with academic stuff.

I called, and cursed when it went straight to voicemail. Not bothering to leave yet another message, I hung up. Calling was pointless, but my need to speak to Ken was growing urgent, especially since I now felt the Board expected me to do so. The toaster popped, and I poured honey on my English muffins, got myself a cup of coffee, and sat at the kitchen island to eat. What could I do?

I checked my watch out of habit and remembered too late that bitch from the Mercy had stolen it. Grumbling, I glanced at the microwave display. 7:24. Two and a half hours before I had to open. I pulled out my phone again and made another call. Juliet was an early riser even on the weekends. The question was, would she answer if she was in the middle of a workout?

She picked up after four rings. "Helena? Is something wrong?"

"No, at least not with me. I was wondering if there were any wards near Meryford University."

"Probably. I'd have to look it up. Is this about Ken Gibbons?"

"He still hasn't called me back, and I'm starting to worry. Would you be willing to ward-step me there this morning? Assuming there's a ward close enough, of course."

"Give me fifteen minutes. I'll call you back."

I tidied the kitchen and the living room while I waited. It was closer to twenty minutes before she called. "There's a warded chapel on the Meryford campus," she said. "It's not used as a chapel anymore, but the wards are intact and not strong enough to prevent ward-stepping. You want to go this morning?"

"He's probably not even there, but I have to check. And maybe someone in his department knows his home number. I haven't been able to find one."

"Why don't I meet you at Abernathy's in a few minutes?

That will give you a few extra minutes in Virginia if you can return straight to work at ten."

I thanked her and ran upstairs to kiss Malcolm goodbye. He stirred briefly, smiled, and went back to sleep. I watched him for a moment, my heart so full I couldn't move. Tomorrow we'd be married. It seemed too wonderful to be real.

Juliet pulled into Abernathy's magically reserved spot two minutes after I arrived. Judy wasn't downstairs yet, and I thought about letting her know what I was doing, but decided to give her a few extra minutes of sleep. I opened the door for Juliet, who wore a belted tan coat open over jeans and a bulky sweater. "Finally the rain's stopped," she said. "Just in time for your wedding."

"Let's hope so," I said. "Thanks again for doing this."

"It's no problem. I'm a little concerned myself. If Dr. Gibbons' knowledge is so valuable, it might make the difference between success and failure. And what if the Mercy decided to go after him?"

"I'm trying not to think that way." I put my arm around Juliet's waist. "I hold on like this?"

Juliet's own arm went around my waist. "Yes. Close your eyes, it helps with the nausea," she said. I dutifully closed my eyes, and immediately my stomach wrenched, trying to turn inside out. I gasped incautiously, but there was no air to fill my lungs, just the stench of hot gunmetal that seemed to cling to my nostrils. I coughed, and suddenly there was air again, sweet, beautiful, muggy air that I sucked in gratefully. Opening my dry, aching eyes, I blinked to rid myself of the gray haze that filled my vision.

Eventually, fuzzy-edged shapes loomed at me through the fog, becoming clearer with every passing second. What I initially thought were pillars were actually stacked crates, neatly piled against the walls of this small room. Scuff marks on the bare wooden floor suggested it had been used for storage for many years. It was so full of crates I couldn't see what color the walls were. The crates almost obscured the door, a bland brown rectangle wedged between stacks.

"Feeling better?" Juliet said. I nodded. "I hope this room isn't locked. I'm really bad at lock picking, even with magic."

The door wasn't locked, but the outer door, reached via a corridor extending several yards from the storage room, was. Juliet sighed and knelt next to the lock. "This could take a few minutes."

"We have some time." I felt remarkably unhurried, now that we were actually at Meryford. I'd need to come up with a story to tell some administrative assistant that would convince her to tell me where to find Ken. Student in need of after-hours tutoring? Did full professors do that sort of thing? I'd only made it through a couple of years of community college before the money ran out, so my experience of college life was limited. Maybe I could say I was supposed to hand in an assignment to him personally. Or pick up some notes from class.

"That's it," Juliet said, standing and brushing off her knees. She opened the door and ushered me out.

Beyond lay a wide open expanse of lawn, green even at this time of year. Concrete paths crossed it, trod by men and women in no hurry to get where they were going. A bronze statue on a tall marble pedestal, its patina green with age, looked beneficently over the quad. It was of a man dressed in what I thought of as Christopher Columbus clothes, complete with baggy hat and a spyglass held to one eye. Was it the Meryford the college was named for? A bronze plaque attached to the pedestal's base was too far away for me to read.

"Where now, fearless leader?" Juliet said.

I pulled up the campus map on my phone and oriented myself. "I think...wow, this is small...it's that way." I pointed toward a couple of low red brick buildings trimmed with classical white pillars. "Social Sciences."

We crossed the quad, sticking to the paths though there were any number of students walking on the grass. I felt it wasn't properly respectful for us to do so, given that we were visitors. The air was cool but not chilly, and my coat that had been perfect in Portland felt too warm here, though not warm enough to take it off. A whiff of fried food came from somewhere nearby, probably the student center whose sign was easily readable off to my right. It was so peaceful I almost wished I were a student there, though the thought didn't last long. I'd been an average student, but I'd never loved school, and it wasn't as if I needed higher education for the job I had now.

The Social Sciences building—buildings; there were two of them—looked cozy rather than intimidating, which is what I'd always thought colleges were supposed to look like. They were built in a style I associated with the South, tall white pillars flanking the white double doors of the entrance. A sloping ramp instead of stairs led to those doors, and a square wheelchair-access button looked out of place next to them. I pushed the doors open and we went inside.

The resemblance to a Southern plantation manor didn't stop at the outside, though the place smelled of fresh paint and not magnolias, which was all my imagination could come up with. The white walls were covered with gilt-framed portraits of cranky-looking men and one very crabby lady, apparently former deans of the social sciences colleges. Short pedestals bearing white marble busts, probably of famous historical figures, circled the round entry. A narrow carpet that didn't cover the whole floor ran down the hallway lined with white doors, and another, identical carpet covered the stairs that rose half a flight, made a right-angle turn, and ended at the floor above. I stopped, unsure where to go. I'd expected a receptionist.

Juliet had walked past me to examine the nearest door. It bore a brass plaque I couldn't read from where I stood. "Main office," she said, and turned the handle.

A middle-aged woman, her hair piled on her head and cat-eye glasses dangling from a string around her neck, looked up when we entered. "Can I help you?" she said. Her accent was thick and syrupy, but her smile was pleasant and suggested it would be her pleasure to help us.

"Do you know if Dr. Gibbons is in?" I said. "I, um, he told me to stop by to pick up some class notes."

"Dr. Gibbons? I'm not sure. You know his office hours are only Tuesdays and Thursdays from two to four." Her pleasant smile became a concerned frown.

"I know, but he said, since it was just to pick them up— maybe he left them here?" I improvised.

"I don't have anything waiting." The woman shuffled papers in a couple of overflowing bins as if the imaginary notes might suddenly appear. "Let me check his office." She drew her sleek black phone toward her, punched a few buttons, and lifted the receiver. "Dr. Gibbons? Oh, you are here. There's a student here who wants to see you. Says she needs to pick up some notes."

I couldn't hear Ken's reply, if he made one, but the woman nodded and said, "Of course." She hung up and said, "You can go on up. He's room 215, on the second floor."

I thanked her and we left the office to ascend the stairs. "That's some good luck, finding him in on a Saturday," Juliet said.

"I think I'm due some good luck, after the week I've had."

"It sucks that you have to work today. Why couldn't the Board give you even one day off?"

I shrugged. It was nothing I hadn't thought of before. "The auguries start to pile up if I get even a little bit behind. It's the job I signed up for."

"I remember the day we met. You'd been the custodian for about five minutes, but you were as confident as if you'd been doing it your whole life."

"It was all an act. I was so overwhelmed, the only thing that saved me was not knowing just how impossible a task it was to be the custodian with no prior training."

"Well, the Board is lucky to have you. Briggs didn't care about his customers and I'm sure the oracle never spoke to him." She was examining the numbers on the doors. "This one."

I knocked twice, then opened the door without waiting for an invitation. Ken knew we were coming, though I was sure he'd be surprised at just who had come to his door. "Ken?" I said. "I'm Helena—"

The office wasn't very big, and the desk and leather chair took up most of the space. A man of below average height began to rise from the chair, then froze. I took in the horrified expression, the bruise spreading across his left temple, the graying black hair shellacked into place, and felt rooted to the spot. "*You!*"

It was my interrogator from the Mercy.

We stared at each other. I was too shocked to move. Ken's expression went from horrified to calculating. Juliet, entering behind me, bumped into my unmoving form and said, "What's wrong?"

"How did you do it?" I breathed.

Ken looked for a moment like he was going to deny everything. Then he sank back into his chair and folded his hands in his lap. "Dr. Ellery altered my voice," he said. This time, he sounded like the man I'd gotten to know over the phone—smooth, totally relaxed, a little condescending. "We couldn't have you figuring it out."

"Helena, what's he talking about?" Juliet said.

I didn't take my eyes off Ken. "He belongs to the Mercy."

Juliet sucked in a startled breath. I said, "You took an awful risk. Suppose I'd seen your picture?"

"A chance worth taking, if I could convince you to switch sides. I don't suppose you're here because you changed your mind?"

"I'm here because you never answered your messages. I thought—" I closed my mouth sharply on more words. How much had I given away to the Mercy in my voicemails to Ken?

Ken's lips twitched in a smug smile. "I've been busy. You Wardens disrupted our plans quite thoroughly. Moving the oracle was a non-trivial task."

"Don't expect me to apologize for that."

Juliet, her voice shaking, said, "What do you mean, he's with the Mercy? Isn't that Ken Gibbons?"

"It's a long story," Ken said, his voice oilier than before, and I itched to slap him and his smug attitude. "But yes, it's true."

"You went through the tests," I said. "Mike Conti said they traumatized you. But you passed."

"Yes, well, if you join after you're tested, surprisingly no one thinks to suspect you," Ken said, his small smile vanishing. "After what I went through, after being treated like a criminal by people I thought respected me, I questioned whether what they believed about the Mercy was accurate. My questioning led me to the truth, and more congenial masters."

"I'm sorry you suffered, but that's no reason to betray your friends."

"So many wrong assumptions in that little statement. Why don't you sit, and we'll talk." He gestured at the chair in front of his desk, and at another one set some distance away.

I remained standing. "It's over for you," I said. "The Wardens will arrest you, and that will be it for the second oracle. It was you, wasn't it, who came up with the plan? You who know so much about the named Neutralities and Elizabeth Abernathy. All that nonsense about time travel—"

"Oh, let's not argue over what's done," Ken said, pushing back from his desk and swiveling his chair around. "Coffee?"

"*Coffee?*" I couldn't believe he was still trying to brazen it out. I still couldn't believe it even when he swiveled back around with a gun in his hand and pointed it at me.

I shrieked and dove for the floor as it went off. The explosion filled the tiny room with deafening sound and the stink of gunpowder. My ears ringing, I sat up in time to see Ken hurdle the desk, still clutching the gun, and shove past Juliet on his way out the door. I leaped to my feet and grabbed her arm. "We have to stop him!"

"Helena," Juliet said, her eyes wide, "he shot me with his coffee mug."

Blood spread across the front of her sweater, lurid red against the pale wheat color of its bulky weave. "Juliet!" I shouted, then caught her as she started to sag. I turned her fall into a more graceful sway and helped her lie on the floor. "Juliet, did he—I mean—stay with me, Juliet!"

She shook her head and closed her eyes, scrabbling at her pocket. "Stop him," she whispered, pulling out her phone. "I'll call…the Wardens…you go after him."

"I can't—"

She clutched my hand. "Can't let the Mercy escape. Go."

I dithered for half a second more, then bolted out the door and down the hall. At the very least, I could follow him until the Wardens got here.

The woman from the administration office was peering out the door as I pounded down the stairs in time to see the front door swing shut. "Was that a *gunshot?*" she demanded.

"Dr. Gibbons shot a student!" I cried. "Call 9-1-1!" Then I was out the door and heading for the quad. Ken's retreating form was halfway across it and accelerating. I put on a burst of speed I hadn't known was in me and followed him. He was fast for a middle-aged academic.

I was gaining on him and feeling a little more confident when he slewed around and shot at me. I screamed, ducked, and zigged to the right. Malcolm had said something once about not running in a straight line when people were shooting at you, but I hadn't paid much attention because we were snuggled together in bed at the time and he'd demonstrated the maneuver with his fingers on my bare stomach, tickling me. More screams came from all sides as people came alert to the sound of gunfire, though none of them seemed to have realized the source. I zagged left, hoping that was the right thing to do, but Ken had turned a corner and disappeared.

I slowed down as I reached the spot. *That* was something I did remember, that running full-tilt around a blind corner was a great way to run into an ambush. I trotted to the corner and peered around. It was a narrower passage between two of the red-brick buildings, with a walkway down its center. Ken hadn't stopped to ambush me; he was most of the way down the walkway and headed for one of the larger buildings, this one of granite and much taller than the rest. I sped after him, ignoring the pain in my side. When this was all over, I was going to start exercising. I wasn't out of shape, but I was in no condition to run this kind of race.

Ken pushed open the building's doors and darted inside. I took the five shallow steps extending half the length of the building's façade at a single leap, then staggered to catch my balance. ARTHUR SMITHSON MEMORIAL LIBRARY, said deeply incised letters on a granite plaque to the right of the doors. Two students came through the doors as I stumbled toward them, and we did an awkward little dance that had me screaming inside with frustration. Finally I found myself inside and cast about frantically for any sight of Ken. He was gone.

I walked forward, examining my surroundings. There were no bookcases visible. Instead, a round atrium floored with marble took up most of the space, lined with drooping ficus plants that looked like they wished spring would get here already. To one side, a circulation desk with checkout terminals blocked access to offices probably for the librarians. On the other side, the atrium gave way to rows of computer terminals, about half of them occupied. Stairs near the center of the room were completely open to view, and if Ken had gone that way, he couldn't have gotten far enough that I wouldn't have seen him.

My eye fell on a door to the left of the circulation desk. *No Admittance*, the sign said, but there was one of those wire-filled glass windows in its center, and beyond it I saw stairs. They looked utilitarian, but more importantly, they looked like an escape route.

I strode casually in the direction of the door, not looking around. I'd learned this not from Malcolm, but from Judy's favorite action movies: if you act like you're supposed to be somewhere, people don't generally challenge you. The brief fear that the door was locked flashed through my head, but I dismissed it. Ken couldn't have made good his escape if it were locked, and it didn't have a deadbolt, so he couldn't have locked it after him.

I stole a glance at the circulation desk. There weren't any librarians behind it, just a couple of students using the self-check stations. Then my hand was on the doorknob, and in another second I was inside.

Ken was long gone, but I felt confident I was on the right track. I hurried up the stairs and around a corner to the half-landing, then up a second flight to another door, also with the glass window. It was locked. I moved on. Halfway up the stairs, I heard a gunshot, and froze, suddenly aware of how stupid I was. I might be able to see his gun despite whatever illusion his magi friends with the Mercy had placed on it—did it still look like a coffee mug?—but that would do me no good if he shot me.

I proceeded up the stairs more cautiously. Three shots. That would be meaningful if I'd known how many he'd started with. I'd only gotten a glimpse of the weapon, and I wasn't very familiar with guns, but it looked smaller than the guns Malcolm used. I hoped that meant it didn't hold many bullets.

I tried the other doors I came across. All were locked. But when I neared the top of the stairs, I saw what Ken had shot at. The final door hung ajar, its knob and lock blown away. I paused below the final landing and took out my phone. If Ken was waiting for me just beyond the door, I'd be stupid to go poking my head through. I wished I had something, anything, that I could use as a decoy.

Malcolm picked up on the third ring. "Forget something, love?"

"Malcolm, Ken is with the Mercy," I said in a low voice, hoping Ken wasn't close enough to hear me. "I went to see him at his office and he's the man who interrogated me when I was captured. The one I hit with the glass oracle. You need to get the Wardens to Meryford University—"

"Helena. Slow down. Are you safe?"

"For now."

"For now?"

"He shot Juliet. I went after him—"

"You did *what?*"

"Shh, he might hear you!"

"Helena, get out of there now!"

"I can't. I have to keep him from getting away."

"You don't. Wait for the Wardens. Where are you?"

"The university library. I don't think he can go anywhere, even if his gun is a coffee mug."

Malcolm didn't respond to this. "Get outside and call 9-1-1 for Juliet. I'll be there as soon as I can. Did you ward-step in?"

"There's an old chapel on the grounds."

"That's something, anyway. Helena, promise me you won't do anything rash."

"I won't. But I can't let him escape. If we capture him, the Mercy won't be able to rebuild their oracle."

"We'll capture him. You've done more than enough." He hung up. I put my phone away and sat on the stairs. Malcolm was right, I'd done enough. Exposing Ken, forcing him to flee...it would get him captured, deprive the Mercy of his skills, and be the beginning of the end for the second oracle. I didn't need to chase him down.

But what if there were a second exit from this floor? There almost had to be, right? Depending on what was kept on the fourth floor, there might even be a freight elevator for hauling books. He might still escape.

I stood and crept up the stairs on hands and knees, edging up to the door. Perfect silence reigned in the stairwell and beyond. I crouched low and grabbed the door, pulling it open slowly. No gunshots sounded. I eased my way through the narrow gap and stopped to calm my breathing. I didn't hear anyone else nearby.

The fourth floor was lit only by skylights, and since the day was overcast, there wasn't much light. Rows and rows of metal bookcases extended as far as I could see in the dimness, all of them crammed with books in orderly lines. Nothing moved. I stood cautiously and took a few steps that put me behind one of the bookcases. The dark Berber carpet underfoot silenced my steps, which reassured me until I remembered Ken would have the same advantage. I moved along the aisle to the end. More bookcases. It was like the most well-ordered maze in the world, with no cunning surprises or cul-de-sacs—just rows and rows of metal shelving units that smelled of dust and ozone.

I sniffed. Definitely ozone. That wasn't a usual library smell. It reminded me of Harriet's glass head shattering on the countertop. The smell of magic. But Ken wasn't a magus, so where was it coming from?

I touched the nearest book, expecting to feel a shock. The book was old, but not in an antique way, just a book that had seen a lot of readers over the years. It felt reassuringly solid despite its cracked spine and worn cover. I wondered if anyone knew it was up here. This couldn't be the library stacks, not the ones in common use, because it was too poorly lit and too dusty. Probably storage. Some of these books might have been here for years, forgotten—

I closed my hand convulsively on the book's spine. Forgotten books. Books no one knew about.

I was in the middle of the Mercy's oracle.

18

I t couldn't be anything else. And it explained why Ken had come here. If he were the oracle's custodian, a theory that made increasingly more sense to me, he could hide inside it until the rest of the Mercy showed up to extract him. Assuming he could get it to activate. They'd had a couple of days—that couldn't possibly be enough time for them to reconstruct the glass sculptures and solve the problem the kidnapped glass magi had described. But he had to be desperate. And maybe there were things we didn't know yet.

But it was impossible, wasn't it? A library had a catalog, some list of contents, anyway, and indeterminacy couldn't function under those conditions. Except…this was like some kind of…of dead book collection, stuff removed from the main collection but not gotten rid of. It was possible none of it was catalogued. At any rate, I felt in my bones my guess was correct. This was where they'd moved the second oracle when the storefront had to be abandoned. No need to move all those books; just find a new collection.

I shuffled down the aisle until I reached the wall, listening closely for the sound of someone else moving around. If I could find the other exit, I could...do what? Block it with my body? My possibly dead body, if Ken saw me first? Malcolm was right. There wasn't anything I could do. I needed to get out of there, get outside and go back to Juliet.

I went back the way I'd come, suppressing a sneeze from all the dust. Fear had my heart pounding in my chest, but even in my fear I was irritated at the Mercy's disregard for the state of the oracle. Okay, granted they hadn't had much time to clean this one up, but the other store had been grimy and uncared-for too. They didn't deserve to have an oracle even if they weren't filthy collaborators.

The aisle seemed to go on forever. I sped up, my desire to get out overriding my desire not to be noticed. Surely I should have come to the exit by now? Cold sweat prickled my temples, an unnamed dread I didn't want to face gathering in the back of my mind. Then I reached the far wall. I hadn't seen a door anywhere. I leaned into the corner where the walls met and took a deep breath. If there was no door, it meant the oracle was active, and I was lost inside it.

Distantly, I heard someone call my name. I panicked and ran, though I didn't know where I was running to. It probably didn't matter. I just had to stay away from Ken. My name sounded again, closer now, and it brought me to my senses. If I ran, he could hear me. But if I could hear him, I'd know where he was to stay away from him. I stood perfectly still and listened.

"Helena, it's not too late," Ken said. He was ahead of me and off to my right, not coming nearer. "What I told you still applies. There's so much we could do if we worked together, two custodians of the oracles."

I kept my mouth shut, though I wanted to argue with him. The last thing I needed was to give away my location.

"You see we've learned to make the oracle active on our terms," Ken went on. "We have your Wardens to thank for that. If they hadn't come bursting in, we wouldn't have had to scramble to get away. It was that scrambling that showed us where we'd gone wrong. We needed to increase the randomness, not control it." He chuckled. "I should send them a fruit basket or something, don't you think?"

His voice was drawing nearer. I backed up and went around a corner I hoped would put more shelves between us. "At any rate, our oracle works. This location is much better than the last, too. So much more convenient for me. Not that I intend to be as busy as you seem to be. I don't know why Abernathy's is so willing to provide auguries for every Tom, Dick, and Sally who comes through its doors. We're going to be far more discerning. Only auguries that will help us fight the Long War."

This location. I wanted to laugh. Ken wouldn't talk so freely about the benefits of this location if he thought they'd have to move again. He didn't intend to cooperate with me. He intended to kill me so I couldn't reveal his secret. I wasn't sure why he thought my death would be enough, not after he'd shot and possibly killed Juliet and certainly not after I'd called Malcolm. Probably he didn't know about the latter. He must be as smug and self-confident as he appeared. Well, it didn't matter. Eventually he'd have to leave the oracle, and then the Wardens would get him. I just had to stay out of his way until that happened.

"I don't know why you're trying to hide," Ken said. "It's not as if you can go anywhere. Come, Helena, let's talk about this."

I moved around another corner, and my toe caught the bottom of one of the metal shelves, making it ring out in a short, dull tone like a muffled bell. "Helena?" Ken said. I heard him running in my direction. I took off the other way, trying to put as much distance between us as I could. Another gunshot exploded far too close to me. So much for being friends.

I reached another wall and darted down the aisle, then ducked low and crouched behind a shelf. This was impossible. Ken had at least two, maybe three more bullets left, but it could be more, and I couldn't count on him continuing to take inaccurate potshots at me. I had to find a way out of here, and fast.

I stilled my breathing and closed my eyes. A distant curse told me Ken had lost track of me again. If I were in Abernathy's, I could walk between the oracles and get out that way. But...this was an oracle, if an irregular one. How much control did I have over it? Sure, I wasn't its custodian, but Harry had said the oracles were essentially identical, so didn't that mean something?

I thought about what I did to enter the oracle without an augury request. It was only a conscious decision in the sense that you tell your hand, for example, to pick up a coffee cup. Your body can't do that on its own. But you don't think through all the steps required; you just...pick it up. I'd tried to explain it to Malcolm, but though he'd seemed to understand, I was sure I hadn't really conveyed the meaning. All I knew was I formed the intention of entering the oracle, and when I walked between the bookcases, I was there. So now I had to figure out if I could do that from where I was, thousands of miles from Abernathy's.

With my breathing calm and regular, I rolled out my

shoulders and stood. This oracle and Abernathy's shared the same space, therefore… I opened my eyes and began to walk back along the aisle by the wall. Between one step and the next, the metal shelves trembled, and then I was surrounded by familiar yellow 2x8s and the smell of lilacs, welcoming me home.

Far too close, Ken screamed in frustration. I ran for the exit, but came up short as the bookcases vanished and I found myself in the middle of the metal maze again. *That's some impressive control,* I thought, focusing inward. Abernathy's appeared again, then vanished. Damn. I had to break Ken's control or I would never get out of this place.

I kept moving, listening for Ken's approach. He'd given up on being stealthy and was cursing loudly and with great imagination. I brought up my memory of my oracle again and held onto it. This time, it stayed. I felt the oracle focusing its attention on me as if in curiosity. Following a well-remembered path, I skidded to a halt in the heart of the oracle. "I need help," I whispered, just in time remembering I didn't want Ken to find me. "That—"

A shudder ran through the store, shaking the bookcases. I braced myself against the reappearance of the metal shelves, but nothing changed. The oracle's attention shifted, and its presence vanished, returning me to the library. Ken stood not fifteen feet from me. His winter-pale skin looked ashen in the dim light, and I smelled vomit. "Stop doing that," he said, his gun hanging forgotten at his side.

"I didn't do anything." The same shudder went through the room, forcing me to grab hold of a shelf or risk being knocked over. Ken crouched and dry-heaved on the carpet, and I almost went to help him before coming to my senses.

Then I felt the oracle again, my oracle. We were still in the library, not Abernathy's, but its presence was unmistakable. Ken wiped his mouth and said, "What the hell is that?"

"It's Abernathy's," I said, "and it—"

The room shuddered again, and this time I did fall, landing hard on my butt. The air felt thick and muggy, though not with humidity. It was like being in a bowl of Jell-O, a sensation I remembered from two years back when I'd dragged Malcolm into the oracle with me to fight a giant invader. It was the sensation of being somewhere I wasn't wanted, of being a piece of grit inside an oyster that wanted to turn me into something it could bear containing. I knew in my heart I was in the presence of the second oracle.

I struggled to get to my feet and held onto the shelf for balance. Ken still lay sprawled on the floor, moving spastically. Abernathy's oracle was still there, I could feel it, but its attention was fully on the second oracle. I staggered across to Ken and fell to my knees beside him. "You have to stop it," I said. "They'll destroy each other."

"Impossible," Ken whispered. "You want to trick me into giving up my edge."

"They can't coexist without mutual annihilation. I'm not lying, Ken. You have to control the second oracle or they'll take us both with them." I was far more worried about losing Abernathy's oracle, but I guessed he wouldn't respond to anything but an appeal to self-preservation.

The air thickened again. It was nearly impossible to breathe. I coughed, drew in as much of a lungful as I could, and pushed myself to my feet. Ken's gun lay a few inches from his hand where it had fallen after his collapse. I kicked it away, hard, and saw it go skittering under a shelf two rows down. "Then I'll do it," I said, though I had no idea what I could do.

I tried to remember how I'd communicated with the oracle

before. It seemed a really bad idea to try to become the oracle at this point, so I cried out, "Can you hear me?"

The air shimmered gold and blue. I felt the oracle's attention on me. I thought, **Like me.** The thought didn't come from me. I tried not to recoil in fear. The oracle didn't frighten me anymore. But having my brain used to produce thoughts that weren't mine was almost too much to take.

I closed my eyes and thought, *What do you mean, like you?*

A pause, then, **Me, and not me. Not you, but me. Like me.**

You mean the other oracle. It's like you?

Alone.

You're not alone. But it was a weak thought. I knew my companionship, as erratic as it necessarily was, couldn't give this extraordinary entity what it wanted.

Like me.

It's not like you! It's a...a thing, a field. Not a creature. And it will destroy you both. You have to stop it.

The image of a sapling appeared in my head. It grew rapidly, as if on extreme fast-forward, until it was a vast oak, thick with emerald leaves and a host of little brown acorns. **Grow. Become life.**

Are you talking about the other one?

I grow. I live. What I was, it is.

The oracle's attention wavered. I stood, stunned with realization. Another shudder went through the building. The two oracles couldn't coexist. One of them had to be destroyed to save the other. And I was damned if I'd let Abernathy's sacrifice itself for the sake of some unthinking field.

"It doesn't deserve to live!" I shouted, forgetting in my terror to think my response. "The Mercy will use it to defeat the Wardens! I know that's something you care about—you can't let it happen—"

Something struck me from behind, and I went down. Ken got a knee in the small of my back, pressing me down. His hands went around my throat. "You can't win," he grated, sounding more like he had back in the Mercy's interrogation shed.

Choking, I thrashed, flailing about. Ken wasn't much bigger than I was, and I managed to worm myself onto my back, my fingers prying desperately at his hands. The air shimmered with gold, surely an effect of oxygen deprivation—or was it? Golden letters swarmed into existence, running over the dusty books like flowing light. Ken didn't notice. His face was dark with anger and his eyes blazed, intent on killing me. Only I saw the books begin to lift from the shelves, floating as if suspended in a golden sea of alphabet soup. One large tome flew at Ken, striking him on the back of that amazing head of hair and making him flinch. His grip loosened marginally, and I drew my knees up and lashed out with my foot, catching him square in the crotch.

I'd never actually seen a man get hit in the groin before, not in real life. Ken made an almost comical expression of pain, and he let go my throat to clutch at himself. I rolled away and ran for it, coughing in the thick air, praying I could stay hidden long enough for…what? I still had no idea what to do.

Don't let it destroy you, I thought as I ran, praying the oracle would listen. *We need you. I need you.*

Life is.

Yes, but you don't have to give yours up for this thing!

Like me.

I felt so tired. *No, it's not like you! Not yet. And neither of you will exist if you don't stop it now!* It was the only thing that made sense. I couldn't destroy it. The glass sculptures that fueled it were miles away. Ken was no help. If I couldn't convince the oracle to save itself, nothing would stop the second oracle from destroying them both.

Like you.

I don't understand.

The air shone gold. In the reflected light, I saw another gleam, but dark, midnight blue, and soft as velvet. It made me want to wrap myself in it and rub its softness against my cheek. The gold wrapped around it, caressing it. The second oracle. I felt nothing from it, no sense of awareness or perception, just a hum against my skin like a cat's purr. It was so beautiful that for a moment, I saw it as Abernathy's did—something alike, something it could understand.

The shining letters twined around the velvet, flowing constantly like streams of liquid gold. The field arched, for all the world like a cat preening itself, but I still felt nothing from it. The room shuddered, and this time some of the shelves fell, striking others and making them teeter. Books cascaded to the floor in a series of erratic thumps, like a dying creature's heartbeat. I realized I was on my knees and leaned against a shelf, pressing my face to its cold metal and feeling tears slick its surface. "Please," I said.

Goodbye.

"*No!*" I screamed, dragging myself up and diving into the center of where the golden letters encircled the midnight blue velvet. Something picked me up and flung me away. I struck one of the metal shelves and cried out in pain, then hit the floor hard enough to knock the breath out of me. Gasping, I dragged myself upright, or at least to my knees.

From where I was, the golden letters were no longer distinguishable as letters. They looked more like slim chains binding the blue velvet, which twisted more rapidly now, bucking as if their touch burned. The vibration increased from a purr to a jackhammer and then went past perception into a mental scream like fingernails on slate. I covered my ears, but it didn't stop the sound. Tears filled my eyes, whether from pain or sorrow, I couldn't tell.

A dark shape rushed past me. Ken ran, staggering, into the center of the field. The chains shifted to avoid touching him. "I won't let you!" he screamed. He set his feet solidly shoulder-width apart and reached out with both hands as if to gather the midnight blue velvet into his arms. It twisted again, and engulfed him, but I could still see him through the folds, as if the velvet were sheer tulle instead. My head aching, I got to my feet and took a step toward him, feeling as if I were once again walking through Jell-O. If he could do it, I could do it, and I would not allow my oracle to sacrifice itself.

Ken grabbed his head with both hands, tearing at his perfect hair. An agonized groan escaped him. I took another step. I was almost close enough to touch him. The golden chains whipped around us, never touching us, but…they were almost herding the velvet field, controlling it. Blood flowed from Ken's ears and the corners of his eyes, and my addled brain realized what he was trying to do. He was trying to become the oracle.

I reached out, stretching my arms to their fullest length, though I had no idea what I could do to stop Ken. If he became the oracle, there was no telling what he'd be capable of, except he would certainly kill me. One more step, and my hand went around his wrist.

The golden chains exploded with light, filling the dark room with a midsummer sunlight that threw everything into stark relief. The velvet field shriveled in on itself, like a puddle of water evaporating at high speed. Ken screamed, arching his back and flinging his arms wide as if he were about to leap off a cliff into some cold pool below. I screamed with him, throwing my arms over my face to shield my eyes. Then, everything just—stopped. Ken's scream cut off abruptly. The light vanished as if it had never been. I lowered my arms to see Ken collapsed on the floor like a boneless thing, the dim light from the skylights making him look ashen. Dead.

I flung myself at him and turned him on his back. He blinked up at me, his chest rising and falling naturally. "Are you all right?" I asked.

He said nothing, just continued to stare, blinking in a regular pattern that made my eyes water. A bit of drool collected at the corner of his mouth, but he didn't lick it away. "Ken," I said, "do you know who I am?"

He was, I thought, with those thoughts that weren't my own. *I am.*

I looked up. The air shimmered again with gold. "I thought—" I began, wiped a tear from my eyes, cleared my throat, and tried again. "You said goodbye."

It passed. Goodbye.

I drew a deep, shuddering breath. "You killed it."

I live. It did not. Dead is not true.

"It's not dead because it wasn't alive. I understand."

A wave of sorrow so profound it was nearly tangible swept over me, and I found myself weeping—for the oracle, for the nameless thing it had destroyed, even for Ken, mindless as he now seemed to be. I wondered if it could be called luck that he hadn't been killed when the oracle he'd tried to become was destroyed.

Home. Home?

I wiped tears from my eyes. "I—no, I should wait here for

the Wardens. I won't be able to pass between the oracles again, huh? Because now there's only—" A horrible thought struck me. "Will they be able to create another one? I know I thought, if Ken were unavailable, they wouldn't have the knowledge, but they've still got all the glass oracle sculptures."

The glowing, shimmering air pulsed once. *No more. Alone.*

"I'm sorry. If there were any way...you know I don't want you to be sad." I suddenly felt dizzy and a little crazy, talking to the air. I understood so little of what the oracle was, and maybe it was presumptuous of me to assign human desires and emotions to something so alien.

A trilling laugh filled the air, the sound of a hundred cascading bells. Something brushed my cheek, feather-light. *Not alone, Helena*, the oracle said, and then it was gone.

19

I sat in the dimness next to Ken, watching him breathe, my mind blank with tiredness. What should I do now? I couldn't leave Ken alone, helpless as he was, but I couldn't get him down the stairs without causing an enormous fuss. So I just sat, hugging my knees, until my phone rang. "Where are you?" Malcolm demanded.

"Fourth floor of the library. There's an access stair next to the circulation desk. It's over, Malcolm. The oracle—Abernathy's—it destroyed the Mercy's oracle. Everything's...actually I guess everything's not all right. Do you know if Juliet...?"

"Juliet was taken to the hospital," Malcolm said. "They were just taking her away when we arrived. I sent Tinsley after her with a couple of paper magi. With luck, they should be able to heal her and spirit her away to Portland. Where is Ken Gibbons? The rumor that he shot her is running strong."

"He's here. He...something happened to him in the

oracles' fight. I think his mind is gone. I don't know what to do."

"Are you all right? You're not hurt?"

"No, just very, very tired. I'll explain everything once we're home again. Can you come for me?"

"I will always come for you," Malcolm said, and hung up.

It felt like a small eternity before I heard footsteps on the stairs. Then Malcolm was beside me, taking me in his arms and holding me close. "I wanted to chastise you for disobeying orders," he said, "but you look as if you've suffered enough. Not to mention you're not obligated to obey me."

"Not until after tomorrow," I said.

"I thought we wrote that part out of our vows."

"True. I did try to leave, but I got trapped in the second oracle."

"Tell me the story later. Right now, you're going back to Portland. Leave the rest of this mess to us."

"Mal, you need to take a look at this," Mike said, his familiar voice startling me out of my reverie. Malcolm squeezed me once, then turned toward Mike, who was kneeling next to Ken. "I'm not getting any reaction out of him. We need a bone magus to look him over, but I think he's suffered serious brain damage."

"That might be for the best," Malcolm said, his voice hard. "Considering what his punishment would otherwise be. He's not faking?"

"I doubt it. But like I said, bone magus."

"I don't see a gun."

"I kicked it away," I said. "It went under one of the shelves. I don't remember which one."

"Don't worry about it, Helena," Malcolm said. "We'll find it."

Someone else helped me to my feet. "Ms. Davies, if you can walk, come with me," a man said. I didn't recognize him, and for about half a second I almost refused, fearing yet another Mercy trap. But I realized in time that was stupid and followed him to the stairs.

We left the library without anyone stopping us, though someone behind the circulation desk looked about to ask us what business we had back there. I was so tired I thought I might fall asleep on my feet. My helper got me going in the right direction, and before I knew it, we were in the old chapel and I felt the now-familiar sense of nausea and dizziness from ward-stepping. When I was able to see again, I felt like crying, because we were back in Abernathy's and Judy was there to support me until I could stand upright.

"You are going to tell me *everything*," she said, propelling me back to the office, "starting with why you went off without telling me *anything*."

"I thought it would just be a quick trip. And you were asleep. It's only been…what time is it?"

"9:44."

"It feels like so much longer. Um…what do you know already?"

"Malcolm called me half an hour ago and said only that Ken Gibbons was a traitor and he was going off to Virginia to rescue you. Again. I've chewed my nails nearly to my elbows with worry."

"I'm sorry. Like I said, I thought it would only take a few minutes. I was worried about Ken not returning my calls and decided to see if I could speak to him in person. So I called Juliet…"

Telling the story, with all Judy's interruptions, still only took about ten minutes. Judy stopped interrupting when I got to the part about the oracle, our oracle, manifesting in the library. When I reached the end, she said, "That's...I don't know what that means. The oracle defended itself? Against the other oracle?"

"Yeah. It was heartbreaking. And it called me by name, Judy. I didn't think it understood humans well enough to know we have names."

"Aren't you frightened that Ken apparently lost his mind trying to become the second oracle? If it happened to him, couldn't it happen to you?"

"It didn't occur to me. I don't think it could, unless the oracle was destroyed while I was connected to it. Or...I don't know. That other oracle was just a thing. Maybe the human brain isn't made to comprehend something like that."

Judy shook her head, her lips taut with disapproval. "I'd still be leery of doing it if I were you."

I sighed. "I wish I could say it's unlikely it will happen again. I've stopped trying to guess what strange things will occur in this place."

A distant banging on the door startled us both. Judy swore. "It's 10:05. Are you going to be all right? Maybe we should close the store for a few hours. You look like you need a rest."

"I'm fine. Or I will be. Besides, the Board is supposed to come by today sometime, and we need to be open when they do."

I put on a cheerful smile as I went to open the door, hoping if I tried hard enough, it might come true. My smile faltered when I saw who was waiting at the door. Not just the usual line of Nicolliens, but four familiar faces: Stirlaugson, Ragsdale, Duwelt, and Harrison. Ragsdale wore a malicious grin. Stirlaugson looked impassive. I swallowed, unlocked the deadbolt, and opened the door. "Sorry about that. I got in...late."

"No excuses," Ragsdale said. He didn't even bother to conceal his pleasure. "The Accords clearly state——"

"I know what the Accords state, Mr. Ragsdale, and as I said, I'm sorry for the delay. I was in Virginia until twenty minutes ago, disposing of the Mercy's oracle." Fatigue, and emotional tiredness, left me incapable of caring about placating the horrible little man.

Stillness spread outward from me, washing over the Board members and touching even those Nicolliens who were too far away to hear my words. "Excuse me?" Stirlaugson said.

"It's a long story, and I'm sure your augury is more important. I certainly wouldn't want to stand around gossiping." I gave Ragsdale a hard stare and was pleased to see him flinch. He recovered quickly.

"If this is your idea of an excuse," he said, "I assure you the Board doesn't make exceptions. I'll be citing you for dereliction of duty, under Article IV, section——"

"Shut up, Timothy," Duwelt said. "Five minutes is hardly dereliction of duty. Ms. Davies, did you say you disposed of the Mercy's oracle? What exactly does that mean?"

"I'm afraid I have to handle the walk-in auguries first according to Article I, Section B, subsection 2, paragraphs iii-vi of the Accords——"

"Never mind that," Stirlaugson said. "Explain."

"It turns out Ken Gibbons belonged to the Mercy," I said, not looking at Ragsdale. "I went to speak to him this morning —*before* opening hours, Mr. Ragsdale—and he shot my friend Juliet and I had to chase him down. And they'd moved the oracle from that storefront I told you about to the top floor of the university library." I swallowed. My mouth was unexpectedly dry. "Ken was the other oracle's custodian. We fought, both the oracles became active, and Abernathy's destroyed its counterpart, leaving Ken brain-damaged and me...very tired."

Again, silence fell. Stirlaugson looked like an ebony statue. Duwelt's smile was almost feline, though I couldn't imagine why. "And your part in this was...?" she said.

"I had to convince our oracle not to let itself be destroyed so the Mercy's oracle could live. It didn't want to destroy it. It said—" An unexpected tear slid down my cheek, and I wiped it away. "It said it was alive, and the other one wasn't, but that it could be. And then it destroyed it."

"Ah," said Stirlaugson. "That's...astonishing. But won't the Mercy simply create another oracle?"

"Abernathy's assures me they can't. I think it would know."

"Then it really is over. Again, I'm astonished. But at this point I should probably learn to expect astonishing things of you, Ms. Davies."

"It's a moving story," Ragsdale said, sneering, "but we should stick to the matter at hand. If you can't manage your life—"

I rounded on him, snarling. "Mr. Ragsdale, I have had enough of your abuse," I said. "I violated the Accords and I freely submitted myself to the Board's judgment. I agreed to the punishment you all determined and I've been nothing but perfectly compliant for over nine months, despite your efforts to catch me in disobedience. I just watched a man's brains be scrambled by an entity your tiny mind could not possibly begin to comprehend. If you think I'm afraid of whatever so-called justice you're able to dish out, think again." I turned to Stirlaugson. "I officially request that Mr. Ragsdale be removed as my liaison with the Board. He's vindictive and mean-spirited and he's making my life hell. Which I don't recall being part of my punishment."

Duwelt's smile grew. Ragsdale sputtered incoherently. "You —" he finally managed.

Stirlaugson held up a hand. "Your request will be taken under consideration, Ms. Davies. Timothy, that was your last warning. Your position on the Board will come under review on Monday. For now, I think you should wait in the car."

Ragsdale was almost purple with rage. He turned and shoved past a couple of people who didn't have the wit to get out of his way and slammed the door behind himself. I gaped after him. "I didn't…I mean, I don't like him, but I didn't want him to lose his position!"

"Timothy has a history of abusing his power," Stirlaugson said. "Very little of that has to do with you. But don't think, if we give you a new liaison, your punishment will be annulled. You still have three months of probation left."

"If it's probation without Mr. Ragsdale breathing down my collar, I can endure it."

Stirlaugson smiled, just the corners of her mouth twitching upward. "You are a remarkable woman, Ms. Davies." She withdrew an augury request slip from her suit pocket, looked at it, and put it away. "Our augury request was just invalidated. The Board thanks you for saving it money. And… congratulations on your wedding. I hope it's a beautiful day."

"Thank you," I said, feeling my knees wobble.

The three other Board members nodded at me in unison, like they'd rehearsed it, and turned to leave. Harrison, who'd remained unexpectedly silent through all of this, was at the end of the line. At the door, he looked back at me and said, "Well done." Then he closed the door behind him.

All the Nicolliens in the room were watching me as if they wanted to ask questions but couldn't decide where to start or, for that matter, who should go first. "Well, form a line, it's not like you don't know how this works," I said. "Everything's going to be fine." I spared a thought for Juliet, who had survived being shot and would definitely be fine. Juliet survived, I survived, Ken...well, he'd survived, but I was sure he wouldn't appreciate it. I could make it through this day, and the rehearsal and dinner, and tomorrow...tomorrow would be wonderful.

Malcolm appeared at the stroke of two in a way that told me he'd been hovering outside waiting for Nicollien time to end. "Juliet is home again, and the good people at the hospital where she was taken are wondering if they imagined her," he said, folding me into his arms and ignoring the Ambrosites waiting patiently for auguries.

"I thought mind control was impossible. Wouldn't you have to, I don't know, fog their memories or something?"

"It is a complicated illusion that involves making half of them believe she was released to a different hospital by the other half. No mind control needed. Fortunately Mike is more than competent at it."

"So he did well? I was afraid he'd lost his confidence, after what happened in Chicago."

"This did much to restore his faith in himself. Thank you for being so welcoming of him. I think this will be good for everyone."

"I'm glad." It was wonderful to be in Malcolm's arms, comforting and safe. "I don't suppose you know what happened to Ken?"

"Surprisingly, we haven't had to spin that story at all. We took him to a more public location to be found and removed the illusion on his gun. Juliet was conscious enough to assert he'd shot her, and there were students on the quad who veri-fied that he'd fired shots into the crowd—" I shuddered, and

Malcolm held me more tightly. "What they will make of his mental condition, I don't know, but I imagine they'll discover he suffered some kind of stroke or aneurysm. They may even believe it was what made him snap. I'm afraid the lack of a victim will complicate things, but we could hardly leave Juliet in an alien city, recovering the hard way."

"So he won't go to trial? I don't see how he could."

"We'll keep him under observation, and if he shows signs of recovering his mental faculties, we will deal with him." Malcolm's voice was cold, and I shuddered again. "But that's a worry for another time."

"I hope it's over. He caused so much damage. I almost wish he could face a tribunal, but really, I'm just as happy he can't help the Mercy anymore."

Malcolm released me to arm's length and studied my face. "You look so tired. Will you be able to endure tonight?"

"I'll have to, won't I?" I stepped away from him and accepted the first augury slip. "At least they're serving my favorite food, so I have something to look forward to."

Most of the people who came in that afternoon didn't want auguries, just to wish me luck on my wedding. Some of them even brought gifts, which I accepted with surprise and delight. Malcolm and I had already set up our household, so it wasn't like we needed the traditional china or toasters, but I was sure our Warden friends would come up with creative ways to congratulate us.

My weariness faded as the day went on. The oracle behaved as if none of the events of the morning had happened, with the same air of distant attention it always had when I brought it an augury request. I could even…well, it wasn't like I was looking forward to encountering Madeleine, but there would be lasagna, and for my last night as a single woman, this wasn't so bad. Malcolm's grand-mère would be there, and she might turn out to be as nice as Malcolm suggested. Everything was going to be fine.

People stopped showing up around 4:30, and I took the time to straighten the books, not reading the titles, just in case. The smell of toasted coconut wafted past me on one of the random breezes that occasionally came from nowhere. I stopped and breathed it in. Maui. Warm, sunny beaches, snorkeling off the coast, making love to the sound of the waves outside our room… I shook my head and moved on. Daydreaming just made it worse.

Distantly I heard the office phone ring. Judy would take the augury request and bring it to me. I went on straightening the shelves and listened to the sound of her approaching footsteps. "The phone's for you," she said, coming around a corner.

"Not an augury request?"

"No, someone named Mangesh Kapoor. He says Conti asked him to contact you."

I couldn't think why Mike would give my name to anyone who didn't just want an augury request. "Weird," I said, dusting off my hands.

Judy, with unusual delicacy, left me alone to take the call. "This is Helena Davies."

"Ms. Davies, my name is Mangesh Kapoor." He had a pleasant voice with a musical Indian accent. "Michael Conti told me you are capable of seeing through illusions."

"I—yes, but—*oh*, you're the one he told me about! The stone magus!"

"Indeed. I would very much like to speak with you in person. Is there a time acceptable to you?"

"Is right now all right? I mean, if you're busy, I understand." For a moment, I suffered brief paranoia; supposing this wasn't the real Mangesh Kapoor? What if this was another Mercy trick? I shook the thought away. The odds against the Mercy having two secret operatives, both of them connected to me, were vanishingly small.

"I confess I hoped you would be available immediately. Have I your permission to enter Abernathy's via its wards?"

"That's fine. Thank you. I'll—see you soon." I hung up and darted for the front counter.

When I arrived, a stranger stood near the front door as if he'd walked in off the street, though I hadn't heard the bells. He was middle-aged, with black hair untouched by gray and light brown skin, the wrinkles on his forehead and at the corners of his eyes the only things that gave away his age. He wore a plum-colored sweatshirt with no logo and faded jeans. He didn't look anything like I imagined a swami to be, though admittedly my imagination began and ended with flowing robes and a turban. "Ms. Davies?" he said. "I am Mangesh Kapoor. Thank you for your welcome." He bowed to me, a formal gesture that *did* fit my mental image.

I thought about returning the bow, decided it would just look stupid, and smiled instead. "It's good to meet you, Mr. Kapoor."

We stood in mutual silence for a moment, then Kapoor said, with a smile, "I am afraid I don't know where to begin. I never believed I would meet anyone like me."

"Me neither. But Mike said you were a disciple of a kind of meditation, and that's why you can see through illusions. Couldn't you teach that?"

Kapoor shook his head. "Mr. Conti is correct that meditation is part of my religious faith. But my ability to see through illusions is something I appear to have been born with. Is that your experience?"

"I…think so. I never encountered many illusions until I became custodian of Abernathy's, so I can't be sure. My parents told me about an encounter I had as a child where I apparently saw a familiar in its true form, but since they didn't know about the Long War, they couldn't have known that's what I experienced." I checked my watch—my spare watch, which still pissed me off. "Why don't we go to the break room to talk? Judy will let me know if anyone comes in."

Sitting at the tiny break room table across from Kapoor, I felt a little more at ease. "I can't even tell if something's under an illusion," I said. "It just fails. Is that what it's like for you?"

Kapoor nodded. "I have learned to follow the cues from those around me, to judge by their reactions what illusion is there. Though of course I have never made it a secret that I have this ability."

"Neither have I—so why didn't anyone tell me about you? Or vice versa?"

"I am a traveling stone magus, specializing in the wards of India and southeast Asia. I rarely come to the United States, and then only by invitation. I knew nothing of Abernathy's current custodian except what everyone does, that she was a stranger to our world until two years ago. I am rather more familiar with the work of Silas Abernathy, who was my predecessor in this calling—no, him and then one other before me."

"I've read Silas's book *Reflections*, so I can picture what you do."

Kapoor's eyes gleamed. "You have it? I have longed to read it. I have only his notes on the wards—they are complex, and we stone magi keep notes on their peculiarities to help those who come after us."

"I would love to give it to you. It's at home, though."

"I should not take your book."

"I've read it so many times I nearly know it by heart. Besides, I think it's fitting that you should have it."

"Then I thank you, Ms. Davies." He leaned back in his chair and looked startled when it gave a little. I really ought to replace these chairs with something more robust and not a hundred years old. "I am curious," he said, "if you were not a Warden your whole life, how you discovered your ability?"

"I thought it was because I was Abernathy's custodian for a long time, but one of the other custodians said Mr. Briggs, the custodian before me, couldn't see through illusions."

"And you are without the marker that indicates one belongs to the Mercy?"

"No, I have it."

Kapoor's eyes narrowed. "You have no memory of some traumatic event that might have triggered it?"

"None."

"And yet it was not triggered by your becoming custodian." He shook his head. "I do not have the marker, and suffered no trauma. I am afraid with only two of us, that is not enough data to draw conclusions. But I cannot think of other questions to ask."

"I read about a man named Aaron Azoulay who died in 1807. He was famous for being able to see through illusions. Famous in his time, anyway."

"So there are, were, at least three of us."

"Yeah. But…maybe it doesn't matter if we don't know why we can."

"Perhaps. I dislike mysteries. And suppose there were something that happened to us that we might duplicate in others? The ability to see through illusions can be useful."

"True." Though at the moment all I could think of was ways in which it was annoying. Still, it had saved my life just this morning, when I saw Ken's gun for what it was. "Maybe we should ask Mr. Wallach his opinion."

"Who is Mr. Wallach?"

"He's a bone magus at the Gunther Node, a scientist. He…has unconventional ideas. But he's smart, and with two of us to examine—"

"I dislike the idea of being examined," Kapoor said with a frown.

"Me too, but if it reveals the truth, wouldn't that be worth it?"

"It could be." Kapoor stood. "I apologize, but I have an appointment in twenty minutes."

"Oh." I felt a little hurt at his abruptness, but then he smiled, and it reassured me that he wasn't blowing me off.

"My schedule is very tight, but I would like to return for that book in a week, if you are truly willing to give it to me," he said. "And I will arrange time to meet with your Mr. Wallach soon."

"Of course. I'll talk to him and see what he thinks. Also, I have a list of other people with spontaneous magical abilities like ours—not seeing through illusions, but other things. Maybe we have things in common that will help explain where our ability came from."

Kapoor's smile broadened. "You are dedicated indeed."

"I don't like mysteries either."

Kapoor bowed again. His body distorted, wavered like an old television screen going out of focus, and was gone.

I stood for a moment watching the place where he'd been. Someone like me. Sure, we neither of us knew where our ability came from, but talking to Kapoor had made it real in a way I hadn't anticipated. And someone who'd followed literally in Silas Abernathy's footsteps! It excited me that I could give him Silas's book, that he'd appreciate it even more than I had.

I checked my watch, trying not to let it irritate me. Forty more minutes, and I could go home. Forty more minutes, and the wedding officially began.

20

"*H**elena!*"

I cringed inwardly. *Calm. Serene.* It was growing harder to hang on to my inner serenity. "Mom, what's wrong?" I managed not to add "now" to the end of that sentence.

"I can't find your brother. Have you seen him?"

"No, I haven't, and that's all right. He's not walking down the aisle, so even if he disappears, no one will notice, right?"

"He ought to be there, though—oh, sweetheart, don't you look beautiful!"

A little bit of my calm returned as I looked at myself once again in the tri-panel mirror ringed with gilded carvings. The gown was the only part of the wedding plans I'd put any actual thought into. It was modeled on Lauren Bacall's wedding gown from *How to Marry a Millionaire*, fitted through the bodice and hips and flaring out from mid-thigh. I'd asked Elle and Veronica to leave off the lace overlay, so it was a beautiful fall of ivory silk from shoulders to hem. With my hair piled high on my head and fastened there with red and cream rosebuds, the antique lace veil draped over the skirt, I looked like something out of a fairy tale. Malcolm would love it. *I* loved it.

"Look, Mom, don't worry," I soothed. "Jake is responsible. He's probably just getting to know some of the young women guests. He knows where he has to be and when—what time is it?"

"5:30."

"Still plenty of time. Why don't you go to your seat? You're more worried than I am."

"I don't know how you've stayed so calm. Everything that can go wrong, has." She made as if to kiss my cheek, apparently decided better of mussing the makeup artist's work, and smiled at me before exiting the little room set aside for the bride. I sighed and carefully sat in the room's one velvet upholstered chair, sweeping my veil aside to avoid crushing it. It was a last-minute addition to the ensemble, but when Malcolm's grand-mère Renee Molyneux offered it to me, I could hardly say no. Not that I wanted to. It was beautiful.

Renee had been a surprise. Tiny, bent, and wrinkled, she looked as if she should be cast in the part of a little old French grandmother in a black dress living somewhere in Provence. But her grip, when I took her offered hand, was firm, her voice strong, and in heavily accented but intelligible English she'd told me I was exactly the kind of woman she'd always hoped Malcolm would end up with. She'd paired this with a sly glance at Madeleine, who'd looked wooden, so I guessed Renee knew all about my fraught relationship with my mother-in-law. Then she'd sat opposite me at the rehearsal dinner and told me stories about Malcolm's childhood that had him incoherent with embarrassment and me delighted at her choice of tales. By the end of the evening, we were fast friends. I hoped she wasn't out there fighting with Madeleine, though that would fit the kind of day I'd been having.

First, the flowers had gone missing. How two vanloads of red roses could simply disappear was a mystery even Deanna Forcier couldn't solve, though at least she hadn't tried to dump the problem on me aside from letting me know there was a teensy problem with the flowers and would white roses be all right? She'd looked so relieved when I nodded that I had to wonder what a bride's normal reaction should be. I couldn't see the point of getting worked up about it and told Deanna so. She'd only replied, "You have no idea."

Then the hotel let us know the honeymoon suite was suddenly unavailable.

Then Ewan, who had to fly in from Seattle that morning, called to say his flight had been cancelled.

Then Viv had come in crying with her head completely covered by a scarf and refused to remove it for ten full minutes. Finally, she took it off, revealing a head of hair that was supposed to be a beautiful platinum blonde to go with the wedding colors of crimson and ivory. Instead, it was pale pink and streaky from her last dye job, making her resemble one of those striped peppermint wheels.

All that happened before four p.m. The wedding was at six.

There was a part of me that felt I would be justified in having hysterics like the heroine of a nineteenth-century novel. Mostly, though, I felt calm. All this show, the flowers and the food and the wedding party and even Viv's hair, didn't matter. All we needed was me, Malcolm, and the offici-ator, and all three of us were present. The officiator, a nice non-denominational minister suggested by Deanna, was as calm and relaxed as I was. He spoke to me briefly before I went to get changed. "You know it's the ceremony that matters," he'd said. "Making vows of your devotion to each other before God and the community. I hope that's what you'll remember years from now, when you remember this day."

"I'm pretty sure I'll remember Viv's hair, too," I'd said, which made him laugh.

I didn't know how all those problems ended up in my lap, but I assumed if Deanna wasn't handling them, she must be dealing with crises I didn't know anything about. That there were worse things going on made a small dent in my calm, but I thought of Malcolm, whom I hadn't seen since noon, and peace filled my heart.

I told the hotel it was too bad about the honeymoon suite, but I was sure we could find an alternative somewhere else that would be thrilled to take the large sum of money I proposed to spend. They gave me an upgrade to the executive penthouse at no extra charge.

I called Ewan and asked him politely why he hadn't ward-stepped here in the first place. He sounded incredibly sheepish when I pointed this out.

I reassured Viv that she didn't look like a dandelion fluff dipped in red paint and reminded her this was *my* day and no one would be looking at her. Which was a total lie, but seemed to comfort her. At least, it got her to stop crying. Then Mike took her aside and did something whose effect I couldn't see, but was apparently enough of an illusion to satisfy everyone else.

Now my brother was missing. I hoped he represented the last of the crises. We were running out of time in which they could happen. Me, Malcolm, the minister. Everything else was gravy.

"Helena," Judy said, poking her head into the room. "The bouquet."

I groaned. "Did it turn into a flock of butterflies and fly away?"

"No," Judy said, her eyes narrowed. "It's here. I wondered if you wanted to look at it. Are you all right?"

"I'm fine. I'm just used to things going wrong at this point. Butterflies would at least be festive."

Judy came fully into the room bearing my bouquet in her hands. It was beautiful, all red roses and white celosia spikes, tied with a huge ivory silk ribbon. "Oh," I said, reaching for it. "It's perfect."

"I'm not supposed to tell you this is version two, after the first one got run over," Judy said, "but I knew you'd find that hilarious."

"*Run over?*" I began to laugh, somewhat helplessly. "That's awful."

"See? You looked like you could use a laugh." She leaned against the wall, then thought better of rumpling her brides-maid's dress. I'd chosen dresses I thought my bridesmaids might be able to wear again, simple red sheaths that managed to flatter both Cynthia's bustiness and Judy's petite frame. Judy's short hair was pinned up on one side by a smaller version of the flower headdress I wore. "Are you just bottling up your anxiety for later? Or are you really this mellow?"

"I just don't feel worried. I mean, what's the worst—no, don't answer that. I may not be tense, but I *am* superstitious."

"Well, everyone's here, including your brother, who I sent off to find your mom. It only started raining about ten minutes ago, which is good because most of the guests are here already. And Deanna found a new DJ."

"That's—we needed a new DJ?"

"Um…maybe I shouldn't have said anything."

I waved that away. "I'm sure someone would have a Bluetooth speaker and an iPod."

Judy stared at me. "You're frightening me. You're sure you're not going to have a panic attack in the middle of your vows?"

"I doubt it."

The door opened again. "Showtime, ladies," Deanna said. She was a tall, well-built woman in her fifties with a deep voice and a charming smile. "Stand up and let's look at you, Helena. Oh, that dress was an *excellent* choice." She fluttered around me, adjusting my hem, spreading the lace veil more carefully across my skirt. I held still, feeling oddly dizzy now that the moment was upon me. All this work for, what, fifteen minutes of ceremony? Or however long it actually took. The rehearsal had gone on much longer. Did I remember the vows I'd written? I did. I took a deep breath and smiled at Deanna. This would be perfect.

The hallway from the bride's room to the reception hall where the ceremony would take place led partly through the mezzanine of the hotel. It was unexpectedly gratifying to see people stop and stare at me—gratifying, and a little embarrassing. "Don't pay them any mind," Deanna whispered. "You are beautiful."

I got the feeling, from how crowded the antechamber was, that the Warwick didn't host a lot of weddings, or at least that it wasn't their primary function. Which made sense, since it was a hotel and not a reception center. But everyone was there, the bridesmaids and groomsmen pairing off as Deanna directed. They looked good. Viv and Ewan were nearly of a height, and really, her hair didn't look *that* awful. More like a streaky white carnation, and everyone liked carnations. She would have been fine even without the illusion. Cynthia made Derrick, with his powerful frame and bulldog-like face, look natural in his tux. And there was Judy taking Mike's arm without even a hint of animosity. They'd been civil to each other the night before, too. I hoped they could become friends.

My father came forward and offered me his arm. "You look extraordinary, Bumblebee," he said, teasing me with my childhood nickname. "I never imagined you'd grow up so lovely."

"Aren't fathers supposed to be horribly overprotective of their daughters? And you seem eager to give me away."

"Such an archaic notion. I'm happy you found someone who makes you look so radiant."

The doors opened, and Judy and Mike began their slow walk down the aisle. I shivered. "Not nervous, are you? Though that would be natural," Dad said.

"No, it's just...I can't believe it's really happening."

"Don't forget that feeling," Dad said. "You'll remember this day for the rest of your life."

The music swelled. Dad and I stepped forward. There was a rush of sound as everyone in the reception hall stood, their eyes focused on me. But all I could see, at the far end of the room, was Malcolm, smiling as fiercely as if we were the only two people in the room.

"You're right," I said, "I will."

"I CAN'T TAKE my shoes off," I murmured to Viv. "I won't be able to get them on again."

"So go barefoot," she murmured back. "You're the bride. Who's going to criticize?"

The dinner was over. The speeches were over. I'd heard everything in a daze, still feeling stunned at how it had all worked out. The ring on my finger, a plain gold band—I didn't want a huge diamond, and I'd switched my engagement ring to my right hand—still felt weird. It was even weirder to look at its mate on Malcolm's hand. I'd thought I felt married already, all those weeks, but the rings brought it all home in a way I'd never expected.

"Helena," Malcolm said, as if he'd addressed me once already. "It's time."

"Oh!" Now I was really glad I hadn't taken off my shoes. Malcolm helped me rise, something I needed with all those skirts, and escorted me to the center of the dance floor. Our first dance as husband and wife. He'd chosen the song and hadn't told me what it was, saying I'd recognize it. As he took me in his arms, the music rose, and I laughed. "'As Time Goes By.' Is this now our song, Rick Blaine?"

"I'll never forget the night we fell asleep watching *Casablanca*. I'd been telling myself for weeks I felt nothing more than mere attraction to you, but that night, I knew I'd been lying to myself."

"I was so embarrassed at having kissed you. I didn't think —you're right, though. That was the night I knew I loved you."

"You have no idea how much I wanted to kiss you in return. And your bedroom was so very close. But it was the wrong time."

"Very wrong. I think, the Accords aside, we managed to do almost everything right."

"As is evidenced by the fact that we're here tonight. I love you, Helena."

"I love you," I said, and kissed him, making a wave of sound rise up all around us.

We danced again, faster this time, then my father claimed me for the traditional father-daughter dance. Then I had to dance with each of the groomsmen, and with my very embarrassed brother, and with Cynthia's partner Ethan, and finally with Harry Keller, who knew steps I'd never heard of and made me look good. Finally I cried mercy and went to sit with Viv, who was also taking a break from dancing. "You're not going to do that thing where you smear cake all over each other's faces, are you?" she said. "I've always hated that."

"No, we think it's stupid and juvenile." I looked around the room. "Where's Judy? I don't want to cut the cake until all three of my bridesmaids are there."

"I don't know. I haven't seen her in a while. She was dancing with Lucas last I saw."

I stood. "I'll go look for her."

"No, you shouldn't have to. I'll go."

"It will give me something to do. I hate sitting in this thing because I can practically hear the silk crying for mercy." I stood and shook out my skirts. "I'll be right back."

I made the circuit of the room, smiling and nodding and accepting congratulations. No Judy anywhere. Probably she was in the bathroom. It occurred to me that *I* needed the bathroom, as nervous as I was of peeing while wearing the fabulous gown. I'd just have to be careful.

Judy wasn't in the bathroom either. I managed my business without getting my skirt or veil wet and went in search of my missing friend. All the little side rooms were locked, except for the bride's room. I opened that door, gasped, and shut it again quickly. Well. So *that* was where Judy had gone. You heard about these things happening at weddings, but I wouldn't have thought—

I returned to Viv's side. She was still seated, rubbing one bare toe against the sole of her other foot as if it ached. "You're not going to believe where I found Judy," I said.

"Where? Let me guess. Outside fooling around with an usher."

"Close. She was in the bride's room. Making out with *Mike Conti.*"

Viv gasped just as I had. "No way. They hate each other."

"I just saw some pretty compelling evidence that says they don't."

Viv absently put her shoes back on. "What should we do?"

"Nothing. They're grownups. If they want to sneak away to make out at my wedding, that's up to them." I was more stunned by this than by anything else that had happened that day. Judy and Mike. Stranger things had happened at weddings. What would William Rasmussen, head of the Nicolliens, think if he knew his daughter had been enthusiastically kissing an Ambrosite hunter? Nothing good. But that, too, was Judy's business and not mine.

All at once the day's exertions caught up with me, and I wished everyone would magically disappear so I could get out of my dress and my increasingly uncomfortable shoes. But there was still the cake, and more dancing, and the throwing of the bouquet, which Pen Wadsworth caught, to the obvious discomfort of her boyfriend. Finally, Malcolm took a good look at my face, clasped my hand, and whispered, "It's time." But even that took time, because we couldn't just slip away upstairs, we had to give everyone a chance to cheer us on.

The second the elevator doors closed on us, I kicked my

266 | MELISSA MCSHANE

shoes off and sighed with pleasure. "Is this a hint that you want me to carry you over the threshold?" Malcolm said.

"No, but it is a hint that a foot rub might ensure the best sex you've ever had as a married man."

Malcolm slipped a card into the reader attached to the elevator panel, then gathered my shoes. "The hotel manager himself gave me this access card," he said. "He was oddly emphatic that we let him know if there is anything we require. Did you say something to him?"

"Only threatened to take our business elsewhere. The Campbell name did the rest. I should feel uncomfortable at throwing your wealth around, but I'm too tired for that."

"If my wealth will get us a comfortable night, I'm not opposed to that."

The elevator doors opened on a vestibule lit by softly glowing sconces that turned its rose and cream décor into a confection of expensive taste. Malcolm opened the door for me. "Welcome, Mrs. Campbell," he said, ushering me inside.

A short hallway led to an exquisite living room with soft chairs and a sofa I wouldn't have minded sleeping on, upholstered in faded blue so perfect it had to represent the highest quality. Off to one side, an executive table surrounded by chairs on wheels doubled as a dining table, with a kitchenette barely visible beyond. Floor to ceiling windows unobscured by curtains gave a breathtaking vista of Portland by night. The rain had stopped, the clouds had vanished, and a half-moon strewed silver across the chair nearest the windows. Soft classical music, nothing I recognized, filled the air. I walked forward, enchanted.

"Helena," Malcolm said, and I turned to see him standing beside an open doorway. "Look at this."

The bedroom beyond wasn't nearly as nice as ours, but for

a hotel room it was still very elegant. What made it perfect was the details. Champagne chilled in a silver urn on the dresser below the window. Bouquets of roses of every color filled the room, with my bouquet—not the special one for throwing, but my own—at the center of the display. The room smelled deliciously of them. The bed's white counterpane was strewn with red rose petals, which I knew was cliché, but I'd always secretly longed for a bed strewn with rose petals, so it only made me smile. The music wasn't as loud in here, but it still made a beautiful background to the perfect suite.

Malcolm put his arms around me. "Like it?"

"Did you arrange all this?"

"More or less. I left it to the manager—just told him I wanted my bride to have one perfect night."

I turned around in his arms to kiss him. "It's beautiful," I said. "But all I need is you."

I WOKE from a delicious slumber to Malcolm sliding out of bed and padding barefoot and, presumably, naked out of the room. I wondered where he was going, but idly, not really caring about the details. Then the cold realization that it was Monday morning sluiced over me, and I sat up, fumbling for the bedside clock. It was white and minimalist and looked like something astronauts might take into space, and it took me a minute to find the readout. I relaxed. It was only eight o'clock. I still had more than an hour before I had to be at work.

Malcolm returned—oh, he was wearing a dressing gown, one apparently supplied by the hotel and very nice. I decided if there was a matching one for me, we'd take them home with us and let the hotel add them to our bill. Or maybe the manager was still feeling so guilty he'd let us have them for free. Malcolm bore a large tray with covered dishes that he set gracefully on his side of the bed. "Breakfast," he said. "I'm sorry you have to go to work. It feels so anticlimactic."

"You're going to work, too, unless things have changed," I pointed out.

"True, but somehow it feels more wrong when it's the bride. Like a mother not getting maternity leave."

"I wish you hadn't said that. What are we going to do when we decide to have children? Haven't any of Abernathy's custodians ever given birth? What did they do?"

"I don't know." Malcolm crunched into a piece of crisp bacon. "It's something you might want to research. Though I don't expect it to matter for a few years."

"No. I've read it's a good idea not to have children right away, to give yourselves time to learn to be a couple. I wonder if that applies to people who live together for years before getting married."

Malcolm shrugged. "It makes sense to me. But it's probably better if you know the answer before it becomes an issue."

I forked up scrambled eggs. "You're so sensible. It's why I married you."

Malcolm's smile became wicked. "That's not what you said last night."

"I don't think anything I say in the throes of passion ought to be held against me."

"Mmm. I think the exact opposite should be true."

"Malcolm, you're going to spill the tray."

"Then let them clean it up." But he moved the tray anyway.

Later, lying comfortably in his arms, I said, "I wish I didn't have to go to work. Do you think they'd fire me right away if I didn't open the store, or wait to hold a tribunal?"

"Let's not find out." Malcolm disentangled himself from me and tossed a dressing gown that did match his own at me. It was silky-soft and smelled like flowers. I was definitely taking it home with me.

We took our time showering and dressing. I smoothed my wedding gown away into its special bag, smiling in memory. Yes, I would only wear it once, but it was a memorable once. Malcolm caught my expression and said, "Not nostalgic already, love?"

"No, just happy."

He drove me directly to Abernathy's, kissed me goodbye, and left me in the rear parking lot, waving to him. The skies were cloudy again, promising rain later that day. I unlocked the back door and let myself in, trying not to feel despondent.

As if in memory of my wedding night, today the store smelled of roses. I dropped my purse on the desk and sifted through the envelopes, already slit open. It wasn't a very big pile. Payment…payment…a notice from the tax accountant that she was ready to set up an appointment… "Judy?"

After a moment, she appeared in the doorway, unusually flushed. "Something wrong?"

I remembered seeing her locked in Mike Conti's arms and blushed myself. "Where did you put the augury requests?"

"There weren't any."

I blinked. "Why aren't there any augury requests?"

"It's weird, isn't it? That's all there was in the mail." She wasn't quite able to meet my eyes, and I wondered if she knew I was the one who'd stumbled across their little rendezvous. She had to know *someone* had opened the door. Or…had he come home with her last night? Was he still upstairs?

"I guess it had to happen sometime." I pulled the putty-colored lump of a phone toward me. "I'm going to call about getting the glass countertop replaced."

"I was sweeping, so I'll…just get back to that." She left as swiftly as she'd arrived. I sighed and punched in the number. She'd talk about it when she was ready. Or never.

At ten o'clock I sat on the stool behind the counter and watched the door. The street outside, normally full of waiting Nicolliens, was empty. I leaned my elbows against the bare plywood and frowned at the door. No mail-in auguries, no Nicolliens…what was going on?

"Is there something I should know about?" I asked Judy, who'd returned from putting the broom away.

"Like what? There's no Warden holiday, if that's what you mean, and Abernathy's doesn't recognize holidays anyway." Judy leaned against the counter, frowning at the door as I was.

"Hmm." I pulled out my phone and scrolled through the contacts. "Freddy Whittaker told me yesterday he was coming in for an augury this morning. He's usually the first one lined up outside the door."

"So he got stuck in traffic. This isn't a mystery."

"I don't know." I dialed his number. "This feels weird. Freddy? It's Helena. Were you planning to come in for an augury today?"

"I was," Freddy said. "I got in my car about half an hour ago to drive over there. Had Vicious leashed and everything. And then I realized I didn't need the augury, after all."

"You figured out the answer?"

"Well…no, not really. More like I just don't need it today. It's not all that urgent."

It had sounded pretty urgent when Freddy had mentioned it to me yesterday—urgent enough that he'd bring it up with the bride at her own wedding. "Oh," I said. "I…guess that makes sense."

"Not really. I hope I didn't put you out or anything."

"Of course not. Have a nice day."

I put my phone in my pocket. "He says he doesn't need it. Like it stopped mattering."

"Since when does that happen?"

"I don't know," I said. "But maybe the oracle does." I hopped off the stool, focused, and walked into the oracle.

The light, blue-tinted, still felt like a storm was coming, but it was brighter, as if the sun was trying harder to shine. "All right, is there something I need to know?" I said, walking briskly through the aisles. "Is there a reason there are no Nicolliens thronging the store this morning? No mail-in auguries? Because that all seems rather suspicious. If something else is wrong…I hope nothing else is wrong."

I came to a stop in the heart of the oracle. I could tell its attention was on me, but in an abstracted way, as if the oracle was reading an interesting book and only half-listening to me. "I know you can communicate with me, and *you* know I want to help you if I can. So why would Freddy Whittaker suddenly lose interest in an augury he was deathly worried about just fourteen hours ago?"

The silence closed in around me, a comfortable silence that should have soothed my spirits. "Okay, maybe I'm wrong. Maybe this is all a weird coincidence. But if you could give me some reassurance, I'd appreciate it."

The bluish light turned faint gold, warm and caressing like the summer sun. I heard rustling and turned in time to see a slim book slipping out from between a couple of thick paperback tomes by James Clavell. It floated across to me, coming to a stop in front of my face. *Destination: Hawaii*, read the title, and pictures of tropical islands decorated the cover. A large brown envelope stuck out from between its pages. I took it, and for a moment it weighed nothing at all. Then it fell into my hands. I opened the front cover to look at the title page.

Helena Davies, No Charge.

I'd half expected that, but it still mystified me. How was this the answer to my question? I removed the envelope, tucked the book under my arm, and unfastened the clasp. It wasn't very bulky, but there were several sheets of paper inside and a standard-sized white envelope.

The first page was a statement from a hotel on Maui—not a statement, a reservation, for a hotel suite for the coming week. The second and third pages were lists of other reservations, for restaurants, for island excursions, even one with a company that did snorkeling tours. I opened the white envelope. Airline tickets, in my name and in Malcolm's, for a flight leaving this afternoon. To Hawaii.

I slid the tickets back into the envelope, my fingers numb. "I can't," I said, my voice barely audible over the roaring in my ears. "You need a custodian. I swore I wouldn't leave."

The oracle's attention never wavered. It might as well have said *Why are you still here? I gave you your answer.*

"But it's impossible," I began, then stopped. If the oracle could destroy another powerful entity without breaking a sweat, so to speak, was it really impossible that it might be able to exert other kinds of control over the world? Like, for example, persuading the world that its auguries could wait?

I shook my head. "The Board will never believe it."

The oracle's attention shifted to the bookcases. A faint blue glow around one of the books intensified into the familiar light of an active augury. I removed it from the shelf and looked inside. *Laverne Stirlaugson, No Charge.* The title was *Busman's*

Honeymoon. "Okay, maybe she will believe it," I said. I clutched the book to my chest along with the envelope. "I'm not sure *I* believe it, but...thank you."

I walked slowly out of the oracle, giving it a chance to change its mind, but nothing happened to strike me down or make the items in my hands vanish. Judy waited somewhat impatiently by the counter. "Well?"

I shook my head. An irrepressible smile spread across my face. "I'll explain everything in a minute. Frankly, *you'll* probably have to do some explaining to Ms. Stirlaugson. But I have to make a phone call first."

I ignored her demands for more of an explanation and called Malcolm. "Are you busy?" I asked.

"No, but shouldn't you be working?"

It was all I could do to keep from skipping in place. "I should have asked, are you busy for the next week?"

"Helena, what are you talking about?"

I felt as if I were flying. "Come pick me up," I said. "We're going on our honeymoon."

Abernathy's will return in
THE BOOK OF WAR

THE AUGURIES, AND MOVIES
REFERENCED

Ken Follett, *On Wings of Eagles*
Virginia Woolf, *To The Lighthouse*
F. Scott Fitzgerald, *This Side of Paradise*
Amy Tan, *The Opposite of Fate*
L.M. Elliott, *A Troubled Peace*
Virginia Hamilton, *The House of Dies Drear*
Jane Smiley, *The All-True Travels and Adventures of Lidie Newton*
Joan Walsh Anglund, *Peace is a Circle of Love*
Dorothy L. Sayers, *Busman's Honeymoon*
How to Marry a Millionaire
Kind Hearts and Coronets

ABOUT THE AUTHOR

In addition to The Last Oracle series, Melissa McShane is the author of The Extraordinaries series, beginning with BURNING BRIGHT, the Crown of Tremontane series, beginning with SERVANT OF THE CROWN, as well as COMPANY OF STRANGERS and many others.

After a childhood spent roaming the United States, she settled in Utah with her husband, four children and a niece, four very needy cats, and a library that continues to grow out of control. She wrote reviews and critical essays for many years before turning to fiction, which is much more fun than anyone ought to be allowed to have.

You can visit her at her website www.melissamcshanewrites.com for more information on other books.

For information on new releases, fun extras, and more, sign up for Melissa's newsletter: http://eepurl.com/brannP

If you enjoyed this book, please consider leaving a review at your favorite online book retailer or Goodreads!

ALSO BY MELISSA MCSHANE

THE CROWN OF TREMONTANE

Servant of the Crown

Exile of the Crown

Rider of the Crown

Agent of the Crown

Voyager of the Crown

Tales of the Crown

THE SAGA OF WILLOW NORTH

Pretender to the Crown

Guardian of the Crown

Champion of the Crown

THE HEIRS OF WILLOW NORTH

Ally of the Crown

Stranger to the Crown (forthcoming)

THE EXTRAORDINARIES

Burning Bright

Wondering Sight

Abounding Might

Whispering Twilight (forthcoming)

THE LAST ORACLE

The Book of Secrets

The Book of Peril

The Book of Mayhem

The Book of Lies

The Book of Betrayal

The Book of Havoc

The Book of Harmony

The Book of War (forthcoming)

COMPANY OF STRANGERS

Company of Strangers

Stone of Inheritance

Mortal Rites

Shifting Loyalties

Sands of Memory

Call of Wizardry

THE CONVERGENCE TRILOGY

The Summoned Mage

The Wandering Mage

The Unconquered Mage

THE BOOKS OF DALANINE

The Smoke-Scented Girl

The God-Touched Man